FULL CIRCLE

Gary Cockaday

HOBART BOOKS

HOBART BOOKS

FULL CIRCLE

ISBN 978-1-914322-15-0

First Published in 2022
by
Hobart Books, Oxfordshire, England

hobartbooks.com

Printed and bound in Great Britain.

Full Circle

By Gary Cockaday

With special thanks to my readers, Laura Culley-Tea & Lee Guyton, and to Paul Martin for initial edits to get the manuscript ready for submission.

A huge thank you to my publishers Hobart Books, especially Adam & David for believing in me and Full Circle. Lastly Mrs C for not complaining too much about the hours spent at my desk.

PART ONE

CHAPTER ONE

June 2016

Sarah knew that this was a bad idea.

That every step was taking her closer to the very bad idea, currently standing against the bar. She had known who he was from the moment he'd entered the room – his reputation, as always, preceding him. James Taylor was the classic bad boy and yet she continued to walk towards him. Her thoughts conflicted… *what are you doing?* – *This is your wedding day!* She knew she should stop, that she should just turn and walk away as fast as she could, to anywhere that took her away from him.

She sensed his energy as she walked towards him – it came off him in waves. She was very aware that she wasn't the only one drawn to him. She'd watched heads turn, both men and women, watching him walk, move, and even stand, but it had been only her that he looked at.

Her.

In that moment of realisation, she had forgotten to breathe. She had forgotten everything, except one thing: she had to get closer to him, to hear him speak, to stand in front of him, to ask him '*why me?*' and more importantly '*what do you want?*' That thought excited her more than it should.

The weekend before she'd been away with the girls – in Ibiza on her hen. There was an awful lot that she couldn't remember about those three days. In fairness, it had been a weekend of wonderful drunken debauchery passing by in a fast-forward, not-sleeping-a-lot haze. One memory returned as she walked, causing her heart to beat a little quicker. They'd played a very noisy game of truth or dare. One of her bridesmaids, one of her *married* bridesmaids, had confessed unashamedly, in reply to a truth question, that James Taylor had been the best shag of her life. A few others had admitted to shagging him – quite a few of them had been married! Most agreed they would shag him again if they could. She remembered thinking *'am I the only one who hasn't?'*

Now, she was walking past her guests, some obviously wanting to talk to her, faces turning, mouths opening, smiles disappearing as she passed. She ignored everyone and everything. Finally, she stood before him, her senses overloading. His smell… his skin… he looked hot – not just visually hot. Dangerous was the word that sprang to mind. She nodded yes when asked 'Do you dance?' letting him take her hand, following him as they stepped onto the edge of the dance floor. Her skin touched his, and she felt a little high, no longer fully in control of her body. A friend caught her eye and laughed, giving her a thumbs-up. One of the friends who'd had the pleasure, one of the friends who would shag him again if she could, and one of the friends who had a husband!

Looking back to her friend, she mouthed 'help,' but her friend laughed before disappearing back into the crowd. She was alone. He pulled her into him. She felt his hands on her waist, and she wrapped hers around his neck as they swayed. Closing her eyes, she hoped no one could see them. Her guests became invisible; only he existed. His body pressed into her, and she groaned as she felt his hand on her bare back, pressing into her, fingers sliding under the edge of her dress. She knew that was way too intimate, but she didn't care, and so she laid her head on his shoulder, breathing in, wanting to kiss him. He pulled her closer, and she felt him against her, felt him hardening, a shiver running through her body.

It was one thing knowing that she should stop him, that she should step back, that she should walk away, but she couldn't. To stop would be to ignore her body, the demanding voices in her head, voices that wanted physical satisfaction, that wanted the cravings to be sated. Was it the Champagne? *For heaven's sake, sort yourself out, you got married this afternoon.* She knew in that moment, why so many of her friends had succumbed. Few would be able to resist the man in front of her.

Time flew by, they had danced through two, maybe three songs when she felt a tap on her shoulder, turning to find her husband asking, 'Would you like to join me outside for a spot of fresh air?' He didn't look happy.

It hadn't really sounded like a question. He grabbed her hand, trying to pull her with him as he turned away, obviously determined to take her outside for what would probably be a severe talking to – one she deserved. James had her other hand. He pulled her to him, whispering, 'I'd like to take you outside… I'd like to rip this dress off you, then I'd like to bend you over my Porsche and fuck you very hard and very fast.'

She left, dragged away by her husband. Looking back, she mouthed, 'I'd like that.'

She left, walking backwards as best she could, but she quickly lost sight of him. She knew he was there, somewhere; she felt empty, bereft as if someone had turned the lights off. She knew she was about to get a proper bollocking, but she didn't care. She'd take the telling off; she'd be a good girl. She'd be or do anything that allowed her to return to him again. Nothing else mattered.

PART TWO

CHAPTER TWO

Three months later

Jackie was sitting in her kitchen, her feet up on the table and a pillow behind her head. These days she found it hard to find a comfy position – sometimes she couldn't. When she couldn't, she would wander aimlessly around the house, moving constantly. Those days were the worst. Currently, she had Radio 2 on; she loved the arts show and would often listen in at bedtime. She found it calming. Recently, ten pm had become her new midnight and time for bed. She had become a lightweight. Bed had become her favourite place and sleeping her favourite thing.

'I need a coffee!' she said aloud, though no one was there to hear her. She would need something if she was going to stay awake until Richard came home. The thought of him returning home made her smile. He'd left the house at seven am – which now seemed an eternity ago – and she'd been alone ever since. She touched her ever-expanding tummy. Only one more trimester to endure before their dreams became reality. They didn't know if they were having a son or a daughter. They hadn't wanted to know when asked the question. After several years of trying, nothing mattered apart from happy and healthy. It became their often-repeated mantra – happy and healthy. What more could a parent want or pray for?

Standing slowly, she arched her back somewhat gingerly, grimacing, her hands on her hips as she groaned. The pain in her lower back had not responded to the paracetamol she'd

4

taken earlier. She rolled her head, hearing the cracking in her neck as her body voiced its displeasure. Being six months pregnant wasn't always fun. Moving to the sink, she filled the kettle, peering through the blinds. Not much could be seen beyond the pale light spilling from the dining room and kitchen windows.

It was the dark borders of her garden that got her attention. There was nothing visible beyond the hedges apart from blackness. Nothing moved. The trees and the bushes were quite still as if nothing existed beyond her home. In daylight, the meadows behind the house were a beautiful place to walk, which they often did, sometimes sitting by a bend in a small river with a flask of hot chocolate in the winter – something cooler, often alcoholic in the summer – but in the dark, it was a very different place. Scary. *I wouldn't want to be out there on my own. Not tonight!*

The kitchen clock seemed to mock her. It was as if time had slowed or stopped. She stood on tiptoes, stretching as she reached for two cups. As she touched a cup, she stopped, standing quite still, listening, trying to mentally rewind the sound she had just heard. Trying to make sense of the noise and standing very still, she listened again. Her head hurting with the effort, the fine hairs on her back now stood to attention. She felt cold; she shivered. It was as if the very air had been sucked out of the house. She blamed the hours of solitude. Being alone for most of the day, her only companion being the incessant noise of daytime TV. Maybe it was that. Maybe it was impending motherhood, but something had her way more jumpy than usual. *Probably caffeine withdrawal.*

Turning slowly, she returned to the kitchen window, rationalising that the sound had to have come from outside. The realisation that she was alone in the house troubled her. For a moment she considered opening the door to take a look – so convinced was she that she had heard something – but instead, she turned the kitchen lights off. With the room plunged into darkness, she looked outside again. Seeing nothing, she laughed, sounding a little crazy even to her. *What did you expect?* The question turned the blood in her veins ice-cold. Later, much later, she would wonder if she had sensed, not heard something.

It was the kettle boiling that broke the spell, and she laughed again, but the laugh sounded forced, even to her. Turning the lights back on, she listened, hoping to hear Richard's car pulling into the driveway. With the lights on she felt better and, if she was honest, a little silly. She shook her head and spooned coffee into both mugs, filling one cup with boiling water before throwing the spoon into the sink. Leaning back against the worktops, she breathed the coffee aroma in.

She loved this room. It had been the last room to be done. It had taken them three years to finish the rest of their house – a four-bedroomed, double-garaged, executive house located in Beetley, a small village on the outskirts of Dereham, a bustling market town. The town was big enough to have everything they needed but small enough that they knew where everything was. Norwich, the county's capital, was just forty minutes away on a good day. Richard had wanted them to live in the country, and this was as good as it got. The best of all worlds. The meadows and woodland behind the house had been the deciding factor, and they'd agreed that it would be a wonderful place to raise a family.

They loved the house. It was one of eight, sitting on a big corner plot, with a paddock garden beyond the family gardens. The house had even come with an elaborate summerhouse with a jacuzzi inside. The views from upstairs were quite spectacular; she loved watching the weather roll in over the meadows, the trees blowing in strong winds. The kitchen had been her vision from start to finish: black ceramics, granite, and marble mixed with commercial quality steel appliances. It had the wow she had envisaged, hoped for; she loved the heated ceramic floors, warm beneath her bare feet. Previously, she would have needed socks and slippers to counter the cold tiles.

She laughed again, but this time it was a warm, throaty laugh – a laugh that had men turning, hoping to find that the girl laughing would look as good as she had sounded. Few were disappointed; most were captivated by what they saw, smiling back, their thoughts often transparent. She'd gotten quite good at turning sometimes clumsy advances into friends. Richard hadn't helped, almost enjoying that other men found his wife attractive. She usually loved the apparent lack of a jealous bone, but just occasionally, she wished he might just stake his claim a little more obviously.

Moving into the lounge, she sat on one of the two white leather armchairs, her legs dangling over the side. She was restless, tired, uncomfortable, and bored. She missed him. The TV sat in the corner almost demanding to be switched on. More and more she missed the noise, the hectic clatter that had been part of every day of her old life as a primary school teacher. Richard had sided with the doctors, advising rest after the last scare. To be fair, she hadn't argued her case too strongly – she wanted this baby – so it was the TV that provided the noise, even if much of it was background. She couldn't abide the multitude of daytime game shows.

Smiling, she remembered his utter joy when finding out that *they* were pregnant, a month before she'd turned thirty. She had wrapped the tester in a small box, leaving it for him to find. Richard was an orphan. She had been shocked, thinking orphanages a relic from the past, not part of 21st Century living. She'd wanted everything to be perfect, to be magical. She'd also lost both her parents, the ache hardly lessened by time. They were their own family.

Mother would have loved Richard, as would her dad. He would have approved of the honest, driven, likeable man that he was. Her mother would have signalled her approval of his rugged good looks with a wink and a whispered confirmation, maybe even followed by a slight dig to her ribs. Richard was a tad taller than the required six feet. He was dark and handsome with a shyness that some mistook, to their cost, for something else – something weak – but with a smile that had many a heart fluttering. He was her rock. She loved him to the stars and back and told him that often, to which he would often reply, 'Ditto'.

Coffee finished, she returned to the kitchen, placing the cup in the sink, again checking the view outside her window. For a moment, she considered calling him, but if he was with a client, he wouldn't answer the phone… so she headed upstairs, hoping a shower might help. Pausing at the top of the stairs, she glanced through the open door to the nursery, checking on Richard's progress with the room. The walls were almost finished – sky blue with puffy white clouds, balloons chasing up the walls, and then the outline of a train with carriages behind. *Perfect,* she thought, *just perfect.*

After showering and drying, she stepped over her discarded clothes – a pair of Richard's sweat pants and one of his white tees – her current favourite clothing. She had a wardrobe full of maternity wear – they'd made multiple trips into the city – but nothing felt so good or looked as good as one of his oversized shirts. Sitting on the bed, she checked the clock again, the time now showing as 10.25… *Where is he?* she wondered for the umpteenth time.

***

Richard waved goodbye to his client. He was a nice enough chap, needing additional funding to expand his garage business in the city. He thought it a good risk, so he felt confident that the underwriters would sign it off. Hanging his suit jacket in the back, he climbed into his car – a base-spec silver BMW 320D – removed his tie, and unbuttoned the top few buttons of his shirt. At last able to breathe, he started the car. He thought about calling home but quickly dismissed the idea as he didn't want to risk waking her. These days she needed all the rest she could get.

It had been a long day already, and he was ready for home. He was lucky that he enjoyed his job, working for NatWest bank as a Senior Relationship Manager. He looked after businesses with turnovers in excess of a million, meaning he often escaped the office. Getting out and meeting people, helping them grow their businesses, was the best part of the job. It was a hard, sometimes stressful job, quite different to how the job used to be. Some of the old-timers talked fondly about liquid lunches and Fridays spent on the golf course. Those were the days when bank managers were respected along with doctors, dentists, and solicitors. These days he had little time for his favourite hobby, and his clubs were gathering dust in the garage. He resolved to find time to play sometime soon.

Driving carefully, as always, he made a hands-free call to his favourite takeaway, ordering a beef curry for him, with no mushrooms, and special fried rice, and then a prawn curry for the boss. He'd freeze hers if she was sleeping. He felt hungry; he knew he wouldn't sleep easily without food. He loved his wife and still couldn't believe his luck. She was as beautiful as she was lovely, a slim, olive-skinned brunette with a passion for life, a five feet three inches powerhouse of a woman. He imagined her curled up on the sofa wanting to be up for his return. Sometimes he had to pinch himself to believe how his life had changed, how perfect it had become.

The city was quiet, and he was driving on autopilot, his mind wandering, recalling the day he'd met her, little knowing that the gorgeous girl standing in the queue waiting to be served would become his wife, the mother of his children. One wouldn't be enough. They'd talked about three or more. He'd been standing at his till – one of five cashiers working that day – when she had walked into the banking hall, and he'd felt his heart thump. He'd checked the queue knowing most of them, calculating the time to serve each one, trying to ensure that he would be the one to serve her. Their eyes met a few times, and he had loved her smile from that moment.

At last, she had approached his till; he was captivated. She was even lovelier closeup, with her brown eyes – intelligent, inquisitive eyes – a very pretty face, framed by straight brown hair that had glistened, and her olive skin. He remembered thinking, Spanish or Italian?

Without realising it, he had processed her transaction without an utterance other than the 'Good morning' greeting. He watched as she had turned and left; she had looked as good from the back as she had the front. He had wanted to run down the street to find her, but customers were queuing. He had berated himself for the rest of the day.

During the next few days, he had taken to walking past her house, a slight diversion to his normal route, hoping to see her again. It had been another week before that had happened, when she'd returned to the bank and walked straight up to his till. He'd cashed her cheque, silently thinking about his opening line, when a red-faced chap had pushed in front with a pile of coin bags muttering, 'Terribly sorry, these weigh a ton – you had finished, hadn't you?'

He'd watched as she had turned away and couldn't take his eyes off her as the man continued, 'Sorry, mate, I'm in a hurry – could you?'

He served the interloper without speaking, his mood only improving when a colleague passed him a note. 'It's from that girl you fancy – the fit one. She wanted me to give you her number. You're a lucky bugger'.

He'd blushed while taking the note.

Stopping at a red light, he turned the stereo on, selecting a CD, fingers soon tapping to the familiar beat of his current favourite album: Queen 2. Feeling a little tired, he opened the window, breathing in the cool night air. A blast of sound behind brought him quickly back to reality. He checked his mirror to find a rather tatty Mini behind him. He raised a hand in apology, easing the car forward through a now-green light to be overtaken by the mini, the occupants saluting with the classic one finger. *Good job I can't lipread,* he thought as they mouthed off at him through the rear window.

The next lights were also red. *Beautifully synchronised – not!* The voice in his head sounded exasperated. He stopped a good distance from the mini, choosing to ignore the continued antics in front of him. Then he spotted the traffic sign ahead...

A47 Westbound CLOSED

'Bollocks... you've got to be kidding me.'

He quickly decided that his best route home was to head for Taverham via Oak Street, then cross-country, adding another chunk of time before he got home. 'Halle-fucking-lujah!'

The lights finally turned green, and he chuckled as the Mini leapt forward with tyres screeching. *Oh, to be young... I'm thirty-three, not fifty-three,* he thought and laughed.

He was happy, a few minutes later, to see the Mini staying on the ring road and not turning left into Oak Street. He hit redial, pausing Queen, intending to call the Chinese to ask that they delay his food order when he heard something. The sound caused him to end the call, a cold chill running from his shoulders to the top of his head. Without hesitation, he pulled over, turning the engine off. He sat still and listened. He heard another scream. Whoever it was sounded terrified, female, and young. He restarted the car and slowly moved forward with his head out of the window, listening.

CHAPTER THREE

Aarav watched Lucy walking down the road, his concern heightening as she stepped into the darkness. It wasn't the walk she faced down the gloomy, littered streets but her destination that concerned him – the place she called home. He was a good man... or at least he tried to be. He loved his family. They were everything to him.

Saanvi, his wife of twenty-seven years, was asleep upstairs. She was three years younger than him, and they'd met and married when she had turned twenty-one. Soon they would trade places as she fired up the ovens ready for the day's baking. Their boys were their world. They had two. Muhammad, the eldest, was currently studying engineering at Imperial College London, and Aryan, his youngest, worked in the family's convenience store when he wasn't at college on a business studies course. Usually, he or Aryan would have walked Lucy home, but tonight, his son was enjoying a night off at the cinema with his friends. This evening, she walked home alone.

Lucy was an easy girl to like, with a sunny disposition – amazing considering her home life. She was difficult to age. He thought she looked eighteen or nineteen, but his wife thought otherwise. She thought she was probably a few years younger; her guess would have put her at fourteen maybe fifteen. Lucy was a very pretty girl with long, blonde hair, but sadly, she was a little slow to be polite – one step behind the world around her was how his wife had described her. He thought his wife might be right, but he had an inkling she was hiding from the world, watching but not participating. He had called social services more than once, but nothing had changed. After a while, they had stopped returning his calls.

Aarav knew where the problem lay. He had served the mother many times until one day he had asked her very politely never to return. To this day he blushed at the language that had followed. So now it was Lucy who shopped for the mother – if you could call cheap booze, fags, coffee, and milk shopping. He had refused to serve her the first time, but she had returned a few minutes later with a cut lip and her mother's ID, so he had reluctantly relented.

He remembered the first time he had walked the girl home to the steps of her house. The street had once been a good street, terraced houses filled with working people. Her house was the only one with a light on, and he had climbed the steps about to knock on the door when it was opened by the mother, Liz Andrews, looking twenty years older than her claimed thirty-something. A street whore, an addict, her face was a roadmap of her life, almost skeletal. He could recall every word exchanged.

'Good evening, Mrs Andrews.'

'What the fuck are you doing here?' she'd demanded, almost shouting the question.

'I thought it best to walk Lucy home. You can't be too safe…'

'Well, you can fuck right off, you self-righteous Paki bastard!'

Aarav had recoiled, taking a step back. He was used to gutter language, but still, it shocked him to the core – the tone, the hatred spat out with every syllable, even more than the choice of words. He watched as she roughly grabbed Lucy, shouting, 'Where's my fucking fags!' before slamming the door in his face, but not before he had glimpsed the hell that lay behind the door… and the slap delivered as they walked away. The very next day, he had called social services for the first time.

Had he had continued watching the road outside his shop, he might have noticed a car slowing, then stopping before turning into the road that Lucy was walking down.

***

James was a little pissed, but that hadn't stopped him from getting into his car, his beloved Porsche, a 997 GT2 RS – a complete beast of a car that had recently been wrapped in a matt black. It had been a graduation gift from the old man, and it was one of the few gifts he'd kept. 620hp delivered through the rear wheels, it was affectionately referred to as a *widow-maker* – not that he intended getting hitched anytime soon. He was having way too much fun enjoying the disappointment on the old bastard's face; almost as much as the why, the whoring, the drinking, and the occasional drug use. He liked to think he wasn't a user, an addict, but most weeks he'd enjoy a smoke, sometimes something a little stronger. However, he drew the line at a bit of social coke – if offered. He'd started smoking the odd joint whilst at Northampton Uni' five years previously. It was nothing short of a miracle that he had graduated, albeit with third-class honours in media studies; his mates had often said he'd have got a first in pulling birds.

'Whoa hang about.' His whiskey-dulled brain sparked into life. *My God she's* – beautiful! He watched the girl cross the road in front of him, the long legs, the bare belly, the flowing hair. He wasn't to know the clothes were hand-me-downs from the mother. The short denim skirt, the cropped T-shirt. He was quite happy to pay for the privilege if needed – he had done so a few times, although admittedly never ever from the street. He didn't give a toss if his shags were enthusiastic amateurs or professionals, married or single. She was mesmerising, truly glorious against the greyness that surrounded her. He wanted her number, he wanted to sit opposite her, he wanted to anticipate kissing her, touching her, and if she was up for it…

14

for a moment his breath caught, as he watched her walking away from him into the darkness.

***

Lucy had meant to go straight home – she had promised that she would. She had learnt the hard way that an unhappy mum was to be avoided at all costs. An unhappy mum would shout at her, maybe even smack her across the back of the head. Luckily, she'd become quite adept at dodging the odd blow.

It wasn't always her fault; Aarav and his son liked to chat, sometimes giving her a chocolate bar. She could feel the bar in her pocket – she was saving it for bedtime, not knowing if they were eating tonight. They didn't eat every night. Sometimes she came home with a bag of fish and chips, sometimes just the chips. Those were good days, when she came home happy, but not every day was a good day. Some days were just bad. She shivered as a gust of wind blew, not hearing the car pull alongside her or hearing the driver saying, 'Hi,' as she stepped off the path, taking her usual shortcut across a patch of wasteland.

***

James followed, his lights illuminating the rough ground ahead. Pulling to a stop, he exited the car in one fluid movement, walking towards her as he again took in the long legs and short skirt – a skirt hinting at what lay beneath the stretched fabric. As she turned to face him, he noticed the flat belly, the full breasts. The girl was just stunning. If she was a pro, he'd pay her well. If she wasn't, he wanted her number. He called to her, 'Slow down, lovely, I only want to talk...' He patted his pocket, checking his wallet was there, an old habit he couldn't break.

***

Lucy could hear him behind her. She panicked and tripped. Pain shooting through her knees and palms, she screamed. She turned to face him, struggling to see past the lights that blinded her, watching as he approached her. Her world had known many unpleasant men – some had stayed an hour, some all night, and a few had even stayed a week or more. She knew he wanted more than the usual look or a touch. He wanted her. It was something she had experienced many times before. Many a night she had gone to her room, barricading herself in, sitting on the floor with her back to the door, waiting to hear the front door open and close. Even then she would continue to sit in silence, waiting sometimes an hour or more just to be sure that her mum's *friend* had actually left.

Scrambling to her feet, she cut her hands on something sharp as she walked backwards. She felt a wire fence sharp against her back. The word *RUN* was repeating in her head, but her legs refused to respond to the urge. The wire was now cutting into her back. She tried to leap past him but tripped again, pain once more shooting through her body.

Suddenly, he had her, she screamed as he reached for her – the sound banging off the walls, a piercing almost animalistic sound that would have you checking that your doors were locked before any thoughts of calling the police.

***

James was panicking, checking the windows of the surrounding houses, trying to keep a hold on her, wishing he was driving home, wishing he was anywhere but where he was. *This is a fucking nightmare.* He had to get her to understand that he was trying to help, but she was kicking and slapping him, her heel jabbing into his shin. The pain was instantaneous, and he let her go. He watched as she crawled away from him, still screaming. He went after her. He had to explain to her that he wasn't trying to hurt her. Somehow, he had to make this right. He tried talking to her in a calm voice, but still she screamed. He tried to get her to her feet as she continued to shout, kick, and punch, and still she screamed. A thought tugged at his consciousness. A thought that made sense of everything, but it disappeared with each scream, each punch and each kick.

Richard had occasionally wondered how he would react if faced with something like this. He had always hoped he would do something, that he wouldn't be one of those people who just walked on by, head down, pretending not to notice. He hoped, believed, that he would make a difference, that he would do the right thing. Pulling over to the curb, he listened, pretty sure the sound had come from his right. He drove slowly, approaching a turning on the right. He slowed and peered down the road.

The road appeared to be deserted, except for a car parked halfway along. He could see no one peering out from behind a curtain, no lights coming on, so… it was down to him. He heard another scream, this time getting a decent fix as to where it was coming from. He drove towards the sound, windows still down, listening as he drove, approaching an area of waste ground that he hadn't known existed. He pulled to a stop behind a parked Porsche. *Nice car,* he thought as he noticed the doors were open, and the engine was running, with huge plumes of exhaust smoke spiralling into the darkness. The driver had also left the lights on.

In the corner, he could see two people illuminated by the Porsche's lights – a man and a girl. The girl was struggling to get away, being held by the bloke. He leapt out of his car without thought to his own safety and ran towards them shouting, unintelligibly, almost primevally as he approached.

***

James watched as the girl's eyes glazed over before she fell slowly to the ground. He turned, hearing the commotion behind him as if a Viking rabble were charging him. On seeing it was just one man, he bent his knees, his feet seeking purchase as he leant into the charge, his assailant bouncing off him, over him. He turned to see him hit the ground hard. He looked for a suitable weapon but couldn't find anything. His attacker lay on the floor, groaning. He watched as the man tried to kneel, then swung his right foot at his head as hard as he could, watching the man's neck snap back, blood spraying into the night air. The girl now sat on the cold ground, her arms around her knees, whimpering. He was breathing in great gulps of cold air, and his body ached. *What the fuck have I done?* he thought. Standing over them, bent double, hands on his knees, he was trying to think of a way out. He could just bugger off but that would be stupid – too many cameras, too much DNA. He realised he was screwed, he understood how this looked, he was caught between a rock and a very hard place.

CHAPTER FOUR

Liz stared at the clock, watching the second hand seemingly pausing every goddamn second. She felt sick, her head fuzzy, her stomach clenched. She hadn't eaten. She hadn't drunk a thing since getting in shortly after 10pm. It had been a crap night; she'd taken a lousy £20 – her payment for a blow job with extras; he'd wanted to touch her tits. It was getting harder to make the money she once had; it was the younger girls raking in the cash. She could feel sweat break out on her forehead, on her back. One moment shivering with cold, the next hot as hell; *I need a goddamn drink, and I need it now.*

Standing slowly, every movement hurting, she grabbed the chipped edges of the battered Formica table to steady herself. The table, like most of the stuff in their house, had been scavenged from the shop at the local dump. The good stuff had been sold years before; she'd pawned the good stuff within days of being dumped by her old man. They had shared some happy times, not many, but the bad memories weren't allowed to intrude very often. When they did, however, they hurt more each time.

Once she had been beautiful. She caught her reflection in a cracked mirror, and her reality returned in a heartbeat – bleached hair needing a cut, a face devoid of makeup. Pushing off from the table, she headed for the front door. The phone rang, and she picked it up, cursed, and then listened. She knew it would be a punter, no one else called her.

'No, I'm not working! Yeah – well fuck you, too!'

Opening the door, she felt the cold air rushing in. She stood in the open doorway pulling her cardi tight – scant protection against the cold. She peered down the street. 'Where the hell are you?' she muttered, thinking, *I'll kill the little bitch when I get my hands on her.*

Hearing shouting down the road, she looked to her left. *Bloody kids.* A group of them often hung around the kids' park down the road. They would hurl abuse at her as she walked to work. *Work...* She laughed hard, wiping bubbling snot away with her sleeve.

A scream could be heard in the distance, and it sounded like a young girl.

Lucy?

Pulling her sweater tighter, she swung the door shut behind her and went to investigate, tripping over the pavement edge. White-hot pain flooded her senses, and she pulled herself to her feet, using the rusting gate to drag herself upright. A curtain twitched – one of her few neighbours – and she smiled and raised a finger in salute. *Nosey bitch.* The curtain stopped moving.

With the aid of garden walls and fences, she made her way – albeit, very slowly – to the waste ground. It hadn't always been abandoned, but the houses that had stood there had been demolished long ago. The promised street improvements hadn't happened – no doubt forgotten, part of a cut-back. She stumbled across the road, not needing to check for cars – few people drove this dead-end street. Even her regulars parked a few streets over. Finally making it to the other side, she stopped, her breathing laboured, and she watched a man wrestling with a girl, then watched as he slapped her. She'd been slapped a few times – more than a few – but to see it was different. Realising it was her Lucy, she ran across the waste ground, tripping over Richard's unseen body.

Swearing loudly, she raised herself into a kneeling position, breathing hard, sweating… Her skin was clammy, her knees on fire. She'd landed on stones, the pain intense. She crawled towards Lucy who was now curled up in a ball, her arms around her chest, sobbing uncontrollably.

***

James watched in complete disbelief as the woman raised the bottle to her mouth, gulping the contents down. For a moment nothing made sense. He felt like he'd stepped into somebody's horror story, an alternative universe, but then he heard the girl sobbing, repeating the one word: Mum. The sound was pitiful, but at least it made sense of the scene in front of him. He knew, instinctively, that he had just two options. The first was to run, to get away from this madness as fast as he could, but the second option appealed more… made more sense. Running would just buy time – and not much of it. Running wouldn't save him.

Getting to his feet, he returned to his car, wincing in pain as he lowered himself into the driver's seat. He reversed and parked behind the BMW. He sat motionless, unthinking, unable to process, staring at the scene before him. Then pulling himself together, he got out of his car, leaving the engine running and the lights on. Next, he pulled a handkerchief from his pocket. Wrapping it around his hand, he went to the BMW, moving it forward and then turning the engine and lights off. Returning to his car, he moved it up against the BMW. He exited his car, again leaving the engine running and the lights on, then he pulled his phone out and dialled 999 as he walked towards the mother who was now unsteadily making her way towards him.

***

Liz approached the man slowly, the bottle clenched in her right hand ready to strike if needed; she was scared but also emboldened, helped by the alcohol coursing through her. Confused, she'd watched as he moved the cars, the penny slowly dropping, finally understanding why – she hoped that the night might yet have a happy ending – a couple of hundred pounds would do very nicely. Payment for her troubles. She wouldn't make a fuss if she was looked after.

Standing a couple of feet away, she smelt the booze on him but also aftershave – the good stuff. She noticed his clothes, dressed in black from head to foot – also expensive stuff, not the crap sold in the supermarkets. He was a good-looking boy! Smiling, her price was rising, completely unaware that he was at the same time *reducing* his offer. He raised a finger to his lips, 'Shhh – police.'

She stepped back, the very thought of the police enough for her to want to leave this place, to go home. They were no friends of hers.

'My name? Sure. James Taylor. My father's Reggie Taylor.'

She stopped, standing quite still, listening. She knew the name. Everyone knew that name, knew the old man – he'd once been something of a local legend. In truth he still was.

'Yep, Sir Reggie Taylor. That's the old man.'

Once upon a time, they'd had some history. It hadn't lasted long, but they had shared a few shags in his car, once in a bed in a cheap hotel down by the river. That image, her as a young girl stepping out, was enough to cause a tear to trail her cheek. Suddenly, she felt dirty, unwashed. She just wanted gone. She wanted to get home. She had a bottle to finish, and tonight she would need all of it to block the pain – the old and the new.

***

The call finished, and he smiled. The story was planted; he was the bloody hero – for once. He looked the woman over, then pulled her close, grabbing her by the arm, grinning as he spoke, his voice barely a whisper. 'This isn't what you think it is. If you're a good girl, I'll look after you.' His grip tightened, causing her to cry out. 'If you're not a good girl, I'll hunt you

22

down. You really don't want to upset me, do you?' She shook her head. 'Now, go look after your daughter, and do yourself a favour, help her get her story straight.'

'Ok…' She started to back away but stopped. 'What's the story?' she asked, her voice dropping.

'You really are a stupid bitch, aren't you?' He stepped towards her; his voice still quiet but menacing. 'I'm the knight in shining armour. That poor bastard' – he indicated the still-prone figure on the ground – 'was trying to rape your daughter. I saved her. Got it?'

'Ow, that hurts!' His fingers were once again digging into her, causing pain to surge through her arm. 'Please, stop. Please… I know what to say. By the time I've finished with her she'll think you're Clark fucking Kent.'

'Good… and remember to be a good girl. I wouldn't want to be you if you aren't…' The threat hung in the air, and he watched her stumbling return to her daughter. He had to bite back a laugh, thinking, *I sound like a right cliché. Pull yourself together for Christ's sake!*

CHAPTER FIVE

Reggie awoke with a start, pulled from a dream that had had him smiling. Sadly, however, the images were already fast disappearing. Sitting up slowly, he kicked the covers off, thinking how sometimes his dreams were infinitely better than his reality. The phone was vibrating across his cabinet, the noise not improving his mood; he was tempted to pick it up and chuck it through the open window. He liked to sleep with a window open so he could listen to the wind howling around the eves. He also liked to sleep through to breakfast – sadly these days, good sleep was hard to come by.

Reaching for the phone, he knew it would either be his sorry excuse for a son or maybe worse, someone calling about his son. They were the calls that cost a lot. The clock beside his bed showed ten twenty-seven pm, and he laughed. *Bloody hell, I'm getting old. Not so long ago I'd have been leaving the house to go and party.* Now, aged seventy-eight, he was often in bed before eleven – sometimes even earlier. Like tonight.

'Frank… FRANK!' he shouted from his doorway as he listened to his son. Soon hearing his old friend run up the stairs he motioned for him to enter. Frank entered the room still dressed. They were the same age, but Frank was not one for an early night – he had discovered a love of cooking, especially baking, late in life, and he would often be found in the kitchen late at night, baking for the following day. Once upon a time he would have opened a bottle of scotch and sat in the large kitchen, keeping him company, chatting about the bad old days, drinking too much, and pinching a hot sausage roll or scone as they came out of the oven. They had shared many such a night.

Maybe he should join him in the kitchen again. They made for an odd couple. Reggie was still the wiry, slightly built man of his youth, whilst Frank was the big man – the man you really didn't want to fall out with.

Frank was mouthing, 'Do you need the car, boss?' He nodded, watching him leave, and then he turned his attention back to James. 'Say nothing until I get there. You hear me? Nothing. Not one bloody word, do you hear me!'

It took no time to dress, and soon he was sitting in the back of the Jag – a lovely Mk II in pristine condition. It was one of three Jags in his collection. *Old habits are hard to break,* he thought, *for me and for Frank. So many journeys together.*

Frank sat upfront, he in the back, and he settled back into his seat with a sigh as they sped down the long drive, the gravel bouncing off the undercarriage. He didn't need trips like this, being dragged out of his bed in the middle of the night, he just wanted to stay home. He loved the house. They'd bought it together, him and his Nancy. She had loved the area, telling him it was very posh and near the sea – her favourite place. She had been so excited, but, in truth, she had been slightly horrified at the thought of thirteen bedrooms, a separate coach house, and the thirty-odd acres until he had convinced her that they could afford cleaners and gardeners – lots of them.

'Staff?' she'd whispered. He had known that one word conveyed a new life for them both. They'd walked, hand in hand, through the parkland, through the trees late into the day, the sun beginning to dip when she had stopped, taking both his hand in hers, raising her face to look him in the eye as if searching his soul, reading his mind, whispering, 'Let's do it.'

Their time together had been way too short, but he still loved coming home and turning into the gates, the drive nearly a mile long, with the house sitting proudly at the end of it.

His mood improved as they neared the city. He loved this city, really loved it, but it was the football club that he loved the most. He was a shareholder with a seat at the table, his badge of respectability hard-won, never to be given up.

The fans didn't care about his past; instead, almost reverently loving the man that he had once been – the hard man, the youth standing in the snake pit and baying for blood, hoping for a rumble outside the ground, especially when the London teams visited. His mates, his gang, always at his side, having his back, the same lads that would still be at his side running the drugs, the whores, and the clubs.

They'd been heady days; he'd built an empire that had operated in three counties. It had been a juggling act, early doors, staying one step ahead of the boys in blue, but ultimately that had been relatively easy, and the fortune amassed was big enough to last three lifetimes. The hard part had been being a dad! Losing his beloved wife, Nancy, to cancer shortly after the lad had turned five had just about destroyed him. The years that had followed had been hard to live.

The boy had become a stranger, looked after by a succession of nannies. They were always good-looking girls – leggy, big-boobed blondes – not one had been over thirty. He'd even bedded a few. A couple of them had hoped to become something more than an old man's comfort on a cold night, only to find their contracts terminated shortly after. It must have been hard on the boy. It had been hard on them all. In truth, he knew Frank had been more of a father than he had. They'd had a chance to reconnect when he had returned from university, but he had preferred the company of his mates. Sometimes he thought it was the glamour surrounding football that had first turned the lad's head, mixing with the players as an equal of sorts – equal spending power and equal appetites, living in their reflected glory.

Glancing out of the window, he was surprised to see they were already nearing the outskirts of the city. He picked up his phone, finding *John H* in his contacts. John wasn't going to be happy, but something told him that tonight he might need the extra insurance of having the DCI on hand. Dick had recently been promoted to Detective Chief Inspector, and Reggie had sent him a congratulatory note inviting him to join him in the director's box as his guest for the game against the old rivals Ipswich – just to remind him that whilst he might have retired, that hadn't changed anything. He'd got enough on Mr Head to last a lifetime of favours.

***

It was John's wife who woke him, with a short, sharp dig to the ribs. She was used to her sleep being ruined – part of the price for marrying an ambitious copper. She didn't feel the need for gentle, not tonight. Tonight, had been a major disappointment. Dick – she wouldn't call him that to his face, but if she was in a bad mood, she was quite happy to think it – had forgotten, not for the first time, that today was, should have been, a special day. Not the big special day – not the wedding anniversary – but the day they had met. Her first day on the job. He was a rising star, and she was a rookie. He had smiled shyly as they spotted each other across the canteen, and they'd married within ten months.

Clinging to sleep as best she could, she listened long enough to have confirmed, please God, that it wasn't one of the kids. She tapped his back to hear a whispered, 'It's work, go back to sleep.'

She rolled over, taking the covers with her and smiling.

***

John stood, shivering as he grabbed his clothes that lay neatly folded on a chair near the bed. He headed for the *en suite*, still listening, not saying much, every second regretting ever meeting the man. Sir Reggie fucking Taylor had one hand on his balls and didn't hesitate to squeeze when needed. He knew he owed him much of his life, his job, his house, the love of his family even, but a lifetime's debt over a moment of madness was…

'Where are you going?' Her voice was husky, a barely awake voice.

'Sorry, I thought you'd be asleep by now?'

'I'm trying.'

'An old... friend needs a hand.'

'Who?'

'Reggie Taylor.'

'Sir Reggie Taylor?' She rolled onto her back, plumping the pillows behind her, her interest obviously aroused. 'What does he need from you?'

'Apparently, it turns out his son has beaten the crap out of someone.'

'That's a surprise... not!' She snorted.

'Well, apparently, he's the hero tonight. Rescued a damsel in distress.'

'So why does he need you?' she asked, her voice laden with suspicion.

That's a very good question. There's a bigger story here for sure.

Reggie Taylor didn't call in a favour for nothing. Half the coppers in Norwich knew the son, knew he was a bit of a handful, so why was tonight the night that Reggie called him? There was more to this, and he wanted to find out what. The truth might finally discharge the debt – at least, he hoped so!

Once in the car, he called the office but hung up before the connection was made, thinking a surprise visit might be a good idea. The younger lads were probably fawning over the old bastard, only knowing the modern truths, the recent history: the football fan, the committee member, and the charities he supported. The older lads knew different. They knew something about the man who had ruled the underbelly of their city, their county, back when the world was black and white. It was frustrating that most of them still talked about the man affectionately, almost reverently.

Reggie had bought his way to respectability, donating some

huge sums to various local good causes, focusing on the very young and the very old. Every charitable act featured in the local press. It was rumoured that he had bought the knighthood with substantial sums paid to the Tories. It wouldn't surprise him if that were true.

***

Frank slowed the car as they approached the wasteland, the streets filled with blue strobing lights. Two police cars parked across the entrance, with an ambulance on the road, its back doors open. Reggie watched a few onlookers being shooed away by one of the cops. He exited the car to be told by the same cop, 'There's nothing for you to see, sir, move on.' Reggie walked towards the gap between the two cars. 'I said...'

'I heard you.'

'Who the... do you think you are?' The missing word hadn't needed vocalising.

'I'm Reggie Taylor.' The acknowledging gasp was audible.

'What can I do for you, sir? asked an older copper before turning to his colleague. 'I'll take this.'

'I've come to talk to my son. I understand that he saved a young girl from a beating?'

'Yes, sir. Of course, sir.'

Passing the cars, he saw paramedics kneeling by a body on the ground, his son talking to a copper, and another was talking to a young girl sat on the ground. Then he saw a woman standing to one side – no doubt the mother his son had referred to as *our star witness*. He watched as she approached him, watching the hope drain step by step as she neared him.

'Are you?'

'Yes, I am. I'm Reggie Taylor.'

She recoiled, taking a step back. 'Reggie…' She grimaced as he took her by the arm, his hand tight.

'Ow, that hurts!'

He helped walk her a few feet away, so they couldn't be overheard.

'Listen to me very carefully. My son tells me that you understand what happened here tonight?'

'Yes,' she whispered, but the nodding head confirmed her acceptance.

'Don't disappoint me. I can be a good friend or the scariest man you've ever met.'

'I know, I know, believe me, I know. I won't… I won't disappoint you. You probably don't remember me…' Her voice trailed away, accepting that she meant nothing to him.

'What about the girl?'

'What about her?'

'Will she be a good girl?' His tone was menacing, implying a world of pain if not.

'You don't need to worry about her, Reggie. She'll do what she's told; she's a flipping brick short that one, if you know…'

Reggie squeezed harder, lowering his voice again to barely a whisper. 'I don't need your fucking life story. Now, be a good girl and go sit with your daughter. I need to talk to my son.'

Beckoning his son over, he decided tonight would be the last time he helped him out. Once this had been put to bed, he'd send him away – somewhere to sort himself out – but then he'd walk, no more money, no more anything. He knew what could have happened here tonight had he not been stopped. His son was out of control. It was time to cut him loose.

CHAPTER SIX

Mickey's shift should have finished hours ago, but instead, he was sitting outside on his favourite step, cigarette in hand, plumes of white-blue smoke spiralling towards the lights. It was hard to hide on the job as everyone knew where he would be; that he liked a smoke, especially if on a late shift. He liked the nights out in the cold with a cup of strong coffee and a cigarette.

It hadn't always been so. A few years back he had a wife – a nice wife, a pregnant wife – and a nice little two-up-two-down, on a nice little city street. Life had been… well, nice. Given the choice, he would have chosen wife and home, but it had turned out that it was she who had the choice, not him, and she had chosen a new life with a new man. The new man, apparently, had a better job, dressed better, and actually wanted to spend time with her. She hadn't said he was better in the sack, but that was what he had heard in his head as she'd listed his many shortcomings.

Since then, he'd lost just about everything else except the job. His biggest weakness – that he would admit to – was that he liked a little punt, online or, rare as it might be these days, at the track. Dogs were his favourite and preferable to the gee-gees. The dogs were honest… beaten-up tracks, ordinary punters, and no need for the fancy stuff. The wins provided momentary relief, the losses left him feeling dirty, unworthy, and often broke.

Earlier he'd taken a call from the boss – apparently, he was happy to find his favourite DI at his desk. He knew that was bollocks. He was no one's favourite anything, and that didn't trouble him in the slightest. He liked what he liked. He did an okay job, and he'd stopped worrying about the stuff he couldn't control a long time ago. His wife had just about beaten the good stuff out of him.

He'd agreed to take the case, couched as needing his *gentle* touch with the old man. He could guess why. Dick didn't leave his bed except for a very good reason. He loved the attention of a story, but Mickey thought there was more to it. There had been rumours about the boss and Sir Reggie Taylor – tales from the old days. He'd bet decent money that the old man had something on him, something good. He'd love to know what.

He lit another smoke from the first. He was in no hurry to return to the interview room. To be honest, he was ready to shake the lad's hand and send him home. He was a hero for saving the girl. Sadly, his sometimes partner, Jo, a DC, aged twenty-five going on forty-something, thought otherwise. Something troubled her gut.

Usually, he liked her gut. He liked the rest of her too. If she wasn't at work, she was in the gym, and it showed. She was the subject of much locker-room banter, but everyone that knew her respected her. She was one of the good guys – a little intense on occasions but trusted. When push came to shove, he'd take Jo over most of the guys he'd worked with.

They made an odd couple. He was the short, fat white bloke, she the beautiful black *poster* girl, the rising star of the force. He ate too much, drank too much, and would admit to having no ambition beyond his pension. She was pretty much his opposite. Everything a cop should be. When promoted to detective constable, her picture had been shared throughout social media. He knew why he enjoyed her company. The question was why did she enjoy his?

It had been obvious that she had been trying to push buttons throughout the interview. It was equally obvious she didn't like either of them. He thought, given the chance, she would love to punch the young Taylor in the mouth, not caring for his arrogance or more probably the way he had looked at her throughout the interview. His eyes had struggled to focus on anything other than her breasts. To be fair, he felt for James. He worked with her a lot, and she could make a black business suit with white blouse look sensational.

Finally finishing the cigarette, he threw the butt away and returned inside, walking past the interview room that he had shown the girl and her mother into once she had been released by the medic and deemed fit to be interviewed. He resolved to wrap these up ASAP. He was ready for an early breakfast with or without *Miss America* – his unvoiced pet name for Jo.

He knocked on the door, opening it as he knocked, beckoning Jo to step out. 'The girl's arrived with her mother,' he announced.

'How are they?'

'The girl… very quiet. The mother not so. Think we've got enough from these two. Send them home.'

'But…'

Dropping his voice to a whisper, he said, 'Jo, just send them home. I've had a call from his highness. We are not to piss off the estimable Reggie Taylor. Apparently, they go back-aways, and we have all we need for now. SOCO seen the lad?'

'Yep.' Her tone remained sullen; her unhappiness was obvious.

'Good. Send them packing, grab a coffee, then come get me.'

'Another smoke?'

'Just a coffee. I'll need that before I sit opposite the old bat next door.'

'That bad?' She laughed as she stepped back into the room, the laugh disappearing as the door closed.

Liz and Lucy were sitting at a table, two empty seats opposite, and the silence was uncomfortable. They'd exchanged words on the way, but Liz had done most of the talking, Lucy listening and nodding her head, as usual, eyes down, mumbling her agreement. All she wanted was to go home, to go to bed and forget everything that had happened… and to wake up to start a new day.

Lucy had been seen by a nurse – a nice lady who had asked lots of questions. Then she had suffered in silence as her cuts were cleaned and treated. Ignoring the 'this may hurt just a little', she had wanted to reply that she could cope with just a little.

It's the slaps at home that hurt – the slaps delivered by my mother!

Looking at her mother, she knew there would be hell to pay once home. She knew her mother's moods, and this wasn't going to have a happy ending. She looked like she needed a drink.

Finally, the door opened, and she listened as they introduced themselves. She was aware of the change in tone from her mother – almost respectful. That surprised her as at home the 'bizzies' were a subject of ridicule or worse. She tried to follow the conversation, the questions, so many questions, and her head hurt as she tried to remember to include the bits her mum had told her to say. Some of it didn't make much sense, but she guessed that they would understand it better than she – they were the adults – so she nodded when needed, and when that wasn't enough, she uttered a barely audible yes or no. Everyone seemed happy with the answers except Jo. She had a feeling that Jo wasn't very happy, but she couldn't worry about her. She had to keep a smile on her mum's face – nothing else mattered.

She wanted to tell them that she hadn't seen much, that it had been dark, that the car lights had blinded her, that she had tried to get away, that she'd tried to hide… that they shouldn't

35

worry about her, she was good at hiding things, forgetting things – she'd had lots of practice – but she stuck to her mother's story using her mother's words as she'd been instructed!

She just wanted to go home.

***

Jackie wasn't the best of early morning risers. She lay on the bed star-fishing, her first thought being: *what time is it?* She listened again.

Not the alarm clock.

She rolled over.

Not the phone.

The ringing continued.

Sleep was hard to shake, nothing made sense, and the ringing wouldn't stop … then the penny dropped.

The front door!

She swung her legs out, standing, then she grabbed her robe, thinking, *you'll pay for this, husband.* She was going to pull his leg for days! She ran down the stairs, pulling her robe on, just happy that he was home.

She couldn't remember fainting, couldn't remember being helped into the kitchen where she now sat, feeling a tad foolish and a little lightheaded. She was worried that she might have to run to the toilet or the sink. She felt nauseous. A cuppa sat on the table in front of her made by the older of the two policemen who were with her in the kitchen. He sat opposite, and the other – the younger one – leaned against the sink. Both watched her. She tried to recall their names, tried to recall what had been said, but she only remembered the word hospital. Richard was in hospital. Just the thought of him in there was enough to break her heart. She realised she was probably in shock.

'Is he going to be okay?'

'I'm afraid that's all we know, ma'am.'

'Can I go to see him?' she asked the older cop.

'Do you have anyone that could accompany you?'

'No, not really… Why do you ask?'

'Well' – she watched as they exchanged a look – 'just thinking that in view of your um…' He looked at her belly.

'Oh, I see… Sure, but nope. I'll get a taxi.'

'We could drop you off.' It was obvious that he regretted offering as soon as the words left his mouth.

'Would you?' Her voice sounded pathetic. Pleading. 'That would be lovely of you. I'll just go and change. Thank you!'

As she climbed the stairs, she began to cry, grabbing hold of the rail to stop herself from sliding to the ground. She felt weak, scared, and vulnerable, her world spinning out of control, but she knew she had to pull herself together for Richard and for the bump.

She touched the bump, drawing some strength from the touch, and started to climb again, praying to a long-forgotten God as she did so.

Dressing quickly – pulling on the sweat pants and T-shirt that she had discarded earlier – she returned to the kitchen, stopping at the bottom of the stairs to listen to the two men having a whispered argument. One of them was not happy about being a *flipping* taxi! That was the younger cop, but she couldn't worry about his feelings. Richard needed her, and she needed to see him ASAP. She needed to see him with her own eyes.

***

James sat in the back of the Jag, his dad riding upfront with Frankie; the Porsche had been collected by Jack, one of his best

37

mates. He loved that Jack had not asked why. Jack was probably taking the long way home – he wouldn't blame him.

He liked Frank; he actually preferred his company to the old man's. Sadly, he'd spent more time with Frank over the years – especially the last few years. He hadn't wanted to ride home with them, but the old man had insisted, and James knew that tone: further argument would be wasted. Any words exchanged would come back to haunt him. The old man's final words were to be obeyed without question.

One day he might have the balls to go his own way. A final 'fuck you Dad'. However, that day was not now. He needed the family name, the family money, but one day… one day he would start again. He had known for some time that he needed to live another life, a different life. This one would kill him, maybe not quickly, but it would kill him, nonetheless. One day.

Closing his eyes, he thought back over the night, the alcoholic fuzziness easing slightly. It was amazing what a visit to the nick did for recovery. Being interviewed by the cops had been a shock to the system. Once home he'd need a little something – if he could lose the old man.

He needed a little alone time. He needed a smoke to take the edge off if he was to find any sleep tonight. He often climbed to the rooftop to sit with a bottle, having a little toke, his favourite spot, sitting under the stars with the pigeons. The best part of the night so far had been sitting opposite Jo. He'd decided early on that he would quite like a bit of Jo.

***

The hospital was a massive shock to Jackie's senses, with the corridors of harsh fluorescent lights, seemingly unending, people everywhere, staff in a hurry, and visitors looking lost, sometimes their own pain obvious. And the noise...

It was obvious that her escorts wished to leave. She wished she had the strength to send them on their way, but until she found Richard, she needed them. Well, one of them. The other could go anytime he wanted.

Finally stopping at a lift, they waited, having summoned it from the second floor needing the third. It seemed to take an eternity. No one spoke, but finally, the doors opened with a ping and a shudder. The empty box behind the doors was not at all welcoming. All three stepped into the lift, the sudden upward lurch adding to the fear growing in her gut. The lift paused, the doors taking a few moments to open as if unsure about letting them out. She knew she was being paranoid, fearing the worst. He was probably sat-up in bed waiting for her, enjoying a cup of tea, flirting with a nurse.

They approached the nurse's station, and she watched as the younger cop strode over to talk to a colleague standing outside someone's room. They talked, heads almost touching, both turning to look in their direction, at her, and she realised… Richard was probably in that room. She started to walk towards them when the older cop gently but firmly took her by the arm.

'Not yet… We need to wait for a doc.'

'But…'

'They won't be long. We'll just get you sat down with a cuppa, and then we'll be off, but the staff here will look after you.'

'OK, thank you… I am so grateful for everything.'

'That's okay, love… just wish we could do more.'

She allowed herself to be escorted to a waiting room, square-foamed, vinyl-covered chairs and a wall-mounted TV playing the news without sound. Thankfully, the room was empty. She doubted she could have sat amongst others. As it was, she was tearing up. She couldn't look at her escorts as they bid her a hurried 'good luck'. She looked around the room again, feeling alone, abandoned, hollow and lost.

The wait seemed to take forever; she'd lost track of time, but it was still pretty dark outside. Finally, she heard footsteps. Feet clad in battered brown brogues, beige chinos, and an oxford blue shirt. *Is this the uniform of hospital doctors around the world?* she thought. She found a friendly face, not unattractive but lined, the stress of the day, the 12-hour shift showing. She had read somewhere about the stupidly long shifts being worked by the surgical staff. He crouched so they faced each other, and she watched him, wondering what was about to be said. What would be the impact on her world?

***

John put his coffee down on Mickey's desk, which was, as always, covered in clutter. Jo's was the neat and tidy neighbour. Pulling open a drawer, he found the bottle… Mickey was such a throwback. He added a slug to his coffee, sipping at the scalding contents, knowing that either or both of them would be arriving soon. As it happened, he didn't have to wait long. He read the body language as they walked towards him. Mickey was happy, Jo was not.

'Hi, boss.'

'How goes it, Mickey?'

'Simple enough…'

'Not really, gov,' Jo interjected. 'I'm not happy. The guy in hospital is a fricking bank manager without a note.' She ploughed on, ignoring the pleading look from Mickey. 'Whereas James is a…'

'Jo.' John paused. Many had made the mistake of thinking him a tad slow, and many of those were now or had been serving time at Her Majesty's pleasure. 'You know who the old man is don't you: Sir Reggie Taylor. Former commission member. His son is a bit of a tearaway, granted, but we've nothing on him. His evidence is supported by the kid and the mother, right?'

'Yes, sir, I get that, but...'

'You've sent the Taylors home, Mickey?'

'Yes, boss.'

'Good. Right, send the girl home. We can re-interview her tomorrow. Any news on our man?'

'Nope, sir. Still unconscious.'

'I want him watched 24/7 until we can interview him. Got it?' Mickey nodded. 'Good. Now, get home both of you. Get some sleep. It's going to be a busy day tomorrow.'

John returned to his office to stand by his one window that overlooked the city hall. He loved the art deco building built in the thirties, standing proudly above the marketplace. Sipping his coffee, his thoughts turned to Reggie. He had a good idea as to why he'd been called in. He was going to have to sort it out with him. He couldn't – wouldn't – be put in this position again. His debt had to be considered settled. He wouldn't look the other way ever again,

***

Jackie sat by Richard's bed. She had begged the nursing staff to let her see him, and they had finally agreed that she could sit by the bed a short while. The cop by the door hadn't been happy but had relented after she had burst into tears when learning why he was outside the door. The nurses had been lovely. They had, very gently, explained why he was being ventilated, and they had entered the room with her, checking she was okay before leaving.

For the past hour, she had been holding his hand as tears fell down her face, praying silently, offering promises of anything – everything – if only He would let her Richard live. She needed him to open his eyes, to tell her that 'hand on heart, this is a huge mistake'.

This can't be happening! she thought as she recalled the many times she had heard other people uttering the same words – both in real life and on TV. Her old reality seemed a million miles away, and soon a new one would dawn. She knew she would have to be brave – braver than she had ever been – and the thought terrified her. He had been her strength; he had been her everything. She knew he was in trouble, that he was unconscious, but she didn't know why. The unknown haunted her. He was the sweetest, loveliest man she'd ever met, but now he lay handcuffed to the bed, with a cop on the door.

Slowly, she lowered herself to the floor, kneeling, his hand still in hers, her head resting on their hands, and she prayed for a happy ending. Whilst praying, she tried to recall her conversation with the doctor. He had said this could take days, weeks, months maybe… She didn't want to think about years or never. She had to believe that her Richard would wake soon.

***

James was waiting for the old man's sermon. He always delivered a stinging rebuke, a summary of his shortcomings, followed by the usual threats. It was always one-sided, always awkward, as if he had forgotten how to talk as a father to a son. Maybe he never had. Maybe he'd never loved him. Memories of once happy times flooded through, but they were mostly images of him and his mum, just the two of them. Very rarely were there three in the picture.

He was kicking himself. He should have stuck to the plan. A few drinks with the boys, then a rendezvous with his latest FWB, the lovely Sarah Horton. She'd recently married one of the old man's mates – a rather boring little man called Edward Horton. James thought him too desperate by far, chasing social acceptance, once again proving that money couldn't buy you class. The wedding invitation had been a surprise. He was aware that his father used his firm and occasionally played golf with him, but that was it. He'd been invited to the whole wedding but had only turned up for the evening reception – and that was only after playing a rather terse message left by the old man threatening murders if he didn't turn up.

The wedding had been, as expected, overblown, but the bar had been free, so he had indulged. He'd lent against the bar, people-watching, hoping to find one worth shagging. His mood had improved after he'd spotted a very pretty little blonde in a red sequined dress – not that there had been a lot of dress. He'd lingered over the legs; she had great legs, nicely in proportion to the rest of her. Maybe another inch would have been perfect, he remembered thinking. Realising that he'd been spotted, he had smiled, beckoning her over.

He'd counted to eight in his head, maintaining eye contact. He'd smiled again as she had taken the first step towards him. He recalled thinking how fit she was, how fuckable she'd looked. He'd liked the slight nervousness as she had neared him, obviously a little pissed.

'Hi, I'm…'

'I know who you are.'

'You have me at a dis…'

'I'm Sarah: Sarah Woods. I mean Horton. I'm the *bride.*'

'Fuck me… you're the bride?'

'Are you asking?' She had a naughty smile, no doubt fuelled by copious amounts of champagne.

'You've married for money then…'

'You're a very bad boy.'

'Do you dance?'

'Do you want to find out?'

James continued to play the pictures in his head. They had danced until interrupted by the husband. Much later he had taken her by the hand, walking her outside, and she had protested a little. He'd pressed her against a brick wall. They had kissed, hard mouths, hungry to taste, and he had whispered to her throughout… his need – his desire – telling her that she had to picture his face later if the old man could get it up. She'd gasped at that, then again as he had dropped to his knees, the gravel hard and sharp. He had pushed her dress up past her waist, kissing the inside of her thighs, removing her panties – white as befitting a wedding. He'd kissed the stretch marks caused by the new elastic, then stood, whispering, 'I'll keep these. I want to picture you amongst your guests naked beneath this dress.' With that, he had walked away, smiling. She, on the other hand, had cried out.

The abrupt stop caused the pause button to be hit. He shifted in his seat. 'So good to be home,' he said under his breath. He opened the door to see the old man striding into the house without a backwards glance.

CHAPTER SEVEN

Lucy woke, opening her eyes slowly, the early morning September sun filling her room. For a moment she felt happy, safe, refreshed. She stretched, ached, and felt pain, the night before returning in a heartbeat. Pinpricks of pain stabbed at her knees and arms. The house was quiet. Her mother was probably passed out in the lounge. She almost hoped she was because that would mean she could run herself a bath – maybe, if she was lucky, a hot bath – without being shouted at.

Standing slowly, she checked her bruises and cuts before making her way to the one window in her room that overlooked the small garden. She loved the garden. It was her space. She'd planted it, with mostly wild flowers; she cared for it. It was a tiny, concreted space with six-foot-high brick walls. It was just big enough to park a family car, more a yard than a garden, but it was a space she had filled with colour. She would sit on her step for hours, whilst her mother slept off the night before, watching the birds feed on the stale bread – bread even she wouldn't eat.

Lucy loved the summer best. She hated winter, but that was probably because they couldn't afford to heat the house – even if the system had worked. The storage heaters were old and expensive to replace. They made do with scavenged wood fires on the worst days, and on the other days, she sat huddled in a duvet, looking forward to summer.

Slipping on a robe – one of her favourite presents ever, the hotel logo embroidered at the left breast – she headed for the bathroom where she cleaned her teeth and ran a bath. The water came out just hot enough. Some days she had to boil a couple of kettles to get the water even lukewarm. She added a tiny splash of the body wash that she'd got for Christmas last year. It was a present from Aarav that she kept hidden in her room. She liked to sit in bubbles.

Once bathed she headed for the kitchen, intent on making a cuppa, and, if there was bread, some toast. It was usually her first job of the day. Her mother wouldn't normally leave her bedroom until lunchtime and only after she'd had at least two steaming cups of what she called builder's tea. She was surprised to not find her in the lounge, passed out from the night before. Shrugging, she turned around and climbed the stairs. Without knocking, she entered her mother's room, coughing as she inhaled the smoke that filled it. She had begged her to quit – or at least to not smoke in the bedroom – but her pleas always fell on deaf ears.

Lucy wanted to turn around and go, just leave, go anywhere. Anywhere would be better than this. *I'm the kid, not the mother.* The cops could be back anytime, so she had to get her ready. Her mother lay on top of the duvet still wearing yesterday's clothes. She stank of cigs, booze, cheap perfume, and sweat. It wasn't nice. She opened the curtains and the window with some difficulty before pulling her mother's boots off, then her jeans before getting her to sit.

'Mum, you have to wake up!' She thought about slapping her.

'Piss off!'

'Mum, the police could be here any time now!'

She watched the painful re-entry into daylight. 'Mum, you have to wake up!'

'Tea. I need tea…'

'I'll go get some. Have we got milk?'

'Don't know.' Her words were slurred, head bent over her neck.

'Have we got money if not?'

'Jesus Christ… do you want me to fucking make it as well as drink it!'

***

Reggie was another early riser. One of the many things he hated about getting old was the lack of sleep, coupled with the sheer impossibility of returning to sleep after a night-time trip to the loo. These days he was often awake before the alarm. As was usual, he remained in bed, enjoying the view from his windows, waiting for Frank to knock on the door and signal that breakfast would be ready in a few minutes. Occasionally, he had suggested that Frank call him to save his old legs having to climb the stairs, but Frank, like him, refused to submit to the notion that they were past it.

So, every morning they indulged with a full English – complete with toast and marmalade – served with several cups of tea each whilst they read the papers, occasionally stopping to put the world to rights. This usually involved much laughter and profanity. Sometimes he thought Frank was the reason he hadn't married again. They worked so well together; they knew each other inside out. Frank would run through walls for him without complaint – just as he would for him.

***

Jo sat in the only half-decent chair, the young WPC accompanying her sitting on the battered sofa, almost disappearing into the over-soft cushions. The room smelt. In reality, the whole house did – cheap perfume trying to cover other smells. The combination wasn't good. Her heart went out to Lucy. Some people didn't deserve kids. If she'd have thought about it, she would have worn yesterday's suit. No one would have spotted the difference. She might be out of uniform, but she'd swapped that for her own version. She had seven very similar, beautifully cut suits hanging in her wardrobe with one wardrobe full of equally similar blouses and shirts.

She was cradling a cuppa. She knew she should have said no when Lucy had asked. All cops knew the cups to decline – it was part of the instinct – and this was one of those cups. She feared what might be lurking at the bottom of the mug if she was to drink from it. She'd only accepted because she couldn't disappoint Lucy, who she knew was desperately trying to make a good impression. She was aware of the impact the girl was having on her. There was something about her that drew you in, made you care. It was an innocence, a lack of guile or agenda, and an obvious desire to please. Whatever it was, it worked. She cared!

Jo liked to see her smile. Her smile was beautiful. It softened her, bringing the girl out. She wondered what normal would do for her, what she could be if she was part of a family, able to dream and chase those dreams. She thought Lucy could be pretty special. She was going to see what she could do. Anything would be better than this.

***

Liz lay in the bath – the bath run by Lucy – and she was in no hurry to get out. She liked to lie, to soak, enjoying the warmth spreading through her old bones. A glass of cheap vodka sat on the edge of the bath. She'd been sipping it slowly, knowing that she would need a little anaesthetic to get through the day. The cops could wait. She really didn't give a flying fuck. She hated her life. She had deserved a better life, had dreamt of a better life… Some days she just wanted to drift away. A tear rolled down her cheek, and she heard a knock at the door.

'Mum, they're here.'

'Tell them they'll have to wait.'

'How long?'

'I don't know, I don't care!'

Closing her eyes, she thought about the call she'd taken from Reggie, still pissed that he'd forgotten her. He hadn't remembered their time together. He had no idea who she was. She'd wanted to shout something; she wanted to matter. In her head, he'd been a boyfriend – one she'd bragged about for a few years. She'd been quite a looker back in the day. She was also angry that he had asked after her daughter, not her. Her anger was only softened by the offered money. The figure was staggeringly huge. Life-changing.

With the money, she could make that long dreamed of move to Spain, a little bar with a flat above. She was almost there. She could feel the sun on her back, the palm trees green against the bright blue skies. She wouldn't miss this life. The only problem was the girl. She'd have to do something with her. She couldn't take her. She didn't fit into the pictures in her head… though, maybe she could clean the place.

Standing reluctantly, she grabbed a towel, noticing her clothes for the day laying on the floor, picked by Lucy: a denim skirt and a white T-shirt with a faded VIRGIN logo. She almost wet herself laughing at that one.

***

James felt surprisingly good. He'd fallen asleep as soon as his head had touched the pillow. The night before, he had spent a couple of hours on the roof. Time enough to have worked his way through a third of a bottle of the single malt favoured by the old man. He had smoked a couple, maybe more, and then retired, finally, ready for sleep.

His phone vibrated, his thumb opening his messages, deleting many without opening or reading, pausing at one from Sarah. Just the one. He liked her self-control…

'Morning, I' Mr No-show I'll forgive you if…'

He liked that. Open-ended, no demands. As he typed, he felt his cock stir.

'If i?' He hit send and didn't have to wait long for a reply.

'If u finally return my panties'

'That might be hard'

'Why?'

'I'm wearing them'

'WTF?!'

'R u alone?'

'Y?'

'Where's the OLD man?' he wrote, chuckling as he sent it.

'London, I think'

'Do u want some co?'

'What here???'

'I want 2 shag you senseless in ur bed'

'Bad boy!!!!!'

'Take that as a yessssssssssssssssssssssssssss'

He had to wait a few seconds…

'Yes'

'Cu in 45 don't get up don't shower I want u as u r'

Jumping up, he headed for the shower. This could be a good day – a very good day. It was true that he liked the sluts, the one-night stands, but every now and then he liked a bit of groundhog.

***

Sarah put the phone down, laying back against the soft pillows. She breathed hard against her palm, sniffing the air.

Think I need to clean my teeth.

She'd promised not to get up. Now, torn between doing as instructed or cleaning her teeth, she considered maybe taking a quick shower or at least having a whore's wash. She wondered if she should put something else on. She'd come to bed in PJ's. She had a drawer full of expensive silk lingerie beside the bed, bought by her husband, no doubt disappointed that she seldom wore any of it. She pulled out a black one-piece – there was nothing to it. She'd wear that for James. Something he could rip off her. That made her mind up. She'd shower and clean her teeth, even if she did nothing else.

Standing in the shower, she wondered why she felt no guilt. She thought it might be that she didn't actually love her husband and hadn't given her heart to him. She knew that if she loved him, she wouldn't be getting ready to jump into bed with another man and her heart wouldn't be banging in anticipation. She'd worked in the office next door to his, so she had known quite a bit about Ed and his firm. She'd listened to the girls gossiping about poor Mrs Horton who'd recently died and how sad poor Mr Horton must be all on his own in a big house with no kids. One day soon after she'd spotted him sitting on a bench by the river on his lunch break. That had been all the excuse she'd needed. Sitting beside him, they'd soon started chatting. Once he'd mentioned his work, she had told him about her abusive ex who was stalking her – a complete bastard who'd kicked her out of his grotty one-bed flat. Ed had immediately offered to help, free of charge of course, just as she knew he would.

Within days, they were dating, and within weeks, they were seeing each other just about every night. Within months, she was sleeping over at weekends, and now they were husband and wife. She'd known that she was using him. She got to live the high life, and he got to parade his trophy, and occasionally, if he was lucky, he got to screw her – something he was eternally grateful about. These days it was James that she pictured whilst with him.

She had always known that one day she would make something of herself. She had endured being the skinny gangly girl at university who had never quite fitted in. Socially awkward. She'd had friends but had spent those years mostly on the fringe of the social pecking order, invited to make up the numbers. In those three years, she'd had two lovers, and both had been pretty inept. Her sex life had been mostly drunken fumbles that had always left her wanting more. They wouldn't recognize her now. She'd filled out, but it had been his money that had improved her wardrobe, and it had been his money that had paid for the visits to various salons who had tweaked and improved her. It might be true that money couldn't buy you love, but it could buy you a hell of a trophy wife.

Old friends had been cast aside and new friends made. Most of those were wives or mistresses of Edward's friends, so girls like her or older. It was a small, tight-knit circle, difficult to break into but easy to be cast out from. The older women were, to be polite, a little disdainful – not that she gave a hoot. The younger girls were just pretentious, tedious, or worse. She'd agreed to the weekly girlie dates to pass the time, to get out of the house. It was a very nice house, a beautifully converted barn, but it was in the middle of nowhere, overlooking empty fields on the edge of Reepham. How she missed the city!

Her reflection confirmed she looked hot. She decided that Ed could buy her as much lingerie as he wanted. She might even text him as much later. She could imagine him excitedly reading the text. *Bless him.*

Her hand slid slowly across her belly. Her skin felt good, smooth, and she parted her legs, her fingers moving under the fine silk, her back arching as she found her clit, sucking in a lungful as she teased herself with sharp nails. She was wet. She was ready for him. She could almost feel him inside her as she lay on the bed, eyes closed as she came, her orgasm crashing through her. She screamed as she felt hands on her ankles, felt herself being pulled down the bed, opening her eyes only to see James standing at the edge of the bed.

'You bastard!'

She watched as he dropped to his knees, then closed her eyes again as he kissed the inside of her thighs, moving slowly up her body, cupping her arse as he licked, kissed, and sucked.

***

James loved these moments. He had room in his life for both the one-night shags and the lovers who lasted a few weeks. Sarah was definitely a lover. He loved her taste, her skin, the wonderful contradiction of haughty nervousness and the exuded wantonness. He slid his hands farther under her, raising her off the bed so that he could kiss, lick, and suck every part of her.

***

Sarah was lost, her feelings already out of control. She knew that this was not normal – her reaction both physically and spiritually. She was already his… his plaything, and she doubted she could say no to him. She felt her arms being pushed up the bed past her head, held there as he teased her nipples, as she begged him to fuck her. She heard the sound of his zip being pulled, felt his jeans being kicked down, and at last, she felt him enter her and cried out.

CHAPTER EIGHT

Steve Woodsmith sat in his car – a rather battered, very dirty, double-cabbed Nissan pick-up. The back seats were strewn with crap, and he was still wearing yesterday's clothes. Sometimes the story was bigger than his need for personal hygiene. He'd driven to this house, Liz's house, after listening to two cops discussing the events of the night before whilst eating breakfast at his favourite pit stop – Route 11 – just down the road from his occasional girlfriend's Attleborough home. He stopped the night whenever he was allowed, preferring it to his tiny studio apartment in the city.

He'd finished his takeaway coffee ages ago and was now rationing his smokes, down to just three. He'd normally buy a packet on the way into work, but today he had driven straight here. Groaning, he lit another, inhaling deeply. To be fair, the only smokes he enjoyed these days were the first and last of the day – or maybe with a pint or even more rarely after sex – the rest were just feeding the need.

Nothing moved. He was happy to wait. As a journalist, he knew all about waiting, chasing the story, hoping for the biggie. This could be his. Big stories didn't routinely make their way to the EDP – the local paper he worked for – but this one shouted front page. He knew the Taylors – *who didn't?* – but the name that had got him all excited was Liz Mack. He knew her, even knew her address, having recently interviewed her on a piece about street prostitution. So, he sat happily waiting for signs of life, knowing that Liz would sell her soul for a few quid, and a story that contained both her and a Taylor might be worth more than a few quid to him. The dream was to get that lucky break, to ride it to the big boys. At twenty-seven, he needed to find that lucky break soon.

His anticipation grew. Once he had the story from Liz, he'd give old man Taylor a chance to add his piece and maybe the wife – he hadn't got her name, so he hoped Liz might know. Failing that, he'd go with what he could get.

At last, the front door opened, and he watched a young girl emerge. 'Thank you, God,' he whispered, thinking she was beautiful and hoping that she was the girl in question. Her picture would be all he needed to sell the story. No wonder Liz had kept her hidden. He checked his appearance in the mirror, sweeping his hand through his thinning hair, removed his glasses needed for driving, and got out of the car. As he walked towards her, she turned to look at him. Her face was breathtakingly beautiful, but there was something else, an innocence, a happiness that belied her surroundings. He needed to capture all of that in a picture.

This is a face for the red tops.

'Hi.' He stopped, realising she looked scared.

'Do you want my mum?'

'Yes, please.'

The urge to follow her as she disappeared into the house was huge. He'd done that a few times, taking the open door as an invitation to enter, but something told him not to, so he waited.

'What do you want?'

It hadn't sounded like a question – more of an accusation – and he turned to see Liz Mack, thinking, *how on God's green Earth did you give birth to that?*

He knew from their first encounter that she would come cheap. She would relish the attention; in her mind, this would be all about her. He had no problem with that. The girl would be the big picture, the mother an inset. The money shot would be James standing with the girl – he could dream. The paper had a pretty decent library on the Taylors, and one always stuck in the memory: James in a tux, a blonde draped either side. That would do. All he needed from the mum was the story and the pics. He wanted to be the first to publish. He'd considered getting the girl to change clothes, but he loved the visual contrast – contradiction.

***

Jackie had reluctantly taken the advice to go and have a coffee, and she was now sitting at a table, coffee cooling, oblivious to everyone around her, unable to think, make decisions. All she could do was wait for Richard to wake up, to sit up and hold her hand, telling her everything would be alright. She couldn't believe some of the things she'd overheard. Some of the things she'd been told. Her Richard wouldn't – couldn't – have done those things. She resolved to return to his side, and if nothing had changed, she would return home. She needed to sleep, if not for her, for their child.

***

Steve turned into the hospital carpark; fingers crossed that he would find a space big enough for the pick-up. He knew from previous visits that finding a space quickly was akin to finding rocking horse teeth. Ahead he saw a car reversing slowly back along the road, its hazards on. He saw why, noticing a car pulling out of a space to his left, so he swung into the space, ignoring the angry blast from the other car. He parked, leaving it unlocked in the vain hope that somebody might nick it, and headed towards the entrance.

Getting the old biddy on reception to give up a ward name had been all too easy, so now he headed up to the third floor, looking for the ITU – the intensive care unit. It was going to be heavily nursed, so getting to him might prove troublesome.

Plan B was probably the best course of action: find him, wait for her, and then follow her out, maybe even to her home.

Turning the corner, he stopped abruptly as he saw a cop sitting outside a room. This must be it he thought, confirmed when a young woman exited hurriedly. He could see the tear-stained face, and he heard the cop wish her what sounded like a sincere 'take care'. Stepping back against the wall, he held his breath as she passed by, her head down. He couldn't see her face, but he hoped he'd get a decent pic later – preferably with a big wet tear rolling down her cheek. He let her get a few yards down the corridor, then he followed her.

***

Reggie took the stairs. If asked, he would happily admit to being a stubborn old bastard. He had to be pissed to take the lift, so it was the stairs – all twenty-six of them. *Better down than up,* he thought. Wonderful smells filtered up to him as he neared the kitchen. Frankie Boy was baking. It was funny how life had changed. If you'd told him that Frankie would turn out to be a first-class cook, he would have laughed so hard he would have wet his pants. Turned out that Frankie Boy was the next Delia Smith. He tasted the air, trying to guess what would be there to tempt him; he hoped for scones with Frank's very own jam and maybe a big dollop of fresh double cream – unless Frankie had some of the clotted stuff hiding in the fridge.

'Coffee, boss?'

Reggie nodded as he lowered himself onto a kitchen chair. 'Sounds good to me, mate.'

The kitchen was huge, with a large oak dining table that could seat fourteen or more. Nothing much had changed in the twenty-five years they had lived in the place. The house still had his wonderful Nancy in it, but nowhere more so than this kitchen. Her domain. For too few years it had been both the centre of the family home and the boardroom. Every one of his inner-circle had loved sitting at this table, Nancy feeding them without interfering in their work, a gentle touch in a hostile, sometimes very angry, often ugly world.

'Need you to pop out later, Frank.'

'No probs…'

'Think we need to make a down payment to the...'

'Mother?'

Reggie smiled. 'Yep… if we can call her that?'

'How much?'

'Make it five. Enough to give her a good time without...'

'A monkey then?'

'Yep, but remind her… one word out of turn and...'

'No probs. Now, do you want a nice scone to go with that coffee?'

'Is the pope Catholic?'

Reggie sat back in his seat. This was his life now; he knew better than most that no one was promised a tomorrow, but if he had one, he'd want freshly baked scones in it.

***

Arriving home, Jackie sat in the car, trying to summon the energy, the inclination, to get out. Finally, she exited and walked to the front door. Yesterday, this had been her home, her sanctuary, maybe even their forever home, but today it felt empty, sad.

How things change.

She needed a bath, she needed to eat, she needed sleep, and if she didn't need it, her baby certainly did. The thought of sleeping filled her with dread. She wouldn't hear the phone if she was sleeping. Sleeping meant waking, and she didn't want to wake only for the horror to slowly seep back in, the ugly truth replaying every time she woke. The house felt empty, abandoned, lonely. Everything was just as she had left it the night before but utterly devoid of life… of happy. She filled the kettle and burst into tears.

The doorbell rang once, then again. 'Who the bloody hell is that?' she said, throwing her hands into the air. Then she paused, not wanting to move. Should she answer it or hide? She stepped back from the window, but the ringing continued. Reluctantly, she went to the door, opening it with the slider on.

'Who are you?'

'I'm a friend of your husband.'

Opening the door slowly, she cautiously peered out…

'What do you want?'

'I'm here to help. Your husband is in a bit of trouble, and I want to help him.'

She opened the door to let him in, even then thinking, *what am I doing? Don't let him in!*

She stood to one side as he entered, his body odour washing over her. She had to fight a gag. She wanted to ask him to leave but lacked the courage. Instead, she hoped he would say his bit and go on his own accord.

***

Frank half-hoped that the house would be empty, that the drive had been wasted. Errands like this were from another time. He wondered how he had ever enjoyed having a word, putting the frighteners on. Once – when he had been one of the scariest men in the county – a visit from him was usually enough to have grown men begging for time. Second visits had been rare, third visits seldom required, and never ever a fourth.

Climbing the steps, he spotted the girl, smiling his best smile. 'Good morning, is your mum in?'

Taking her slight nod as confirmation, he pushed the door open, shouting a little louder than he had intended: 'Liz?'

***

James admired the view. Her arse was poetry – he assumed as a result of her recently acquired passion for riding. The thought caused his flagging cock to start to harden again as he pictured her in jodhpurs and boots. They'd shagged twice already. Could he complete the hat-trick? He checked his bored meter. Did he want to shag the delectable, recently married Sarah Horton again or pop into the city for a cold one? Life was tough. Too many choices.

***

Liz couldn't remember being happier. She was counting the notes for the third time – she hadn't dared count them in front of Frank. She'd listened to his warnings, understanding the threats made should she or Lucy become a problem. Frank had stood there suited and booted, his huge frame filling the room. She would have agreed to anything he wanted. Frank was not a man to be crossed.

She wondered how much more money would be headed her way – thousands rather than hundreds. Maybe as much as ten thousand. Her good fortune needed to be celebrated. She needed a drink, a proper drink at a pub, so she made for her bedroom. The floor was soon covered with clothing deemed unsuitable for the occasion. Finally settling on a mid-blue strappy summer dress that just about contained her tits, she sat in front of the chipped mirror applying makeup before shaking her hair free. *Not bad,* she thought. *Not too bad at all.* Stuffing the money into her purse, she left without a backwards glance, heading for the pub.

The Golden Star had been her local in a previous life. An old-fashioned boozer, it was famous for its real ales and home-cooked food. It had been a long time since she had eaten properly, something served on a plate. Life felt good. This was how it should be. She decided on ale-battered fish & chips with a pint of lager tops to wash it down. With the order placed, she scanned the pub, not recognizing anyone. There were a few old-boy regulars, but most looked like desk jockeys on a lunch break. She picked a table for two away from the door.

Once the food arrived, she almost fainted with joy – it smelt wonderful. She was lost in the moment, no thoughts of... well, anything. She decided this must be what normal felt like. She covered the food with salt and vinegar and lashings of tomato sauce before spearing a big fat chip on her fork...

'What's a nice girl like you doing here?'

Groaning, she prepared a put down – something polite to suit her surroundings. Like *piss off... please*.

'Danny?' In a heartbeat, her mood changed. This was the man, Danny Jones himself, who'd played her like a fucking fiddle. She'd fallen in love with a married man, gotten herself pregnant, lost her job, and ended up sleeping on a mate's sofa. Danny had taken her in and looked after her right up until the day Lucy had turned one. Danny had changed, almost overnight – as soon as the coke supply ran out. In a matter of days, she went from girlfriend to whore as he became her pimp. She'd had to *work* to earn her drugs – the coke costing her just about everything: her soul, her hopes, and her dreams. That sordid, toxic relationship had continued for a few years until her looks had faded, her dependency costing more than she earned. One day he'd just kicked her out.

What the fuck does he want...

'Can I sit?'

'Sure.' She wasn't going to say no. He could be an evil bastard; her short-lived joy began to dissipate.

They sat for a while not saying much, pretending to be like everyone else, talking about the weather, the food... he even pinched a few chips, his stubby fingers slavering them in the tomato sauce before stuffing them into his tiny mouth. She wondered how she had ever thought him handsome, but once she had. Now he looked like a used car salesman: cheap suit, awful shirt, no tie, hairy chest showing, and carrying a few extra pounds.

'So, what do you want?' she'd finally asked.

'What makes you think I want something?'

'You always want something!' It had come out a tad regretful, almost playful. She hated herself for even suggesting that she might still miss the old life – she might, she probably did – but no way did she want him to know that!

'Listen, babe' – he leaned in, talking quietly – 'I had a nice little result last night. Four winners. A nice little earner.' It had been a good night, a once-a-year win, his only regret was the pittance that he'd placed on the first bet. The cash was spread across all his pockets. Two pockets already accounted for, a backstreet bookie, a man not to be messed with, and his landlord who was threatening eviction. 'I saw you and thought it might be fun to pop over to watch the gee-gees this after'?' He paused. 'We could party after; I've got some of the good stuff back at the flat.'

To her surprise, she found herself standing, agreeing to spend the afternoon with him... not thinking about anything else other than having a good time. She deserved a good time. Not once had she thought about Lucy.

***

The windowsill was biting into her upper thigh, her hands pushed above her head hard against the glass as she felt her legs being eased apart, his breath hot on her neck. She moaned as he nipped her skin with little bites, whispering in her ear. She bent at the waist, pushing her arse into his groin, eyes shut. 'Fuck me! Just fucking fuck me...'

***

James took a step back, admiring the view. She looked glorious. She'd dressed for lunch, her dress now stretched tight across her beautiful arse. He had always thought that he was a leg man, but she was converting him. She was facing the window, Salle Church in the distance. He took her hands, raising them above her head, whispering, 'Keep them there – don't move!'

He stepped back, and she kept her hands above her head. 'Good girl.' She needed tying. He looked around, removing the cord from her dressing gown and flinging it over the curtain pole. Then he tied her hands, stretching her, her toes finding the floor. Her reflection in the window surprising him. *Wooo!* His cock hardened. He yanked her zipper down, his hands reaching around her, freeing her beautiful tits, feeling their heaviness in his hands.

Something caught James's eye as he felt her familiar heat, her wetness. He paused, realising somebody was coming up the drive, one of his dad's best mates – her husband. He entered her hard, causing her to gasp, then moan… thinking how this could get interesting. The ink was hardly dry on the wedding licence, and here she was, his wife, naked for all the world to see. He pulled back on her hair and turned her face, kissing her hard, her eyes shut, words… sounds coming out of her mouth, guttural sounds. She wouldn't hear the old man until he got to the bedroom door. He knew she was close to orgasm – he could feel the wave starting, threatening to engulf her. He fucked her harder, hands on her hips. She couldn't break free even if she wanted to.

***

Jackie stood by the door, waiting for Steve to come back, to leave. She couldn't wait to get rid of him. The house smelled – she would need to open the windows to air the place. She wanted a bath… a cuppa… a padded room where she could scream. He'd been upstairs a long time. Nothing made much sense. Steve had introduced himself as a friend but had bombarded her with questions. Finally, he had admitted that he was a journalist. The thought had sickened her, and she'd agreed to the photo just to get rid of him, but she had felt stupid being photographed in the back garden. Just as she had thought, *Thank God, he's going,* he had asked to use the bathroom. She had watched him take the stairs, ignoring her. 'We have a cloakroom downstairs.'

***

Edward stood in the doorway, immobile, incapable of speech. Short of breath, he'd run up the stairs, leaving his car running when he had spotted his wife almost naked, her tits banging against their bedroom window. When he had first pulled into the drive, he had thought she was waving to him, the vision etched into his brain, but then he had seen a man standing behind her. It had taken a few moments for him to process the reality that his wife was having sex with someone. Once at the door he had realised that someone was James-bloody-Taylor, and he wasn't going to stop, wasn't going to run, and wasn't going to explain or apologise as he carried on screwing his oblivious slut of a wife in front of him.

Fighting the urge to turn and run, he stared transfixed at the sight, noticing the sweat on her back, the redness at her wrists, the size of him, the sounds she was making, completely unaware of his presence. Wondering would she stop even if she knew he was here. His emotions were all over the place. It was as if he were watching a sleazy porn show. This wasn't his wife. This wasn't the woman he'd made love to on the beach whilst on honeymoon. This wasn't the woman who made him feel young again, the woman who'd given him a glorious second chance at happiness.

In a heartbeat, he was broken, desolate, and dead inside. He turned, catching the bastard's eye, a sardonic smile on his face. Anger spilt, took hold, and his heart felt like it was going to explode. Thinking this was what absolute heartbreak must feel like, he left, going to his study. Flinging the door open, he went to his desk, pulling open every draw, throwing the contents to the floor. Finally, he found it – his father's prized Walther P38. The old man had said, despite his hatred of the Krauts, that this was the best handgun used in the war. He took the gun with trembling hands, checking through tear-filled eyes that he had a round in the chamber. He recalled, somewhat bizarrely, his father telling him that the gun had a double-action trigger, so it was safe to have one in the chamber.

***

James gripped her hips as he pounded back and forth, his own orgasm fast approaching. She'd come at least once – maybe twice. Sometimes it was difficult to tell. She was pretty noisy and pretty vocal. He liked that, hearing her caught between a whimper and a scream.

***

Reggie was sitting at a desk in his third favourite room of the house – his study. The first was the kitchen, the second his bedroom. The study was on the first floor, and it overlooked the massive gardens. The upkeep cost a fortune, but it was worth every penny on days like this, bathed in sunshine. The newspapers lay on the floor having been read from cover to cover, and his coffee cup sat empty. Swivelling in his chair, he looked outside wondering if he should take a walk to wake himself up or just sit back, succumbing to sleep.

***

Pulling his jeans up, James thought it might be best to bugger off and leave the newlyweds to… to do what, he had no idea. How did they move on from this shit – she didn't even know the old boy was in the house. Torn between watching and staying, he watched her leave the room just about wearing the dress that she'd been wearing as she had greeted him earlier, but just the dress. Her underwear lay on the floor, close to the window; he squashed his feet into his shoes, pulling on his shirt, deciding to leave.

Intent on showering, Sarah headed for the bathroom next door, stopping when she heard, 'Bloody answering machine.' She paused, her mind questioning… A chill ran through her. *Shit, he's home! How long has he been home? Does he know? If he does, why is he in his study? Who is he talking to?*

All these questions took only moments to ask. Was she ready for the answers? She crept down the stairs, her heart thumping. She heard, 'Sorry, old boy, but I had to call you. I don't know what to do.'

Without thinking, she stepped into the room, his study. He sat behind his desk, his head in his hands. On hearing her enter, he looked up…

'Why?' His tone seemed more than a little anguished.

He knows. Shit!

'Why not!' she spat, her arms trying to cover herself.

'You whore!' he shouted.

'I'm *his* whore!' As she said it, she wondered why she was being so evil. Why could she not say sorry, ask forgiveness, but in some deep dark corner of her mind, she knew why. They couldn't turn the clock back on this. It wouldn't be forgotten or forgiven, and she knew that she wouldn't stop. She couldn't give him up, so it was best to be cruel to be kind – at least, that was her hope.

'Get out! GET OUT of my house!' he shouted as he stood, picking up the gun as he did, brandishing it at her, his hand shaking with the weight… 'GET OUT! GET OUT!' She walked over, standing before him, shouting, 'Don't worry! I'm going! And I won't be back! Ever!'

With that, she turned and walked.

***

He watched her leave, unable to move or speak. He'd never felt so alone. Returning to his desk, he sat down, defeated, broken, his world in tatters. Sobbing, he felt humiliated. He looked at the gun in his hand, turning it over, looking at it as if for the first time, wondering how long he had been holding it. Then, without further thought, he raised it to his temple and pulled the trigger.

***

Reggie tried to resist the gentle attempts to wake him. He knew Frank was only following orders. He was the one who had asked him not to let him doze off for too long, especially during a mealtime. It was difficult enough to sleep through a night without catnaps, but it was almost impossible if he rested his eyes for too long during the day. The dream had been a good one: he'd been playing golf, walking up to the ball laying a few feet from the pin. He'd laid up beautifully off the tee, then hit a high wedge to the green, up and over the trees standing guard. Some of his mates tried to drive the green, but not him. A nice little 5 wood off the tee, a big wedge, and then the hope to need the putter just once maybe twice.

'Cuppa tea there for you, Reg.'

'Thanks, Frankie. What would I do...'

'Starve probably,' he uttered with a laugh. 'Also, a nice teacake.'

'You having one?'

'Had mine downstairs – fresh out of the oven. You were soundo, boss. I thought it best to leave you awhile.'

'Thank you.'

Reggie sat up, the tea cake's aroma tantalising him, when his phone beeped indicating someone had left a message. He quickly decided that whoever it was, they could wait until he'd drunk his tea and eaten his cake.

After finishing the delicious teacake, he hit play and listened to the message left by Eddie. He then played it again, thinking it seemed strange. Something about his old friend's tone had seemed troubled, so he picked the phone up and dialled, getting his answering machine. He left a message asking him to call back and added that he hoped he was okay. He then tried his mobile without joy.

Wondering what to do, he played the message again. Eddie was upset, his voice racked with emotion and something else. Without further hesitation, he pulled out his wallet, removing Mickey's card and dialled his number.

'Is that Michael?'

'It is.'

'Hello, Mickey, it's Reggie Taylor.'

'What can I do for you, *sir*?'

The emphasis on the *sir* was not lost on Reggie or the respect implied from a very tired Mickey, judging by the sound of his voice. Reggie told the story as best he could, admitting that he had no reason to suspect anything untoward. Mickey had agreed to get a car over to the property ASAP. Thanking him, he then called Frank, telling him to get the car ready.

The drive wouldn't take long – about forty minutes. Frank had a heavy right foot when needed, so they could be there in thirty. Reggie updated him as they went. Pulling into the drive, he was pleasantly surprised to see a police car already parked, the occupants standing by the car, one on the radio listening intently. Reggie exited the car and approached the other cop.

'Good day, sir, and who might you be?'

'Reggie – Reggie Taylor. I'm a friend of the owner, Ed Horton.'

'Ah, yes. You called this in?'

'Yes.'

'Why?'

'Have you checked the house?'

'We've walked around it; there is no sign of damage or forced entry.'

'Have you been inside?'

'Not yet. We were waiting for the okay to do so, we can't see any reason to be alarmed.'

'I know where he hides a key.' Reggie headed for the porch, ignoring the request that he wait. Finding the key laying under a pot, he let himself in.

'Sir!'

Reggie shouted, 'Ed! ED!' stopping as he found a note laying on the floor, slightly creased. He stooped to pick it up.

Hi Honey

Decided to go shopping as you're away for a couple of days!!!

Miss you loads – food in the fridge if you are home b4 me

I'll call you later.

Lots of love

Sarah xxx

PS I'll try to spend lots

Passing the note to the cop closest to him, he continued walking around the house, shouting out, his voice betraying his ever-growing concern for his old chum.

'Sir… Reggie… I think it best we wait for…' He stopped speaking.

'No… NO! Nooo! WHY?… You daft bugger; you silly old...'

He stood in the doorway. It was obvious that Ed was dead. His body lay sprawled over the desk with a huge hole in his head. There was blood splatter above and behind him; a gun lay on the desk.

***

James lay in bed, listening to Sarah showering. They'd arrived an hour ago, booking a room at The Savoy on the way down. They hadn't talked since leaving Norwich. She'd retreated from any contact – verbal or physical – and to be honest, he'd been happy to just sit in first class, watching the world go by.

Her car was parked in the multi-storey by the train station, and his had been left at Rose Lane a short walk from the station. They'd each bought their tickets online so they could just walk on. He wasn't concerned – the daft old twat had taken a gun to his head, blowing his brains out. They hadn't been anywhere near him at the time, so no worries about the evidence. Sarah had been a mess, hysterical, he'd had to slap her, shock her into something resembling silence.

The plan had been quick to form. They had to get out and get out now. He packed a bag for her and dictated a note for her to write whilst he made the bed, leaving the room tidy. Then he had dragged her out of the house. He'd thought it a good idea for him to drive to the train station the long way round, going to Norwich via the Fakenham Road, the road he would take from home, her taking the shorter direct route. Lovers meeting at the station. The note would buy them time – a day or two. Time to prepare for the shitshow that would be waiting for her. It had been obvious to him that she needed to be somewhere else; he had no idea what she might say or do.

***

Mickey parked alongside the patrol car.

'Nice house.'

'Lottery win for you and me.'

'Chance would be…'

Both he and Jo got out of the car, his exit more laboured than hers. She didn't look like she'd only slept three to four hours, whereas he felt like one of the walking dead.

'What have we got?'

Mickey listened to the uniform whilst Jo handed over the protective clothing needed to enter the house. SOCO was on the way but held up in traffic. Mickey spotted Reggie sitting on a bench by the back door in what he thought was the front garden, so he headed over.

'Hi, Reggie.'

Reggie raised his head. He looked distraught.

'Don't get up.' Mickey sat beside him. 'What can you tell me?'

'I don't know. Not much. He called and left me a message. Well, part of a message.'

'Did you keep that message?'

'Yes, I did – at least, I think I did. I hope I did.'

'How did he seem, sound?'

'In the message or...'

'Both.'

'Never happier. He'd come through some tough times, but he re-married recently to a lovely girl.'

'What about the message? How'd he sound?'

'Not good; something was troubling him. He sounded upset, which is why I came straight here.'

'Any money worries?'

'Nope, he is – was – a solicitor. He had a nice little practice, a small office in the close by the cathedral. He was also doing a few voluntary shifts at the Citizens Advice place in the city. He liked to give something back.'

'So, you can't think of any reason? What's the new wife like?'

'Sarah? Lovely girl. Devoted to Ed. She's going to be...'

'Are you able to contact her?'

Reggie paused, thinking. 'I've no idea. I don't have her number. I have no idea where she might be. She said shopping in the note, but that could be anywhere.'

'Note? What note?'

'I gave it to your colleague. Sarah said she was going shopping.'

Jo joined them. 'What we thinking?'

'No bloody idea. We're going to have to leave someone by the gate – if we can't find Sarah – to wait for her.'

'Have you tried his phone?'

'It's secured. Needs his thumbprint… and no, we can't!'

The three of them wandered back to Reggie's car. Mickey felt sorry for the poor old boy – he'd aged overnight. Gone was the polished 'I'm in charge' demeanour, replaced by an overwhelmed, emotional, old man – no doubt all too aware of his own mortality. A common reaction when faced with death.

***

Liz looked around as Danny pulled to a stop. She wasn't so pissed that she didn't know she was playing with fire. Exes are exes for a reason, and she had a thousand reasons why this one should be nothing more than a bad memory. The trouble was that he had been his charming self all afternoon. Nothing had been too much trouble, and he'd even kept a happy face when losing big. She was pretty convinced they had returned home with less than they had left with – a lot less.

The door opened, and there he stood with that silly smile. He held out his hand. 'My lady.' She took it, letting him pull her out of the car. She hid her disappointment at the surroundings – a rundown block of flats, and what seemed like a graveyard for clapped-out bangers. Cars were abandoned everywhere. Her hopes for something a little posher were instantly dashed. In her head, he had lived in an apartment by the river, maybe the penthouse. She knew the river area well. It had been her patch when she'd first walked the streets. It was very different now, very expensive, and the girls who worked those streets for years had moved elsewhere.

They climbed the stairs to the third floor, and she laughed. *Well, at least he lives on the top floor… the penthouse.* The flat was dark, the furniture was not much better than hers, but the view from the lounge window was over the city. The view she decided was the best bit so far.

'Penny for 'em.'

'Nothing really. Just thinking about what might have been. What might have been if you hadn't been such a… such a dick.'

He laughed loudly. 'Me too, hon. I think about it… about you… a lot.'

A little groan escaped her lips as she felt his hands pulling her dress up as he kissed her neck. 'We shouldn't…'

His hands found her skin, her panties, and she groaned again. 'I should know better. I've read the book, and I've got the bleeding T-shirt.' She turned, kissing him. 'Please don't be a fucking twat this time.'

***

73

Danny lay in bed as Liz snored beside him. *I must be bloody desperate*, he thought – which he was. He resolved to speak to her in the morning whilst she was still in a good mood. He had a few pills that would put her in a good mood – albeit short-lived – and he would have enough time to convince her that they should get a little boozer with her money, start a new life in the country – a long-held dream of his. She'd like that, the stupid cow. He also thought that they could up the ante and have a word with the old boy. A smile crossed his face. Salvation was at hand, and life was good.

He just needed time. Time and money.

***

Jackie was once more sitting by Richard's bed, telling herself that no news was good news. She was thinking about what the doc had said – the one with kind eyes. He had gently told her off, reminding her that she would be no good to Richard if she was worn out. He'd been looking at the bump whilst talking to her. She could read his mind on that subject. She knew she looked a mess; Richard's pants and tees might be acceptable clothing at home or for popping to the local shop, but not for sitting by the bed.

At some point, she had stopped praying for him to open his eyes. The doctors said he could awaken any time. There had been moments when she'd begun to dread that moment rather than wish for it, always immediately feeling guilty that she could think such a thing. Her thoughts had become a noisy, confused, conflicted battleground. Sometimes the voice of hope shouted loudest, that he would wake as her Richard shouting his innocence, but there were times when the other voice, the nasty, snide voice, whispered: *But what if he doesn't?*

***

Reggie sat in bed, cupping a mug of hot chocolate, a rare treat, in his hands. He tried not to drink too late. He had learned to his cost that drinking past ten pm caused him to wake in the dark, needing to pee. He hated stumbling to the loo, still clinging to sleep, knowing even as he walked, that by the time he got back into his bed, the duvet would have cooled, and sleep would sometimes be hard to find again. Many a night he had lain still, trying to convince himself that rest was almost as good as sleep.

It was the girl that troubled him. An innocent amongst those who weren't. She deserved better, much better. He might call the social in the morning to see if anything could be done. It was the mother who really worried him. He'd known her for a short while. In her day, she'd been a looker, an up-for-it type of girl – great fun whilst it had lasted. It was never going to be anything other than what it had been. Fun without commitment. He laughed gently. She'd been ahead of her times... the original friends with benefits girl.

The truth was that even then he'd preferred a more peaceful home life. It was a welcome and much-needed contrast to his working days. Nancy had been the perfect wife. She was a school teacher when they'd met, the girl next door, pretty with a gentle touch... He put the cup down and switched off the light, thinking about his Nancy, about days gone by. Sleep came quickly.

***

Lucy picked up her supper plate, the sauce evidencing the beans on toast eaten earlier; this wasn't the first time she'd been left home alone overnight, and it wouldn't be the last. Her mother kept odd hours, sometimes disappearing for days. She turned the TV off as she headed to the kitchen to wash up the plate and cutlery. Once she had tidied up, she checked the battered fridge, which was almost empty. Same with the storage cupboards. She'd had to cut off the blue bits in the bread to make her toast earlier. She opened an old biscuit tin, which was where they kept the shopping money. No notes, and less than five pounds in change. It was enough to get her through tomorrow and maybe another day if she was careful.

CHAPTER NINE

James lay quite still, caught between sleep and the need to get up and to eat. Images from the night before, fragments sparking, flooded his mind. She was – had been – incredible! Opening his eyes, he found her fast asleep. She looked even lovelier asleep. An innocence lost once awake. *Bloody hell,* he thought, *I care about her. What has happened to me?* He'd gone to sleep spending her money, imagining the fun they could have travelling the world together, and he had woken up in a sodding romance novel!

The night before, somewhere between their second and third fuck, they had lain entwined, laughingly drunk on the best of Champagne, the debris of a room service pizza on the floor. They'd discussed their future – once her inheritance landed. A new life somewhere far away. They hadn't decided where, but the vista would include white sand, palm trees, and blue seas and skies with a white-washed villa close to a beach. He thought the image intoxicating and had fallen asleep living the dream. They both had.

Reaching for his phone, he checked his messages. Nothing caught his eye, apart from the time: 9:57. At some point, they would have to head home and face the music. Coming here had been an instinctive reaction, but it had been the right thing for her, giving her time to sort her head out, so she would be ready to return to face the questions. He felt her leg touch his, her skin soft, warm… She turned into him, her breasts against his chest. She was waking, slowly.

All too soon he would see her recalling reality. He vowed to be there for her – this morning and all the mornings to come.

The night before, he had learnt something of her past. Edward had been her lifeline in an otherwise screwed-up world. She'd hit rock-bottom before meeting him and had a dark side that had got her into trouble a few times. Faced with such honesty, he had responded, to his surprise, with revelations about his own life, and his needs and desires had raised her excitement. She had come loudly, and at the time, he had wondered what pictures in her mind had caused her to scream as she climaxed. He'd had to cover her mouth whilst he sought his own release.

***

Lucy was in a happy place. She liked Danny, having met him earlier. They'd arrived in a blur of excited conversation, the introductions made, shouted from room to room whilst they'd both changed into something suitable for shopping. Lucy had been intrigued as to how mum's old boyfriend had become her new boyfriend. He was unlike any other boyfriend, old or new. He was a joker, who smiled and laughed a lot, as did her mum. Anyone that could get her mum into a good mood was okay with Lucy.

They had been in the mall for an hour, and they'd had muffins from McDonald's for breakfast. She had a bag with a T-shirt in it – a new T-shirt. She couldn't remember the last time she'd got something new, something unworn by anyone else. It had come off the sale rail, but she didn't care. It was new, and it was hers.

The future looked good… sounded good. She hadn't meant to listen in to their conversations, but she had got bits of it. The new start – a nice little boozer with a flat above. Lots said about the old man and his money. She had listened to her mum saying something about being careful. Danny didn't know him like she did. Lucy didn't want anything to spoil the day. They'd come home loud and noisy, and she'd forgiven her mum for leaving her the moment she saw just how happy she was.

***

Jackie was another waking to reality. She was normally an early riser, but she had got to bed late, and sleep had been hard to find. The greasy bucket of chicken and chips bought on the way home hadn't helped, the chicken looking like it had been fried more than once. She'd forced down two pieces with the lukewarm coke, and her stomach was now paying the price. If it had been left to her, she would have stayed by Richard's side, but she'd promised his nurse that she would go home and eat. She'd said many things. Some she could recall, some not. The message had been to hope for the best but prepare for the worst and not to forget that she was a mother-to-be. She needed rest, and she needed to eat. She was told if she wasn't careful, she could finish up in the bed next door.

Sitting up, she reached for her phone, her mouth dry, shocked to find it was late morning. Flicking through Facebook, she ignored the few notifications, scrolling through all sorts of nonsense, the trivia of other people's lives. She vowed never again to laugh at the trivia, the food plates, the look-how-wonderful-my-life-is posts. She craved normal.

As she scrolled, a local paper headline made her catch her breath. 'Suspect Banker in COMA.' She opened the page. The few seconds it took to upload seemed to take forever. The pictures caught her eye – one of her! 'You bastard! You complete and utter bastard!'

She checked the headline again, noting the credit was given to Steve Woodsmith. She read the editorial several times. Each time her anger rose as did her disbelief. *How could he? The bastard!*

She looked at the other pictures. James Taylor, the hero of the hour. It was Lucy Mack that caused her to shed the first tear. She touched her image. She was a pretty girl, and her heart went out to her as she read something about her life. Then, lastly, there was her Richard. The image wasn't good. She knew the photo well. It was one of several on the table in the hall. *You bastard!*

Standing quite still, with anger flooding her body, she was unsure what to do next; her mind screamed contradictory thoughts. One moment the urge to flee was overwhelming. The urge to run was powerful. The need to protect her child was paramount, and the nasty little voice whispered, *You don't know him... not really. He could have done this. You know he could. He's a man after all!*

She wondered if she was losing her mind. Picking her phone up again, she deleted her Facebook account and her Instagram – she didn't need to see the nastiness, the worst of people.

Once done, she headed for the shower. She needed to scrub herself clean. Once clean, she would think very carefully about her options. She hoped – wanted – to believe her Richard. The Richard she knew. To stand with him. To fight the world, hand in hand. That's what she hoped, but the doubt, the possibility lingered, and she felt guilty. She felt dirty and more than a little frightened.

***

Reggie sat in the conservatory, his coffee barely touched, the paper laying on his lap. He'd read the editorial twice, concluding that James would be found to be the hero in the court of public opinion. He felt a little sorry for the other chap, but he'd learned long ago to banish such feelings.

Thoughts of his old friend soon dampened even the tiniest of happy thoughts. He couldn't imagine what would have caused him to take his own life. Sadly, he was getting used to the passing of friends. You didn't get to his age without losing a few.

Lost in his own sense of mortality, he had what he would later call an epiphany, resolving to sell everything apart from the house. He had enough to last several lives. He couldn't possibly spend it all, and one thing he was certain about was that he wouldn't waste another penny on his son. It was time for the boy to make his own way. It would be the making of him – he hoped!

Looking around the splendour of the formal gardens, a tribute to the two old boys who tended them, he knew that he was a lucky man. This house and the acres of parkland and woodland beyond the gardens were more than enough for anyone. He got to his feet, intending to find the gardeners, wish them a good morning, and thank them for their efforts when he heard the front door slam shut. He paused for a few seconds, wondering if it was James or Frank. Believing it to be his son, he headed inside.

***

Liz sat outside the coffee shop, grateful for the opportunity to sit and rest her feet, hoping the double espresso hit would recharge her batteries. The morning had started off as fun, but she was now very much fed up with window shopping. She wanted to spend real money – her money! Danny had convinced her that they would be able to get more out of the old man. They had him over a barrel with his trousers down.

She forced a smile as Lucy returned with Danny a step behind, each carrying a tray. She wouldn't have smiled if she had known that Danny had just spent the last of his winnings on cake and coffee. It was his last throw of the dice, his investment in their future. She would have been unhappier still if she had known that he had taken a call whilst queuing. It had been a call from his bookie – a man who would have hunted him down had he not answered. Danny sat opposite her, a smile crossing his face…

'You okay?'

'I'm good. I was thinking today's a good day for you to call the old man.'

'Why me; couldn't you?'

'Not really, my love. He doesn't know me. It needs to be you.'

'Who are you calling, Mum?' Lucy asked.

'Never you mind. This is grownup talk, drink your shake.'

'I'll tell you what to say. You'll be fine. You can charm the honey out of bees.'

Liz laughed. He had the knack of making her feel better about herself. She'd talk to him later, convince him to make the call, and with that thought she started to dream about the future. Dreaming was easier when you had money. Her life had been without dreams for so long… so any dream was good. It was easy to picture the two of them working behind a bar, pulling pints and serving good, honest grub to happy, appreciative locals. Not once did she think about Lucy or the hard graft it took to run a pub.

***

Sarah's emotions were all over the place. She knew she had to do this. She had to go home, but she had a good idea as to what was waiting for her. James had prepared her well. She would almost certainly be greeted by a cop in a car, parked facing the entrance and waiting for her to arrive, and they would be looking for a reaction from her.

It was another sunny day, and she was starting to feel uncomfortably hot – overheating even – so she shrugged her coat off with some difficulty. She needed to get a grip and calm down; she was overthinking everything.

James had said it was best to think one step at a time and focus on the funeral. That would be easy enough; she knew she could play the grieving widow. *Breathe.* Next up would be the will. How hard would it be to sit through that? She knew everything was coming to her. He'd come home one day, excited to tell her that he had drawn up a new will. 'It was her or the cats' home'. Everything else was just time – time for them to get to know each other.

It was working, and she felt better. He'd also told her to think about something happy when stressed, something calming, something that would give her time to relax, time to consider her response. So, she pictured white-washed villas and deep-red sunsets over cobbled streets and tiled plazas with quaint restaurants, noisy bars, and shops. Lots of shops. All she had to do was to make it through the shit-show, and the future looked wonderful.

As always when thinking about James, her mind returned to the sex. She hadn't thought herself a sensuous woman. She enjoyed a good shag, but her past sex life had been more about endurance than enjoyment. James had shown her that sex could be wonderful, sometimes even making her blush, her body betraying her excitement at the mere thought of some of the suggested games whispered into her ear as he fucked her, causing her to respond ever more passionately.

Coming in from Reepham, the driveway was blind. She couldn't see anyone as she indicated left, turning into the drive. Ahead was a police car – just as James had said there would be. Sarah parked in her usual place, Ed's car beside her. She sucked in a deep breath, thinking, *we can do this.* She opened her door, her attention focused on the young cop who moments before had been enjoying a crafty smoke. He got out of the car as she walked towards him, then she took a few steps before tripping. She'd remembered James telling her to make an impression, to cry if she could before they broke the news, then that would be the memory. That would change the conversation. As she fell, she screamed, 'Noooo!' She felt someone lift her, asking if she was okay. She had to stop a smile. If only James could see her now. He would be so proud of her.

Her performance would have the young cop later telling Mickey, 'You should have seen her, boss. Heartbroken she was.'

Replacing the phone, Jackie grabbed her coat and bag. For once she had made a bit of an effort, wearing one of the few maternity summer dresses she owned – a light blue dress with bare shoulders. Richard had liked this dress, so she wore it for him. Looking in the mirror for the first time in days, she put the jacket and bag down to find a scrunchie in her bag, before pulling her hair into a ponytail. Checking her appearance, she thought, *Good enough. They can't say I haven't tried.* She'd even applied a little makeup.

Summoning the courage to face the day, she walked to the front door whilst retrieving her car keys. Opening the door, she stepped out into a burst of bright white flashes and people shouting. The combination was overwhelming. She wanted to retreat back into the safety and quiet of her home, but the door had swung shut behind her. At a loss as to what to do, her instinct kicked in, and she forced her way through to her car, where the world was a little less surreal. The car started first time – *thank you, God* – and she selected reverse. She moved onto the road, trusting that the press would get out of her way.

The press scattered, still shouting, still taking pictures as she floored the accelerator – wanting to get away, as far away as she could. Her phone rang, and she answered it, listening to the nurse updating her, trying not to cry.

***

Answering the old man's phone wasn't something James would normally do, but the ringing was driving him nuts. He called out, 'Dad!' without reply, so he entered his study to find the phone on his desk. Picking it up he saw his dad at the far end of the garden, sitting on a bench, looking lost in thought.

'Hello?'

'Hello... is that Reggie – Mr Taylor?'

'Who's calling?'

84

'You probably don't remember me… I'm Danny Jones.'

'Who?' Searching for a pen and paper, he scribbled the name down.

'Um… Danny Jones – I'm Liz's boyfriend.'

'Who the fuck is Liz?'

'Okay, right. She's… um… Lucy's mother. The girl that your… um… was attacked.'

'How is little Lucy?'

'What? She's fine. Anyways, the reason I'm calling is…'

'Yes, why am I talking to you and not the mother?'

'Well, I um… *we* think you're getting us on the cheap. That we deserve more.'

'You do, do you? You could be right.' James's tone had changed, sensing what was coming. He could hear the desperation in the man's voice; he decided he needed to manage the conversation.

'Yep. We want double what you've offered.'

James thought for a moment, checking his dad was still on the bench. 'I'll call you back.'

'When?'

'You're a little desperate, aren't you?'

Danny's voice dropped to a whisper, and James thought he heard him walking as he waited for a reply.

'To be honest…'

'Go on…'

'I'm being chased on a debt, and they're not the sort of people to piss about.'

'Who?' He had realised that Danny didn't like silence, that he felt the need to speak.

'Why do...'

'Look, mate, I'm getting a little bored. Who do you owe the fucking money to? I can buy you some time.'

'Okay, it's Bob – Bob Carpenter... his friends call him Chippy... but he's not...'

'I'll call you back. Don't call me again, not on this phone. Not ever. Goodbye.'

James terminated the call, clearing the last call from his father's phone, having quickly scribbled the number down first. Checking everything was as he found it, he left the room chuckling.

***

Reggie sat on one of the many garden benches, grateful for the chance to rest. This was one of his favourite spots, hidden from the world. A place where he could think, ponder about life, make sense of it – if sense could be found. His thoughts once again turned to Ed, asking **why** for the umpteenth time. So many whys. Why didn't he ask for help? Why had he taken his own life? Why had he blown his brains out, and why so soon after the wedding. Why? His own morbidity troubled him. He was a man very much aware of his own clock running down – his dead friends outnumbered his still breathing friends, he found making new friends hard – he found new people insipid, uninteresting. His legacy meant nothing beyond the grave. If he was to leave something good behind, something that would last, he had better make it happen sooner rather than later.

***

James was sitting outside in his car, and he punched in the numbers.

'Is that Danny?'

'Yes – yes, it is. Um, can I take you outside?'

James could hear the hope in his voice mixed with fear. It was a bad combination. He could imagine Danny right now, fingers crossed, praying silently, hoping for a life-changing moment, a maximum return from minimal effort moment.

'So, we've been thinking…'

'Really?'

James was surprised to hear his voice. He hadn't meant to vocalise his thoughts. 'Look, pal, I'll keep this simple. Be home tonight at eight. Send the kid out somewhere. Just you and the mother – okay?'

'Yep, no probs. Will you have the cash?'

'Yes.'

'All of it?'

'Yes.' He could hear the questions not being asked in the silence. 'Make no mistake, this is a one and only payment. Make the mistake of coming back for more and you'll wish you hadn't! Agreed?'

'Agreed.'

Ending the call, James sat in his car, considering his options, knowing only one would work for him. Only one had a conclusion that he could live with. He had until 8pm to find Chippy. It would be cheaper to cover that payment on certain conditions being met than concede to the attempted blackmail. He knew who to call to get the info – another old mate of the old man's. There was a risk keeping this from him, but they had to disappear. He knew they would be back once the money ran out, and now there were two of them. Removing the problem permanently was the only option.

***

Jackie stopped outside Richard's room, feeling quite nauseous, the urge to run, to hide quite overwhelming. She took a deep breath... This was the moment of truth – the moment she had prayed for. Now that it faced her, she almost yearned for the time before waking. Her head bent in one more silent prayer, she slowed her breathing down, fighting for calm.

On arrival, one of the nurses had told her that a doctor wanted to speak to her, and she would find her in the waiting area – a room she knew well. She hadn't had to wait long as she was soon joined by a Doctor Meadows, who sat beside her. She'd listened to the good news whilst dreading the bad. She ticked the list off in her head. He had scored well in every test – eyes, verbal, and motor – and the prognosis was good. Very good. However, he wasn't out of the woods yet; she would have to be patient. She knew that.

Opening the door, she stopped to peer through the gap. He looked to be sleeping, and disappointment mixed with relief crashed through her. She walked slowly towards him, sitting by his bed, all the time telling herself off. Feeling guilty, she took his hand and settled in for the wait. Soon enough she would hear his first words. Soon enough she would see his truth in his eyes. For the first time, she feared what that might be.

The doc had said that he was probably going to have good and bad days – some days he would take a few steps forward, and some days not. He could surprise them... but maybe not. She found some comfort in that. She had time – they had time – and she'd stay by his bed all night if she had to, just to hear him tell her that he loved her. She watched his breathing. It was the first time he'd breathed without the tube since he'd been admitted, and that was progress. The monitors by the bed beeped with lines pulsing across the screen, and she drew comfort from those. He was alive, and he was coming back to her. Thanking God, she cried.

CHAPTER TEN

Parking a few streets away, James sat motionless. Nothing was moving; he sat in silence. He knew he could still call this off – one call would do that – but he also knew that these two were a problem. Left alone they could haunt him for years. He would become their personal banker, whenever times were tough. They had to be put down. He tried to slow his breathing, his senses heightening, his gut churning, and then finally, he opened the door, sucking in lungfuls of fresh air and fearing he might throw up.

He didn't know what to do next. He was tempted to pull out again and drive anywhere – home even. He had no one to blame; he'd set this in motion. He checked the street, and all was quiet. It felt strange to be back here, surreal even. He hoped tonight would be the end of it. It had to end. Now!

His phone buzzed, and he looked to see it was a text from Sarah, inviting him to pop over. He liked the girl; he liked her a lot. A great fuck, with no agenda. He hoped they had a future.

Lighting a cigarette, he got out, leaning against the Porsche and inhaling deeply, he wondered again if this was a good idea. *Too late now, pal. Way too late.*

He headed towards the house, past the waste ground and a grubby transit van. *Probably occupied by the people I'm shortly going to text.*

Standing in the shadows, he watched Lucy step out of the house. He removed his phone, selected messages, and typed: **'she's left, let's do this.'**

He hit send knowing that he would very shortly be joined by some very motivated men. Not the sort of men you would want to answer the door to. It was sad, he thought, how cheap life could be – especially the ending of life. The cost for what was about to happen was settling the twat's debt. A few grand. Pocket money really. He'd spent more on a good weekend – way more!

Hearing footsteps, he turned and watched as three men approached. They were silent, not talking, almost ghost-like, and he felt a strange comfort thinking this probably wasn't their first rodeo. One was a big guy – the one in the middle – and he was a step ahead of the other two. Obviously, he was the alpha. The man-in-charge. The other two, to be fair, looked… well, normal. The one to his left was a big fat guy, and the other was short but solid. The alpha was so visually stereotypical that James had to bite back on a laugh. Obviously, he worked out, and equally obvious was the fact that he liked tattoo parlours. All three of them were in jeans, T-shirts, and boots – big working men's boots. James could guess why…

'You James?' asked the man in the middle. The alpha.

'Yep.'

'Got the money?'

James reached into his back pocket, removing an envelope which he handed to him. He watched as he checked the contents.

'That'll do.'

They walked past him, heading down the street.

'Wait up.'

They stopped, turning.

'I'm coming with you.'

'That's not a good idea, son.'

'Yeah, leave it to the experts,' added the fat guy.

James quickly closed the gap. 'Listen pal, I've paid for a ringside seat.'

'Your call, mate, but don't say I didn't...'

James led the way, knocking on the door that soon opened. James watched the joy on Danny's face quickly replaced by confusion, then fear as he realised that James hadn't come alone. The alpha pushed past him, slamming Danny into the wall. 'Where is she?'

'In the kitchen.'

The alpha passed Danny to the other two who grabbed an arm each, both taking a turn to hit him hard in the gut, causing Danny to buckle, only staying on his feet because he was being held upright. The alpha headed down the hall, followed by James. Liz stood in the kitchen by the sink, and as she turned to see them, a scream caught in her throat.

'What the...?'

The question would never be answered. The alpha walked over to her, punching her in the face. One punch and she fell to the floor, her legs giving way. He could hear a muffled scream behind him and the faint smell of piss.

James felt a little dirty – not the hoped-for reaction. He knew something of the old man's past, but he couldn't see any glory in this. He felt the need to throw up, but pride wouldn't let him leave until the job was done.

***

Danny felt numb, incapable of thought. It was as if he had left his body. He couldn't see a way out, couldn't see an ending that didn't involve pain – and lots of it. The thought of what might happen terrified him. He tried to tell himself that his imagination was worse than anything they could do to him, that they would do, but he knew that was a lie. He knew there would be no happy ending, for her or him. It was him that he was most worried about.

'Forget the money, please… we won't be a problem. I won't be a problem. I promise! It's her you want. She's the one you need to sort out, not me – let me go, please. You'll never hear from me again, I promise.'

He'd intended making more promises, but the alpha backhanded him, the force of the slap sending bright white sparks crashing and exploding inside his head. He wasn't a softy – he'd hurt a few people over the years – but that had been nothing like this. Nothing so fucking scary as this was. Another slap followed, this time to his left. It was an open-handed slap, but the reaction was the same – more sparking, more white light, and more pain.

There were no words, and each blow hit in silence. It was the silence that was scary. He watched Liz trying to stand. *Why the fuck did I get involved with that?* he thought.

She fell back to the floor, pulling a shelving unit with her, the noise deafening. The fat one pulled her up by her hair, and she screamed. He sat her on a chair, covering her mouth with his hand. He watched, glassy-eyed, as another one of them opened a bag and removed a syringe, scattering the contents on the floor. Then he got it, the penny dropped, thinking, *Fuck it, just let them. Just let them do it.*

The alpha knelt in front of him, and Danny listened as he whispered in his ear, 'You can walk away from this. All you have to do is inject the bitch. It's her we want, not you.' He held out a hand, taking the syringe being offered. For a moment he considered stabbing him and making a run for it. For a moment he even considered injecting himself, but without further thought, he walked over to Liz.

Bending so his face was level with hers, he mumbled, 'I'm sorry. I'm so very sorry.'

Her eyes were questioning, pleading, and her body shook, rattling against the chair as she bucked, trying to break free from the fat guy who held her arms behind the chair. Danny stuck the needle in and pushed hard. Once injected, she slid to the floor sobbing, gut-wrenching, animalistic sounds coming from her mouth. He sat on the floor, holding her, afraid to look at anyone. He prayed hard, knowing that it would be his turn next. He hadn't believed that he could walk. He hadn't believed that when the words had been whispered into his ear.

***

James was very disappointed. He felt nothing. No joy, no relief, no nothing. He'd expected a reaction, something, anything other than this numbness – the woman would be dead shortly, his troubles dying with her. He watched as she almost hummed, no doubt enjoying the rush that would end with her last breath. He turned towards the alpha. 'I'll leave him with you,' he muttered, and with that, he left, needing to see Sarah even if just for a hug, craving life, craving goodness.

Once outside he paused, reaching for a smoke, inhaling deeply after lighting. The smoke hitting his lungs, he headed to his car, his pace quickening with each step. He wanted to drive, to leave this behind him.

***

Frank stood in the kitchen looking outside as he prepared a pot of tea. Reggie liked his tea strong and sweet. He found him sat in his study, head bowed, lost in thought. Frank had a pretty good idea of what was troubling him. Losing a mate at their age was tough, hard to bear – a stark reminder of your own place in the world.

Frank felt a cold shiver run down his back as he recalled the day his life had almost ended. They'd been kids larking about by the river one hot summer, diving and looking for treasure. His feet had caught in some reeds, and he hadn't been able to break free. He'd panicked, kicking out when Reggie had dived in to save him. He'd freed him, dragging him kicking and spluttering to the surface. Reggie could be a right royal pain in the arse sometimes, but he owed him everything.

CHAPTER ELEVEN

Jo was typing, her fingers clenching, suspended in mid-air, another bloody report almost finished. She was tired, and the air was stifling, oppressive, not helping her battered sense of humour. Mickey sat at his desk looking bored.

'That's me done for the day. Fancy a quick one?' he asked, pushing his chair back before standing.

'You wish,' she said but with a smile, thinking, *I really do need to take you shopping.* His suit hung off him, shapeless. *Probably bought from a bloody supermarket along with his bread, cheese, and microwaveable meals.* The shirt and brown brogues looked equally worn and just as cheap.

'Come on, it's been a shite day. We deserve a quick one or three.'

'Okay, but not The Coach. I've seen enough of the boys.'

'Okay, I give in this once. You choose,' he said with exaggerated deference.

Jo stood, locking her computer and grabbing her jacket as she left with Mickey. The walk didn't take them long. Her favourite wine bar was just along the road past the building that once housed the city's lunatics. *Appropriate,* she thought. *Shame the doors aren't still open!*

Mickey ordered a couple of malts with a couple of lagers, and Jo took the whisky and downed it.

'Whoa, slow down.'

'Two more of these please, mate.'

They took their drinks to one of the sofas, for a moment just sitting in silence.

'It's the girl I feel sorry for,' Jo started.

'I know. Poor little bugger. Fancy going home to that.'

'I'd have done a runner faced with that. I wonder where she is?'

'The scary thing is that if we hadn't met her, we wouldn't be looking for her.'

They had spent the previous night driving the streets looking for any sign of her. It was now all over the news. They'd had numerous sightings, with no joy. She'd wondered how many girls were lost walking the streets, how many babies were about to be born to unknowing fathers, and how many wives were about to take a lover. At the time she'd blamed the job. The job did that to you, it kept playing with you, with your sanity – making you doubt anything, everything unless you saw it. It was the job that had you imagining the goings-on behind closed doors!

'You okay?' she asked.

'What?' asked Mickey.

'You look upset?'

'Nope.' He sighed.

'Look, I don't want to reaffirm your thinking that I'm a cold-hearted bitch.'

'Please don't shatter that illusion,' he replied playfully.

'She'll go to a better place when we find her.'

'You think?'

'Yep. The mother was a whore, a druggie, an alcoholic…'

'I know that. I meant… do you think we'll find her?'

Jo considered the question. She knew what Mickey was suggesting. She hoped the girl was hiding. The other option was... 'My turn. Same again?'

She didn't wait for an answer.

Mickey watched her walk to the bar. It wasn't a hard thing to do, and he was always aware without looking that he wasn't the only one enjoying the view. He was also very much aware that some would turn to see where she had come from, finding him, and probably thinking 'you lucky bugger' before concluding their thought with 'he's punching'.

For a moment he thought about a change in lifestyle – lose a bit of weight, buy a few clothes – but he knew the good intentions never lasted beyond the next drink or the next meal.

***

Jackie knelt by his bed, his hand cradled in hers, tears pooling in her eyes as she prayed, begging the man upstairs to return him to her whole. Once her words were finished, she rose a little, kissing his hand. For a moment she felt him stir, mumbling. She stood, her heart beating furiously, and waited. Finally, he opened his eyes for a moment, then again, longer this time. He seemed to be waking, staring at her, his lips moving. She bent closer, trying to understand him, gradually working out what was being said.

'Who are you?'

***

James took the back roads to Reepham, driving slowly, very aware that he was delaying his arrival. He hadn't spoken to her for two days. He had made the same journey the night before, thinking he needed her, but he had turned around just short of the town, feeling damaged and dirty, wanting to hide from the world awhile.

Jack had rescued him, finding him stumbling between bars. He had taken him home, put him to bed, and he'd spent the day at Jack's feeling sorry for himself, his head hurting with every movement, his phone vibrating often... which he ignored. He knew he needed to be in a better place before he spoke to her.

***

Sarah had fallen asleep on the couch – the same couch she had slept on the night before. She had been unable to sleep upstairs, so she had come downstairs, dragging the duvet with her. It had been hard to find sleep; she was unable to switch off. She couldn't find a feeling, an emotion. She knew she should have felt something, anything, other than just numb. A never-ending nothingness. She'd tried picturing the villa, the beaches where she hoped her future lay, but nothing had worked. Her thoughts remained scrambled, keeping her from sleep. It was true that she hadn't loved him, but he had been a nice guy, and he had loved her. He deserved something more than she felt – which was nothing.

She woke with a start. She was being kissed. She sat up.

'You bastard! Why didn't you call me? I called and called, but you wouldn't answer. I needed you!'

'Shhh' – he pulled her to him – 'I'm here now.' They hugged, and she cried, but this time with some happy tears mixed in with the sad ones. He moved her hair from her face, and she felt his lips touch hers, soft, gentle, then probing and demanding. She kissed him back hard, her hands reaching for him, reaching for his belt which she pulled undone, then pulling his jeans apart and reaching for him. She heard a sound, a triumphant sound as she touched him, held him. She felt herself being turned onto her knees and her panties being moved to one side. She paused, breath held, waiting for him to enter her, to fuck her. She felt his cock gently probing. She wanted to

99

bend back into him, to take his cock, but he held her hair in one hand, pulled tight.

'Fuck me… please!' *I need to forget – everything.*

'As you wish…'

Her body responded, and she felt the heat course through her, her muscles contracting, pulsing, throbbing. She buried her face into the cushions, screaming with joy, knowing that she would soon explode on his cock.

***

This was one of Reggie's favourite parts of the day. Frank was in the kitchen preparing a late supper, whilst he watched the news with a small whiskey. The news, especially the local news, was one of his favourite programs. His attention heightened when the presenter introduced a double death in the city with pictures of Liz and a man he thought he recognized, a face from the past. The presenter went on to say that a girl was still missing, age unknown, but she was believed to be a late teen. The screen was soon full of Lucy. She looked beautiful but sad. It was one of those pictures where you immediately understood the saying that the eyes revealed everything. A picture that made an impression; a face you wouldn't forget. Her smile didn't reach her eyes – they were sad, sorrowful almost, accepting that this was her lot.

'Frank! FRANK!'

A few seconds later he appeared, drying his hands on a towel. 'Yes, boss?'

'Get the car.'

'Okay. Do you want the Jag?'

'No, the Range Rover.'

'What about supper?'

'Turn it off. We could be out awhile.'

Reggie collected his jacket, checking he had his phone – he would need that tonight. He had a few calls to make. Overdose be damned, somebody had taken them out. He would find out who. If they had the girl, they'd better start praying.

Having brought Frank up to speed, he called John Head.

'John, it's...'

'Reggie, I know who you are. What can I do for you?' His tone was polite, but it was obvious that he wasn't overjoyed to be hearing from him.

'I wanted to thank you for your help the other night.'

'No problem. Have you heard about the girl's mother?'

'Nope,' he lied.

'She's dead. An overdose I'm told, but...'

'But?'

'This is between us, and this is our last conversation on this subject. Agreed?'

'Go on.'

'She wasn't alone.'

'Not the girl?'

'No, not the girl. The girl's missing. We think she found them and did a runner. Poor little sod.'

'You don't think she's been taken?'

'I doubt it, Reggie, this isn't London. We're looking for her.'

'What will happen when you find her?'

'I imagine she'll be taken into care.'

'Care? How old is she?'

'Her records are patchy – very patchy. You wouldn't think it possible in this day and age, but we think in the fifteen to eighteen range.'

'Eighteen? But the papers are saying fourteen to fifteen.'

'That's what we thought too from interviews. We really don't know; she's off the grid.'

'Who'll be responsible for her once she's found?'

'My best guess would be children's services at County Hall. Well, at least until they can prove her age. Anyway, why the interest? Thought you'd be more interested in the mother?'

Reggie pondered before responding. He didn't know why, but there was something about the girl, he just didn't know what. He felt drawn to her, wanting to protect her. *Why? I don't know her,* he thought. 'Oh, you mean her evidence? I assume you have her statement?'

'We do.'

'Well, that's okay, isn't it?'

'Should be. The other fella has woken up.'

Without pausing, Reggie asked, 'What has he said?

'Not much. He's lost his memory… apparently.'

Convenient? Does that help him?'

'Who can tell. There are some who might think it helps, others not. Nothing to stop us taking him to trial, but this is a model citizen with an impeccable record.'

Reggie heard the inflections, the emphasis placed on each word, and he quickly thanked John and hung up. He scrolled through his contacts, wondering who to call next. This was going to be a long night, but he wanted to find the girl.

CHAPTER TWELVE

Sarah awoke with a stiff neck – the joy of yet another night sleeping on the couch. For a moment she forgot what had to be done today. James had left during the night, apparently thinking it best not to be caught together yet. The room smelt of him. The smell of sex hanging. Then it hit her. Today was the day that she had to go to Ed's solicitors to listen to the reading of the will. She knew what was coming. Ed had no kids or siblings; she was all he had.

Once showered, she selected a fairly conservative beige suit, and then with make-up minimally applied, she headed for the city. Soon, she was sitting in a rather formal, uninviting waiting room, waiting for a Ms Stephanie Randall to find her. She hadn't waited long before she stood, hearing her name called, shaking the proffered hand whilst at the same time appraising the woman in front of her: thirty-something, attractive, but stern in appearance. *This is going to be a right laugh,* she thought. *She doesn't like me much.*

The building was something of a rabbit warren – lots of small offices off long corridors. When open, the doorways revealed battered desks with a couple of what looked like comfy chairs and book-filled shelving. The look was repeated in each open room. *It's so blinking quiet,* she thought, *like a morgue.* Finally, entering a rather small but tidy office, a replica of those she had peered into, she took the indicated seat, thanking her for the sincere best wishes. Once seated, she waited, and then finally, Ms Randall opened a file, pausing as if reading for the first time.

'I think we can dispense with some of the formalities. Ed – Mr Horton – was quite specific in his instructions, wanting us to get this done as quickly as possible should he pass. As you might know, our firms had a very close relationship. I knew your husband very well.' She looked quite emotional for a second, then with forced good humour, she added, 'So I was quite honoured to be named as an executor.'

Sarah had drifted during the preamble but focused once she heard the house and worldly goods mentioned – it seemed she now owned the family home. She valued that at about five hundred thousand, and, in addition, she owned three mortgaged buy-to-lets currently rented out, several bank accounts, and of course, the pension and life insurance…

'Will they pay out for suicide?' she asked slightly incredulously, her voice rising.

'We have checked, and yes, they will,' said Ms Randall, her tone implying that she hadn't yet warmed to her.

Sarah was trying to calculate the amount coming her way. 'Do you have a value for… um… everything?'

'Not quite. We await property valuations, but I would suggest something in excess of a million … maybe more.

'What about inheritance tax?' she asked, her concern obvious.

'Well, as everything has been left to you – apart from a small gift to a cats' home…' She stopped as Sarah laughed.

Sarah couldn't help herself. He'd not forgotten the cats' home. She laughed until she cried, taking the tissue offered by Ms Randall, who appeared to be softening in her attitude to her.

'Thank you.'

'Are you okay for me to finish?'

Sarah nodded, thinking, *Oh, yes, please. I just want to get out of here.* 'It was the cats' home that got me. That was his little joke – our little joke.' *Why am I telling her this?*

'Do you have the death certificate?'

'Yes.'

'That's good. You need to go to see your bankers with that. They will transfer everything to your name, and you can continue to draw cash, so don't worry about emptying the accounts before you go.'

Sarah thought, *Ouch! You bitch! She really doesn't like me. I bet she hoped she'd be the next Mrs Horton.* 'So, what's the time frame? I want to sell everything ASAP.' *Game, set, and match.*

Ms Randall sat back in her chair. 'Well, as I mentioned, we've rushed this meeting through as Ed told me that he wanted us to talk to you as soon as possible, should anything happen. The insurance pay-out should be thirty to sixty days, but probate given the size of the estate can take three to six months, but again, we will push. You have the bank accounts to see you through.'

Sarah stood, ready to leave, hand extended.

'There is one more thing, Mrs Horton.'

'Yes?'

'Ed's business. Would you be interested in us making an offer to buy?'

Sarah thought for a moment. 'Yes, please, but make it quick.' With that, she left.

***

It was six fifty-five pm, and Vicky Harper was still sat behind her desk – a desk she'd occupied since being appointed to her current role as a Senior Social Worker, part of the FAST team working in the county. Childcare had been her life – looking after those that needed someone to care about them, about their lives. She'd been in the job since leaving university some thirty-five years previously.

Really, she should be home by now. Her cats would probably ignore her when she finally walked through the door. They were like that, quite capable of ignoring her, even once she'd put food in their bowls. Living alone, apart from her three rescue cats, she was often the last to leave. The others had husbands and families to juggle alongside a tough and often demanding workload, so she didn't usually mind being the last one working, but occasionally it grated as if her life was less important than theirs.

Replacing the phone, she almost jumped for joy. She'd found a place for the girl, albeit short-term. It would do for now. They'd found her hiding in the city college – not a bad choice. She'd been safe, with something to eat. Hiding in plain sight. Vicky finished the notes, making a call to her colleagues who would drive the girl to the house. When the phone rang again, she sighed and picked it up.

'Hello. Can I help you?'

'I hope you can. I'm Reggie Taylor.'

'How can I help you, Mr Taylor?'

'I'm enquiring after Lucy – the girl found at the college. I believe she's under your care?'

'She is. Are you family?'

'Um… no, but…'

'I'm so very sorry, Mr Taylor, but I can't help you, I am sorry. Good day.'

Vicky hung up the phone and sat back wondering why he'd called if he wasn't family. Families were complicated, she knew that as well as anyone. Perhaps better than most. In part, it was why she had vowed to keep her life simple. Standing, she turned the computer off, tugged on her jacket, and left after switching the lights off, grateful to say goodbye to the place for the weekend, even if there was no one to say goodbye to her.

As she left, she replayed the conversation with Reggie, regretting her rather perfunctory responses – with hindsight she could have had a conversation without it being a problem. She should have listened to him, however much she'd longed to be home with her feet up.

***

James had wanted to visit Sarah, but he thought it best not to tempt fate. The old man knew she'd been to the solicitors today, and he might be tempted to pop in to check on her. Sarah had been disappointed but understood. She hadn't put up much of a fight; she'd sounded tired... very tired.

Faced with going home, maybe bumping into the old man, or staying out, he picked staying out. He was now sat in Platinum Lace – a lap dancing bar he and the boys often popped into to enjoy a few beers, watch the girls, and sometimes even buy a dance, if not for themselves for each other, which usually caused much laughter. He loved the honesty of the place; it was what it was, nothing more, nothing less. He'd called most of them, hoping they would jump at the chance of a night out.

The music throbbed, and he sat in one of the comfy chairs by the stage. His mates knew where to find him. A bottle of overpriced champagne sat beside him, cooling. The girls knew who he was, and they knew not to crowd. Not to sell. He would find them if required.

He spotted a newbie, a pretty little thing, he smiled, indicating the chair beside him. She walked towards him all rolling hips; his cock stirred. Suddenly, the room filled with noise as the boys arrived. She had been about to sit on the vacant chair now filled by Dave with Jack taking another chair. James indicated his lap, not knowing that Kieran and Tom had just arrived. Tom jumped from behind to sit on his lap, giving him a hug and a big wet kiss. *I love these boys.*

Sometime later they found themselves in Turtle Bay, more than a little worse for wear. Tom had gone home already – the price to pay for being a footballer. He played for the Norwich U23 team but was expected to breakthrough into the first team sometime soon. As Tom left, they were joined by Lee and Jay – friends of Jack he hadn't met before.

James's attention wandered. Scanning the bar, he spotted a blonde. *Not a natural blonde,* he thought, but she was very well put together. *She's not been hit by the ugly tree,* he thought and laughed. She had great legs – *long* legs – her jeans moulded to her skin. She had a wonderful arse, and her tits looked hard, firm. Tight skin. *She's been under the knife,* he thought. She turned, maybe her sixth sense telling her that she was being scrutinised.

Good face, he thought, *and nice smile.* It reached her eyes. A little too much makeup, but that failed to hide a good bone structure. *She'd be a looker without all the crap,* he thought as her eyes held his. He liked a girl that could lock on. He counted to nine and still she looked, unblinking, her smile growing by the second.

He moved in, aware that his mates would be watching his progress. They were good-looking lads but lacked his don't-give-a-fuck approach; within a few minutes, they would be shaking their heads wondering how he got away with it as they watched him walk her out, with his hand on her waist, guiding her through the busy bar to the door. Time would tell if this was a fifteen-minute alleyway shag or if they had lost him for the night.

The drive to her flat took a while – driving was proving to be interesting and something of a challenge. He drove slowly, not wanting to attract attention, his cock in her mouth, her directions clear but short. It seemed nothing would distract her.

'We're here. I think.'

She raised her head. 'Yep.' Then she returned to his cock.

'Don't you want to go in?'

'Nope.'

James leant back, pushing against the seat, close to orgasm. He watched a couple of girls walk by, laughing. He smiled back, they waved, he came.

She sat up, wiping her mouth with the back of her hand. 'Thanks for the lift.'

'Where are you going?'

'Home.'

'Do you want me to...'

'Nope, I don't think my boyfriend would be very happy.'

'Your boyfriend?'

She stepped out of the car, laughing. 'See you sometime... maybe.'

James bit on his first reply. 'Yeah maybe. Be good.' He watched her go, laughing, enjoying the view. He decided he liked her. Once she was inside, he started the car and headed for home. The roads were pretty empty, so he was soon back. Once parked, he sat on the steps, lighting a cigarette. Inhaling deeply as the world slept, he was soon relaxed. It had been a good night, and for once, he felt tired and ready for bed. Like the old man, he had trouble sleeping. He assumed the old man was just suffering from getting old, whilst his sleep issues were probably lifestyle.

**

Reggie sat in his study, the door open so he could see anyone walking past. He'd heard his son arrive and was ready for him. He knew he had to do this. It was time to cut the cord – the money cord. Sink or swim!

109

'James, in here please.' He watched his son pause. He sensed that he wanted to walk by, to ignore him, but he finally looked at him. He looked resigned. Tired. Finally, he joined him.

'Hi, Pops.'

'Sit.'

He watched his son sit, the look of indignation crossing his face followed by concern, then something else. A look he hadn't seen before – a dash of fear. *This is going to be harder than I thought; I should have done this a long time ago,* he thought.

'What's going on?'

Reggie paused, looking at his son as if for the first time – as a stranger might. He was an enigma. A handsome boy, he was a talented sportsman with county caps across several sports. He was also an intelligent lad – his school reports were testimony to that. Most concluded with 'one of the brightest students in his year, but he needs to apply some hard work to his undoubted intelligence in order to get the most out of his time with us'.

'I've been thinking about your future.'

'So, have I, *Pops*.' The inflection on the *Pops* was obviously intended to annoy.

'Good to hear. What conclusions have you come to?'

James sat up. 'Dad. Can I still call you Dad? He continued, not waiting for a reply, his voice changing, hardening. 'It's a little late for you to act like a father, and more than a little late for me being a son, your son anyways. Once this trial is over, I intend to leave this poxy country and start again. I don't know where. Maybe Mexico. See something of the world.'

'How much is this going to cost me?' Reggie regretted the words and his tone the moment he spoke.

James stood. 'Not one fucking penny, Dad. Not one penny.' With that, he left the room without a backwards glance.

Reggie watched him go, aware of two things: one, he could yet retrieve this. He could call him back, and with a few words, he could offer a simple but sincere apology to save the day, to prevent this ugliness from happening. Two, he had never felt so alone as he did right at this moment, knowing he wouldn't call him back – not yet anyway.

The house reverberated with the sound of doors slamming, and he slumped back in his chair behind his desk. The first desk he'd bought, it had followed him from his first proper office – a portacabin in a scrapyard – to here. It was the only thing that had followed him. The only thing to have survived. He'd kept it so that he wouldn't forget why he lived the life he now enjoyed. His study was one of his favourite rooms in the place, adorned with very expensive artwork and photographs of his Nancy. One of his favourite pics was the three of them, and he stared at this picture now. They'd been so happy, so very happy. His Nancy had been the joy in both their lives. For a moment he thought about going to his son but decided that he needed to let him be his own man, to stand on his own two feet – or was that him being delusional or just the stubborn old bastard that he knew he could be?

He found some comfort thinking that he'd be back sometime soon, once the money ran out – hopefully, a better man than he was now – and then he'd pick up the pieces. He hoped that they might finally find some peace. He wanted to be proud of his son, and he wanted his son to be proud of him, to maybe even love each other a little as a father and son should love.

CHAPTER THIRTEEN

Sleep had evaded Sarah again. She'd tossed and turned on the sofa most of the night – or so it had seemed – and her headache hadn't responded to the paracetamol she had taken a couple of hours earlier. Thinking she might be dehydrated, she'd forced a couple of glasses of water down, and now she needed to pee.

Sunlight was beginning to peek through the gaps in the curtains as she made her way to the downstairs loo. No sooner had she sat down, she heard a gentle knock on the front door. 'You've got be kidding me,' she uttered. Standing, she grabbed a piece of tissue to dry herself before making for the door, the gentle but persistent knocking continuing.

The door, once opened, revealed a dishevelled James. 'What are you doing here? I thought you said we had to be careful?'

James entered, kissing her hello as he passed. 'We do, but I fell out with the old man last night.'

'How, why, what happened?'

'Time for that later. Come here.'

Sarah felt herself pulled, his hands on her skin, hot to the touch.

'I need to shower, clean my teeth.'

Her words were ignored as he pulled her top off, his hand inside her underwear. She tried pushing him off. 'I really do need to wash!'

'You can wash after.'

Laying back on the couch, she felt something sharp against her skin. It took a few seconds to remember her attempt at poetry the night before. She had to hide that; she would be mortified if he read her attempts.

No words were needed that night

We danced until the light

Lovers at first sight

She'd quite liked the opening. The memory of that night – her wedding night – was powerful, but she had crossed through many attempts to finish it. She found it with her hand behind her back, crushing it into a ball before forcing it down between the cushions.

Another thought kicked in as she began to respond to James. Today was the day she had to meet with the local funeral director to discuss the... Assuming she received permission to have his body released to her? She prayed that they would. She wanted this over and done with ASAP. She wanted a small funeral; his will had asked that he be buried beside his former wife if she survived him. That hadn't hurt her. It wasn't meant to.

'Hello, where are you?'

'Sorry, I just remembered that I have to meet with the funeral people today.' To her surprise, James stopped, pulling her close for a hug, saying, 'Poor baby. You go and shower. I'll make us a coffee.'

She hugged him back, kissing him. 'Thanks, babe.'

'I'll fuck you tonight,' James said with a laugh.

'Promise?'

'Promise!'

***

113

Jackie was another early riser... although to be truthful, sleep had been hard to come by. She'd gone to the hospital the day before – as she had every day – to be told that Richard had asked not to have visitors and that had included her. She had thrown her toys out, stung by the rejection. The gems had included: 'I'm not a fucking visitor, I'm his wife.' The nurses had been brilliant. They had shown her to an empty room and had made her a cuppa, only letting her leave when they were happy that she had calmed down.

Today, she hoped for a better day. She had resolved to go to the hospital as normal, not phoning ahead to check or ask. She left the house after showering, grateful to find that the press had moved on to some other wretched person whose story needed telling. She prayed as she drove. Praying at least gave her some comfort that she was doing something, and more importantly, praying gave her much-needed respite from actually thinking.

Her world was ever changed. She knew that at some deep level, going forward, tomorrow, the day after, nothing would ever be quite the same as last week – a week she had lived innocently without concern, or at least without big heart-breaking, life-shattering concerns.

***

Lucy was sitting in her room by the open window. The view wasn't much to look at – other people's back gardens, a few trampolines indicating that families lived there, with occasional excited, screaming heads popping over fences and some kids playing with parents. Some were neat and tidy, some unkempt, with grass way too long to cut, but every house looked like a home. She glanced around her room. It was neat and tidy, but it wasn't her room. She was borrowing it. She couldn't stay here, even if she wanted to, and she didn't want to.

The night before, she'd overheard a conversation as she had left the communal bathroom. Claire, the woman looking after her, was talking and had mentioned her name. She'd crept to the top of the stairs to listen.

'Vicky, I don't know, she's not... How can I put it?' The woman had listened for a few seconds. 'If I guessed, I'd say she needs help – specialist help. I can put a roof over her head, but I can't...' Again, she had paused. 'Okay, but I can't keep her here long. Please find something for her, something better – something long-term.' After a few seconds, she continued, 'Shit, I'd forgotten about the funeral. Who's sorting that out? A pauper's funeral? Poor little love.'

Lucy had crept back along the hallway, opening the bedroom door very carefully. Once inside, she'd sobbed, her heart broken. Nobody wanted her. Her mother hadn't. No one had.

She looked around her room. She hadn't brought much with her, but she placed the few possessions into her rucksack very carefully, then left very quietly by the backdoor. Without a plan, with no idea as to what to do next, she was angry with her mother, she was angry with the world, and she was lost. She was reacting without thinking, making decisions as she walked.

***

Richard opened his eyes reluctantly. His room was sterile, his thoughts jumbled, and his mouth dry – so dry he couldn't raise saliva to moisten his lips. He raised his head, trying to find his water. The beige plastic cup was just within reach if he stretched as far as the handcuffs would allow, and he drank greedily, soon emptying it. The jug was most definitely out of reach. So far, his movement had been restricted to having his head raised so that he could drink. He craved a McDonald's – a Big Mac with a banana milkshake. He loved the Big Mac sauce. *How could he remember that?* How could he remember the taste of a Big Mac, when so much else couldn't be recalled? His doctors had explained everything to him, but still, it was frustrating. Gradually and reluctantly, his thoughts drifted to the proverbial elephant in the room.

The police wanted to interview him. The handcuffs had rather given that away and he'd seen the copper by his door. The thought that he might be that man scared him. He remembered nothing of that night! He knew he had a wife – a very pregnant wife – but again that was news to him. He'd been told that she had sat by his bed every day, every night. He had felt awful asking not to see her yesterday, but he had needed time – time to think. He hoped to wake up each day finding his memory restored, so that he could look at her knowing his truth. So much of his life was a mystery. He'd lain awake wondering what sort of husband he was. Was he a good husband? Was she a good wife? Did he have a lover? He hoped not. Did she?

There was a gentle knock on the door. 'Come in,' he replied, regretting the invitation as soon as had said it. He wished he had feigned sleep.

'Good morning,' the nurse said. 'How are we today?' Without waiting for a reply, she added, 'Your wife is here, and she would like to sit with you if that's okay?'

Richard nodded, watching her. She was a new nurse. He hadn't seen her before. She looked nice – very nice – but nervous. *Am I that scary?*

'Could you refill my water please?' he asked, watching her as she did so. He looked for her name badge. Hannah. He watched as she left. He liked her. She was nicer than many, but his usual morning nurse – Netty, the name on her badge – was his favourite. A no-nonsense, straight-talking woman with a lovely smile. He settled back into the pillows, and each second felt like an eternity, wishing he could just stop time or better still turn it back. Finally, she entered, his wife, his heart breaking at the sight of her. He knew one thing without a doubt: this woman loved him. She seemed so lovely. Maybe he wasn't all bad, and he hung his future on that thought.

It was obvious that she had no idea how scared he was. Just thinking about her scared him, but that feeling, that apprehension, sky-rocketed when she was in the same room. He'd seen the look of love every time she'd walked through the door, every time she had stepped up to his bed or sat on it. He'd seen the unasked questions every time she had taken his hand in hers, every time she'd looked into his eyes. It was soul-destroying; it was wearying.

'Darling, are you okay? Do you need a nurse?'

'No, I'm fine.' He wanted to pull his hand away.

He knew that they both knew that was a lie, but he couldn't cope with more than one conversation at a time. He looked at her face. She was very beautiful. He had tried and failed to recall her face during the night. Any image he had pulled had paled with the reality. He'd like to see her after she had slept through the night. He could see the stress, the tiredness around her eyes. He was the reason – of that he had no doubt whatsoever. He liked how she looked and how she smiled. He liked the dress she was wearing; she deserved the best of everything he thought. For a moment he felt hope. He hoped that he would be found innocent, that he would recover his memory. He wanted to feel how it would be to share a life with this woman, deserving to be loved by her.

Another knock at the door came, and another nurse poked her head in. 'I'm so sorry, but the… um… police need to talk to your husband.'

Richard watched her stand, catching a glimpse of the couple by the door. They made an odd couple. She was really beautiful, whilst he was anything but. He assumed from the suits that they were detectives. Jackie stood, squeezing his hand. 'I'll go get a coffee.'

He watched her leave as the two cops approached his bed. They looked very serious, and he doubted they were here with good news.

***

Parking outside the funeral parlour, Sarah turned the engine off, breathing in deeply. She was dreading this, but it was down to her to make the arrangements. Reggie had offered to help, to join her today, but she had thanked him for the very kind offer, saying this was something she had to do alone. In truth, spending time alone with her lover's dad, who happened to be her dead husband's best mate, wasn't something she was ready for. *Way too complicated!* She almost shuddered at the thought.

To placate him, she had accepted his offer to hold the wake at the big house, thinking it would be easier to leave Reggie's early than leave her own home, the grieving widow needing her space. Ed had always called it the big house. Reggie had proven to be a good friend, supportive and caring. He'd speeded up the inquest procedures, getting a coroner's order to release the body. She hoped his son might be as wonderful one day – once he was ready to become a man.

As she got out of the car, she remembered James whispering in her ear, 'It would be fun to drag you up to my room for a quickie whilst the old man holds court.' That wouldn't be happening now. She shook her head, trying to shake off that image. She needed a head free from James for the next hour or so. He was intoxicating but dangerous. Some of the things he whispered in her ear whilst fucking were scary but exciting!

The night before he had said something about releasing her inner slut.

***

Reggie sat in the garden room. His breakfast, prepared by Frank, sat on the table beside him, the toast untouched, the teapot cooling. He'd been listening to Radio Norfolk, shocked to hear that Lucy had gone missing again.

Standing slowly, thinking that getting old wasn't fun, he went to find Frank, determined that he wouldn't rest until he found her. The question was: *What will you do with her once you've found her?*

The girl needed a chance, a life. Could he give her that? He didn't have much of a track record in looking after anyone save himself, but he knew that he had to try. He was compelled to by guilt or...

He couldn't find the words. The need to become involved, to do something, couldn't be ignored. He had to find her quickly. The mother was being buried in a few days. He had considered paying for a decent burial once he had found out that she was having a pauper's funeral, but he had concluded that he shouldn't draw any further attention to himself.

***

Finally, she watched the two cops leave his room. Deciding not to wait – she had thought he might need a little time to recover – she headed in. He was lying on the bed, his arms crossed and covering his eyes. She ached for him.

He glanced left. 'Get out,' he said with a whisper.

'Richard.' She went to his side, taking his hand in hers.

'Please, just get out. Please.'

'Richard, please… it's not true. Whatever they've told you, it's not true. You couldn't have – you wouldn't have. I know you, you're a good man.'

'Get out.' This time he was louder, the pain evident in every syllable.

'Richard, please…'

'GET OUT! LEAVE ME! … Please, just go.' He shook her hands off, rolling over away from her. 'Please, just leave me alone. Just leave me alone.' The last few words she barely heard.

Jackie stood, her eyes full of tears, undecided as to what she should do, torn between staying and leaving. She knew he needed to be on his own, whilst she needed to stay by his side and hold his hand, willing his memory to return so he could know the man that he was – the man she loved. She turned and left, hardly able to see through the tears. She headed for the lift, ignoring the nurse who was trying to attract her attention.

***

The drive to the girl's house didn't take long. They parked outside. They'd come in the Range Rover, its darkened windows keeping them hidden from nosey neighbours. Reggie stayed in the car whilst Frank checked the house out.

'No joy?'

'Nothing. The house is a shithole.'

'Poor little love. Did you try the neighbours?'

'Most of the street is empty, Reggie. I don't think she's here; she'll be somewhere she feels safe – somewhere she can hide. She's not coming back here anytime soon.'

'Right, let's get going. We can check out the college. She might have gone back. I'll make some calls while you drive.'

Frank started the car, making a five-point turn before facing the way out. Reggie pulled out his phone, trying to think who to call. None of the agencies would talk to him. They probably weren't doing anything other than waiting for a phone to ring. 'Stop, Frank. Go right. I want to try the shop we just passed; they might know the girl.' Frank turned right, stopping by the shop. Reggie climbed out of the car, standing for a moment, arching his back. His body felt stiff, aching. He looked at the shop, hoping that they did know her. Perhaps they would have an idea where she might be.

***

Aarav saw a car pull up. He had always loved the sheer size of the Range Rover. He had often fantasised about the cars he would buy if he'd won the jackpot, and a Range Rover was a constant choice in his top three. This one looked like it had every extra going. His interest piqued when he saw the old chap exit the car, then seeming to check out his shop before walking to the door.

'Good day, sir. How may I help you?' He watched as the man paused, looking around the shop… then at him. He hoped that he was impressed by what he saw.

'I hope you can.' The man removed his wallet to show him a newspaper cutting. 'I'm sorry, I haven't introduced myself. I'm Reggie Taylor, I'm trying to find this young lady. Lucy – Lucy Mack.'

Aarav took the piece of paper. 'Such a lovely girl. She comes to my shop often for her mother. Ah, where are my manners?' He held his hand out. 'I'm Aarav, and this is my shop,' he said proudly. Reggie offered his hand. The handshake was firm. He decided he quite liked Reggie Taylor.

'Have you seen her?'

Aarav knew he had a decision to make – whether to trust this man or not. The girl needed help – more help than he could give her. 'What do you want her for?'

Without hesitation, Reggie replied, 'I knew the girl's mother – many years ago – but I met her again recently. My son saved Lucy from a beating the other night. I just want to take her home to get her off the streets – somewhere she can be safe.'

Feeling happy that she had this man looking for her, Aarav replied, 'There's a park at the end of the road – Wensum Park.

There's a chance she might be there. I think she goes there a lot in the summer. It's a nice place to sit and think. I was going to take a look there myself once my son returned.'

***

Reggie took Aarav's hand again, thanking him and acknowledging the good luck wishes as he left. He had a destination. He had hope. He got into the car quickly, telling Frank where to go, urging him to drive quickly. The drive didn't take long – they could have walked. There was nowhere to park, so Reggie got out. 'Park it anywhere. Park it in the middle of the street if you have to, then come find me.'

'Reggie, for God's sake. Give me five. Let's park, and I'll come with you.'

'No time, old friend.' With that, he was through the gates. He hadn't been to the park for decades, but he recalled it was quite narrow and long, and there was a pavilion. There were a few people walking dogs, and he approached one, showing them her picture and confirming he was the girl's grandfather when asked. He liked the old dear's attitude more than he did the rat on the lead. He liked big dogs, proper dogs, not something the size of his foot that wouldn't stop yapping.

'I saw a girl like her on a bench over there.' She raised a bony hand to point towards the end of the park.

Reggie thanked her and set off, adding, 'If you see an old boy in a suit running this way, can you send him to me?'

Reggie was struggling for breath by the time he made it to the end of the gardens. The autumn sun now quite low in the sky, he saw the bench ahead – an empty bench. He walked to the bench and sat down, reaching for his handkerchief to mop his brow. He was breathing hard. 'I'm getting too old for this.' His phone rang and he answered, breathlessly managing, 'I'm at the end of the park…'

'Are you okay?' a voice asked.

Glancing up, he smiled and then chuckled. 'I am now, sweetheart. Please... please sit with me for a moment.'

'Are you sure you're okay?'

'I'm good. We've been looking for you.'

'Why?' She sounded nervous. Scared.

He saw Frank approaching and held out a hand to pause him. She turned to look and seemed ready to run. He knew the next few minutes were incredibly important for her, maybe for him too, he acknowledged. He had to get this right – not just for now but for tomorrow and the tomorrows to follow.

'I'm an old friend of your mother's. I knew her many years ago: I bumped into her recently.' He was relieved to see Lucy sit beside him, a few feet away but on the same bench. 'She asked me to promise that I would look after you if anything happened to her, that you had no one to look after you if anything did.' Reggie turned to face her. 'I know you're scared, you have nowhere to go, and you don't know who to trust.'

'I trust Aarav,' she said with a whisper.

'Aarav?'

'He owns the shop I go to. He's a nice man.'

'Okay, I've met him, and you're right. He is a very nice man. In fact, it was Aarav who told me how to find you.'

'He did?'

At that point, Frank joined them, although still standing a few feet away. By the look of him, he'd run the whole way too.

'You okay, Reggie?'

'Yep, we're good thanks, Frank.'

'Who is he?' she whispered. She looked ready to run again.

'He's my best mate. He looks after me – cooks and drives, that sort of thing.' Reggie leaned towards her to narrow the gap,

123

whispering, 'He's actually a very nice man and not half as scary as he looks.' He was relieved to see her smile. Reggie sat back. The next few days were going to be hard for her – a mother to bury and a new life to start. He'd do the best he could.

'You don't have anywhere to live, do you?'

'Nope.' She started crying, and Reggie put his arm around her. She leaned in, which he took as a good sign. The other option would have been two old men trying to catch her.

'Frank and I live in a big house near the sea. We'd like you to stay for a few days.'

She turned towards him. 'A few days?'

'You can stop as long as you want – forever if you want. That will be your decision, won't it, Frank.'

Frank nodded.

'If you want, we can walk to the shop so you can speak to your friend who will get me checked out – a quick Google should do it.'

'Are you famous?'

Reggie belly laughed. 'No, not very.' He stood. 'Well, maybe just a little. Come on, lovely, let's go back to the shop. We can speak with your friend.' After a moment's hesitation, she stood.

Reggie followed Frank. He held his hand out to her, and when she took it, he knew in that moment that he would do whatever was needed to see she had the best life possible. He felt something – an emotion he couldn't label. He felt teary. He walked one step at a time, feeling for her hand in his, each touch telling him that his life would be forever changed.

***

James had been drinking for much of the afternoon. He had left the house soon after Sarah had departed. There was nothing he hated as much as boredom, so he found himself sat at a bar

– at one of his favourite city centre haunts. His interest was focused on a rather pretty blonde sitting by the bar. He liked the cowboy boots, the tight faded blue shorts, and the white T. He wondered how she would taste… how she would kiss… and he intended to find out. She glanced over from time to time, catching his eye and smiling.

Finally, she accepted his offer to join him. He watched as she walked towards him. She had a great walk – very sensual. She sat beside him, he imagined her naked, well, almost naked – she could keep the boots on! Her eyes were beautiful, soft brown with hints of green, and they sparkled. She looked naughty, up for anything.

'Hi, I'm Vanessa.'

'Hi, Vanessa, I'm James. How about we go somewhere nicer?'

'I'd love to, but my shift starts at six.'

'That gives us about twenty-five minutes.'

'You don't hang about do you?' she said, laughing.

'Not if I see something I want.'

'Do you see something you want?'

'Yes.'

'Do you always get what you want?'

'Not always… mostly, but not always.'

'What if I'm not that type of girl?'

'I'm hoping you're not!'

'Follow me,' she said without hesitation. Standing, she headed to the back of the bar, and James followed her through a couple of rooms to a small courtyard, the cigarette butts suggesting it was used by the staff. She climbed a fire escape ladder, and he stood admiring the view. She had a great arse.

He followed her to a small flat roof and approached her as she backed against a brick wall. He stood in front of her, reaching for her shorts, pulling her to him.

***

Sarah eased herself into a very hot bath, a large G&T with lots of ice close by. She had, initially, been disappointed to return to an empty home, but she was now enjoying the peace and quiet. It had been a strange sort of day. Her husband – her dead husband, *I'm too young to be a widow* – was to be buried Monday week. She had left a message for Reggie, but unusually, he hadn't yet returned her call. She hoped he didn't call too late. Knowing James, he would probably have her answer the phone mid-shag; she laughed at the thought. Her new lover, her 'friends with benefits' boyfriend, sometimes scared her. He was a self-confessed hedonist. That word had sounded delicious to her. It was true he lived for the moment, for the 'high', without thought to consequence. For an overthinker, that was quite intoxicating!

***

Lucy gasped when she saw the Range Rover. 'Is that your car?'

'One of them. I have a few. Too many really.'

'Can I sit in the front, please?'

'Sure. Frank, I'll drive. You sit in the back.'

Frank looked surprised; it had been a while since Reggie had driven anywhere, but he opened a back door.

'Right. I need you to guide me to Aarav's shop, please.'

A few minutes later, they pulled up outside the shop. Reggie followed her in, listening as Lucy explained that she was going home with him. He saw the questioning look pass across Aarav's face.

'It's okay. I'll take very good care of her.'

'I know you will. I know who you are. I looked you up on Google.'

Reggie and Lucy both laughed. 'I would have looked after her, you know; she could have slept here until something was sorted.'

'You're a good man, and I thank you. Lucy thanks you.' He then turned to Lucy. 'Right, young lady, are you ready?' He watched as she hugged Aarav, whose awkwardness soon melted with him hugging her back, and then they finally stepped apart. Lucy picked up her bag – a scruffy, tiny bag that contained everything she owned. Well, he was going to change that. He was going to change everything for her. Reggie took Aarav's hand, looking him in the eye. 'I'll see she pops back to see you sometime soon. That's a promise.'

Lucy climbed into the front.

'Are you driving home too, boss?'

'I think I might.'

With Frank in the back, they headed off. Reggie couldn't wait to see her face when she saw what home looked like. Once home he'd call Dick or Mickey. That could be a problem he thought, but he'd worry about that later. For now, having her safe was all that mattered. He resolved to do the best thing for her – whatever that might be.

**

Lucy sat back in her seat, the drive through the city giving her time to think, to adjust. Just a few moments ago she had been terrified. She'd had no future, no one to care for her. Nowhere to sleep.

She listened to Frank and Reggie talk – their plans for tonight, for supper, for tomorrow. They were going shopping for her; she needed clothes. They sounded happy. Happy for her.

Soon they were leaving the city behind them; she shed a tear for her old life, for her mother, for the...

She turned to look at the fields and woodlands that they sped by, resolving to never forget the past. She made that promise several times, but she had to try to enjoy this new life. It was alien to her, but something told her she could trust Reggie and Frank. She heard the indicator, felt the car slow, and saw a long road ahead – a curving road with huge gardens on either side. Farther ahead, she could see a massive house. She counted twenty windows. They stopped beside a huge fountain, and Reggie opened her door. She got out, unable to take it all in.

'Is this…'

'It's home, sweetheart. Let's go in.'

Frank opened the front door, and she stepped into a hallway twice as big as her old house. She didn't know what to say next. She looked behind her, taking a last look at the grounds.

'Who's hungry?' asked Frank.

'I am,' she replied.

'Let me show you my kitchen. You're going to love it. You can be my sous-chef.'

'What's a sous-chef?'

Reggie watched them walking side by side, chatting away, and he smiled. Life was going to be very different going forward – for all of them. He couldn't believe how this girl had coped with everything that had happened to her. Just surviving the life that she had lived was pretty incredible.

Frank was in the kitchen warming up some scones, and the kettle was on. Lucy was sitting at the table. She looked tired, ready to drop. Only adrenaline would be keeping her going, he assumed.

'Right, young lady, once Frank's filled you up, we need to find you a room and some clean clothes.'

Lucy nodded.

'I know just the room. It has a lovely view over the gardens.'

'Thank you.'

'We are going to have to take you shopping tomorrow.'

Lucy didn't know what to think. She liked Reggie and Frank and felt safe with them. Her biggest worry was that the dreaded, hated *social* might come and get her to take her somewhere else. Somewhere horrible. She'd always know her old life wasn't normal; she'd seen enough TV soaps to know that much. She'd also known that she wasn't thick like her mother had often shouted. She wasn't stupid. It had been easier to hide herself to try to stay invisible, not to be seen, and not to be noticed!

'So, I can stay here?' she whispered.

'That's up to you, but let's not worry about that for now. I think you need to take a few days out. I have lots to sort.' His voice softened. 'We need to let the police and social services know that we have found you. I'll call them in a mo'.'

'They might want to take me away?' The thought scared her.

'I promise you this is your home if you want it. Frank and I will look after you as best we can, but we want what's best for you. I'm hoping you want to stay here awhile. For as long as you want. You can stay here forever if you want to. It's entirely your decision.'

She couldn't take everything in. Without thinking, she hugged him, squeezing hard, her eyes filling with tears. Had she looked up she would have seen two old men also looking a little emotional.

***

They climbed the stairs together, side by side.

'Are you ready to see your room?'

She nodded.

'I'm in the bedroom to your right, and Frank is at the other end. Your room is ahead in what we call bedroom number six.' He stood beside the door. 'After you,' he said, watching as she opened the door with some trepidation. He didn't know what would happen next, but he had prepared himself for both extremes. He would have understood any reaction. The poor girl must be worn out, scared... Only recently she had found her mother dead and had hidden from the world, thinking, believing that no one cared for her. She had been driven to a foster home, knowing nothing. Her trust in him blew him away. How'd this girl survive her life?

Lucy looked into the room, and her first impression was that it looked like the rooms in the magazines her mum used to read. It was huge. She heard Reggie say something about redecorating it and getting new furniture and stuff, but this room was... it needed a big word to do it justice. She turned to hug him. 'It's magnificent!' She walked to the window, and the garden outside was just about visible in the fading light. She turned, scanning the room, looking into each corner, spotting a door on the opposite wall. 'What's through there?' she asked, pointing.

'That's your study. We'll get you a computer and a TV. Beyond that is your bathroom. I'll leave you to settle in. I'll pop back with some clothes if that's okay? I think we can find you something?'

He saw the nod.

'Are you very hungry or just very tired?'

Another nod.

'Right... that's good. I'll get Frank to get a full English on. Can you eat breakfast for tea?'

Another nod. This time she smiled.

'Good. We'll eat in say half an hour. I'll get Frank to shout 'tea up' when we're ready.'

Another nod.

He turned to leave, pausing by the door. 'I hope we can make you very happy here. Please treat this as your home.'

Lucy walked into the room next door – the study – and laughed. She then turned to check out the bathroom. She couldn't believe she had her own bathroom. She touched the matching towels, all so very soft to the touch. She wanted a bath – she *needed* a bath. Hearing a knock on her door, she went to answer it, finding Frank holding what looked like a pair of sweatpants, a T-shirt, and a hoodie.

'Hope these will work until we can get to the shops. They're probably a bit big, but at least they're nice and clean.'

'Thank you, Frank.'

'Oh, you're very welcome. Reggie said something about a fry up. You hungry?'

'Yes.' She turned to go, then stopped. 'Frank, would it be okay for me to have a bath before tea?'

'Absolutely. Take your time, sweetheart. We'll wait for you to come down. It won't take me five minutes to sort out a spot of supper.'

'Thank you, Frank.'

'My pleasure, sweetheart. I'll shut the door.'

Lucy placed the clothes on the bed before returning to the bathroom to run a bath. She left her clothes neatly folded on the floor. She would take them downstairs to wash after her bath. Once in it, she noticed several bottles of bath salts and liquids. She picked one which claimed to be relaxing and added it to her bath. Liking the cloud of bubbles, she stepped into the bath, then slowly lowered herself down. Once her body had got used to the hot water, she pushed herself up the bath. For a moment the world stopped, and she closed her eyes, tears forming, and cried for both her old life and her new one.

***

James pulled into Sarah's drive. He'd called her on the way to say he was hungry and did she have anything in the house worth eating. She had sounded tired, so he'd picked up a huge takeaway on the way over, the smells tormenting him as he drove. He sat in the car for a moment, thinking about life, his future. She was definitely a good short-term solution – soon to be cashed up, a looker, a great lay, a wild side to be played with and a need to travel the world.

Yep, she'll do for now. We can travel the world together until the money runs out.

Happy to see her standing in the open doorway, he smiled and waved. They'd eat first, then he needed a shower. In truth, he probably needed the shower first, but the food smelt too good. He hugged her, then stepped into the lounge. Spotting that she'd lit a few candles, placing them on the coffee table with plates and cutlery, he smiled. A lager had been poured for him, and she had opened a bottle of red. He sensed she needed to chat to unload about her day, and he made a note to find time for her later, after they'd eaten, after he'd showered, and for certain, after he'd fucked her. They could talk after!

***

Jackie had never felt so alone, so lost, so numb. She had lost track of time. She really didn't know what day it was. One of the nurses, Netty, had set her down. Netty was a lovely woman who had told her, quite firmly, that she had to rest and take some time out – not just for her, but also for her baby. She couldn't continue as she was. She knew the nurse had been thinking of her – of them – so she sat holding a cooling cuppa, the TV in the corner. She hadn't watched any TV for a few days now as she didn't want to risk catching the local news.

The baby moved… a gentle kick.

Not long to go now, she thought. It could be a December baby – maybe even a Christmas baby. She started to cry, hugging her belly. She made the bump a promise to keep their family together, but what if Richard was guilty? What if he went to prison? Could they, the three of them, survive prison? She made a promise that tomorrow she would stay away from the hospital. She needed a day off, a day to recharge. The nurse was right.

***

Sarah couldn't believe that they were about to eat the takeaway in bed. James had taken everything through to the best guest room downstairs, including the candles. Bless him. She had bathed upstairs – it was the best bathroom in the house, with a roll top bath and great views over the fields and woods beyond – but she still couldn't sleep in the old master room. It was one thing to sit in the lounge, to use the bathroom, but she could not, would not, sleep in what had been their bed. Their bedroom. That had been a different life. A life she wanted to forget – had to forget – if she was to move on.

James was showering. She had insisted that he took a quick shower. He would have to shower before she let him anywhere near her. Now, she lay on the bed, suddenly ravenous, the take-out smelling wonderful. She was tempted to nibble. He had said to start without him, after all. Finally, he joined her, wearing just a towel pulled tight around his waist. She made a playful grab for him.

'After supper.'

'But I want you now.'

James ignored her, opening various trays of delicious Chinese. Selecting a king prawn, he offered it to her, and she took a bite.

'Yum!'

She took the rest, the sweet chilli sauce dribbling down her chin.

'More! I want more!'

He offered her another prawn, and she took it whole, licking his fingers clean.

'More. More!'

She watched James pour her a glass of wine, and he took a long gulp from the bottle.

'Me!'

He held the bottle in front of her mouth, and she took a mouthful before watching him eat. Soon they were feeding each other by hand, pausing only to drink from the bottle. She felt happy; she felt complete. She wouldn't change a thing right now. This was … She didn't know how to describe it. This was a new feeling, a new experience, unlike anything that had gone before it. She loved how he lived – without fear, without thought to consequence. Everyone should experience this once. This was the life she was meant to live.

'Take your top off.'

'Why?' she asked, thinking she must have spilt something on it.

'I want to cover your tits in this sauce, then lick it off.'

Feeling a little giddy, she removed her top, every sense overloading. She watched him select a container, dribbling the still-warm sauce on her tits. She lay back with eyes closed, feeling every lick, every touch. She felt herself being turned onto her knees. She pushed back into him, leaned into him, moaning when he whispered what he had planned. She sucked his fingers into her mouth, listening to him telling her that one day soon she would experience her first threesome. Imagine what two cocks could do to her. She came hard – harder than she'd ever come before. She collapsed onto the bed, aware that he hadn't finished.

James smiled. He was enjoying the view. She was naked, her sweat-glazed skin warm beneath him. He took his cock, gently stroking her pussy with it. He had felt her physical response to his words, and he knew that she was ready to play, to step outside of the bedroom. To him, sex was a game to be played, to be explored. He was confident that, in time, she would make an excellent partner.

CHAPTER FOURTEEN

It was a beautiful day. One of those classically British autumnal Sunday mornings when the world seemed a little better, a little brighter. Earlier Reggie had called the police, speaking to Jo, ostensibly to check that Dick had passed on the news that they had found her and that she was safe, adding that he would be talking with social services next. He wasn't usually over-fond of the cops, but he quite liked Jo.

Jo had confirmed that he needed to talk to a Ms Harper, giving him her mobile number – once he had explained why he needed it. During the call, she had mentioned that the mother was being buried this week – a pauper's funeral. He had been surprised at the date, thinking it might take longer than the usual week to ten days, but Jo had advised that the coroner hadn't asked for an inquest following the post mortem. She had explained that they found the cause of death to be an overdose.

She had said, somewhat bitterly, 'That druggie alcoholic street whores were not worth the expense.'

He thought she might be quoting someone else. He had assured her that he would contact the funeral directors to sort a few things and would pay for a decent send-off, adding that he and Lucy would attend. He knew the news would be hard to take. Death was one thing, but watching a loved one, especially a family member, a parent, being buried was a final painful acceptance that life was forever changed.

He heard Frank on the stairs, and soon the door opened. 'Morning, boss.' Frank entered carrying a tray with breakfast and a copy of both the Telegraph and the Sun – his guilty secret.

He wouldn't read the papers during the week, but Sundays were special – and a little different!

'Been busy?'

'Phone calls, Frank, just a few calls.' His voice softened. 'The mother's being buried this week; we need to sort a few things.'

'Just let me know.'

'Will do. Is she up yet?'

'Don't think so. I'll knock on the door and ask if she wants a cuppa, maybe breakfast in bed?'

'I think she'd probably rather eat downstairs?'

'You might be right.'

'Actually, I think it would be nice if we all eat downstairs. Let's make it a rule going forward. We eat together. It'll give us time to talk.'

That's if she wants to stay.

'Excellent; I'll go make her a cuppa.'

Reggie watched him go, thinking that even Frank had a spring in his step this morning. She had that effect on you, he thought. He too was looking forward to spending the day with her. He hated shopping, but they had promised to do so today, and so they would. He would wake her if needed. Reggie hated shopping almost as much as he hated funerals, and he had two to go to – one this week, and his old mate the week after. One of the hardest things about getting old was the ever-increasing number of funerals he had to attend. When it was his turn, he just wanted a swift, no-nonsense goodbye and a plot under a tree overlooking a lake – his tree, his lake.

***

Lucy stood in front of one of her bedroom windows, enjoying the view. She thought the garden was beautiful but huge. The woods in the distance were part of the estate, as was the coach house. Frank had woken her earlier with a cup of tea, happily answering her many questions about the house and the grounds. Apparently, Reggie owned just about everything that you could see from the house. Thirty acres of gardens, woodland, and lakes. It was as unreal to her as anything could be, as far removed from her understanding of what might be as a trip to the moon or Disney.

After breakfast, she wanted to explore, to walk from one end of the estate to the other. It was only after Frank shouted 'breakfast' that she realised how hungry she was. Frank had suggested a full English, so she took the stairs quickly, still shocked at how many doors she passed. *I could get lost in this place.*

The kitchen smelt wonderful, and the table was laid. She was happy that they were eating in the kitchen. She'd seen a dining room on the way down, and the table was massive. She'd bet you could sit twenty around that table.

'Where do I sit?'

'Anywhere you want, love.'

Selecting a seat on the far side so she could watch Frank cooking, she checked out the table. Lots of sauces, a rack of toast with jams and marmalades, and a pot of tea. Her taste buds kicked into overdrive as she saw the plate put in front of her.

'Thanks, Frank. This is the best breakfast I've ever seen. Can we do this every day?'

'Do what every day?'

Lucy spun round to see Reggie standing in the doorway.

'Hello, Reggie.'

'Mind if I join you?'

'Nope, that would be nice. You too, Frank. Let's all eat together.'

'That's what we thought.'

The breakfast tasted as good as it looked, and she was soon clearing the plate, listening to their plans for the day. She couldn't believe that they were going to take her shopping for new clothes, new bedding, new everything. It was going to be a busy day. She felt a little nervous. She hadn't experienced anything like this before, but she felt safe with them. She was still apprehensive about the future, but something told her that it would be way better than her old life. Guilt swept through her; she felt bad for being happy.

***

Reggie watched Frank and Lucy chatting away nineteen to the dozen. She worried him. He knew behind the happy smile that she would be thinking about the other stuff, that he would have to find time, the right time, to sit with her and talk about her feelings. The biggie would be the upcoming funeral, but today would be all about the shopping.

Shortly before coming down to the kitchen, he'd spoken with Ms Harper – a nice enough woman. She was slightly surprised at hearing from him on a Sunday.

He had mentioned John Head early in the conversation, for once not calling him 'Dick'. They'd chatted about Lucy. They didn't have much – no records, no history except an anonymous call a couple of years back that had revealed nothing. She had agreed it was pretty shocking.

It was the birth certificate that troubled him the most. He didn't need to talk to his lawyers to know that this could be a big issue. If he could prove her old enough, if he could prove she was sixteen, this was her home for as long as she wanted it. However, if they couldn't do so, he could have a fight on his hands. He would start with the hospitals. Even if she hadn't registered the birth, they would have a record of her somewhere… *wouldn't they?*

***

Jackie had been true to her word. Any thoughts about going to the hospital quickly banished, she'd kept herself busy with housework, and now every surface glistened. The washing machine and tumble dryer were both working overtime. The next job was to go online and order the shopping. Supplies were low, and the fridge was almost empty. She would normally drive to one of the local supermarkets, but she couldn't bring herself to do that. So, for only the second time in her life, she would place the order online.

Five minutes later, she was sitting at the table, coffee by her side, scrolling through the fruit section, selecting bananas, apples, and grapes. She stared at the screen for a good while, unable to make a decision as to what to order next. She walked every aisle when shopping in the real world. Shopping online wasn't working for her – she had to see it, see the shelves. Nothing made sense, her world was crashing, and she couldn't even order the bloody shopping without losing the plot. Standing, she threw the laptop against a wall, screaming as she did so before collapsing, sobbing her heart out. Her world seemed bleak… dark. She knew she had to stand to function, but the effort seemed beyond her. She just wanted to hide, to disappear, to find the secret to turn back time or to wake up knowing this had been nothing more than a bad dream.

The doorbell rang, and she lifted her head as the ringing continued. *Who could that be?*

She went to the curtains and peeked outside to see Gaby, a casual friend, married to a rather gorgeous chap called Jon. They'd met a few times but hadn't become close friends. *Why are you here?* she thought. She looked to the drive to find it empty. The press had moved on. *Thank God.*

She went to the door to find Gaby gone but found a bunch of flowers with a card lying on the floor. She picked them up and returned inside. She put the flowers in the sink to sort them later but opened the card. She smiled at the offer of help – the first such offer since the news had broken. She had been grateful for the solitude. They had friends – of course, they had friends – just not that many. They had been enough for each other. They'd mixed socially with colleagues, and that had been enough social interaction for them both, but now she felt alone. If Gaby was the only one to show up, they were pretty much on their own, and if he was guilty, she would have to start again. That thought terrified her. Not the starting again... but if he was guilty!

What would she do if he was? She knew the house was heavily mortgaged. They'd agreed to go all in, to buy a futureproof house – one that would look after them for years to come. Maybe forever? As to savings, she had no idea. She left that to Richard. She thought it might be prudent to visit the bank tomorrow to get some cash. Best to be prepared for whatever happened next. If he was found guilty, if he went to prison, she would need to make a life for herself and the *bump*. They wouldn't be able to keep this house, that much was for sure.

***

Sarah crept into the kitchen to find James standing at the sink, drinking a cuppa and seemingly lost in thought, wearing only black boxers. She moved silently to stand behind him, simultaneously kissing the back of his neck and sliding her hands into his boxers.

'We need to talk,' he grunted.

'I know,' she said laughing, feeling his cock start to grow as she cupped his balls.

'We have plans to make my love. Things to do.' He turned to face her.

'Yep, but can we fuck first?'

'You're insatiable, you know that?' he said sternly.

'Does that mean you like me?' she said, laughing.

'I think I more than like you.'

Looking into his eyes, she asked, 'Do you?' and kissed him hard.

***

It had been a very good day, thought Reggie. He had to turn away when thinking how much his Nancy would have loved a day like today. His beloved wife had always wanted a girl. She had often complained, albeit in jest, that she was surrounded by too much testosterone. Thank God she hadn't known the whole truth. Today, however, would have had her happy and proud.

It had been Lucy's day, her enjoyment obvious. He hoped, even for a short time, that she might have forgotten the bad stuff. She'd been a little overwhelmed, to begin with, but she had soon settled in, quickly relaxing with Frank's help – who was a surprisingly good personal shopper, especially when it came to colours and fabrics.

It hadn't been long before they had to return to the car to drop off the bags before heading back to the shops. The shop assistants had been mostly wonderful when it came to the clothes. One, in particular – a lovely woman called Maureen, who seemed to take a shine to them – had certainly spotted their need for help. A teenage girl shopping with two old codgers had caught her eye. He'd quite liked Maureen. He had wondered if Lucy would be up for more shopping next weekend.

They were now in her room, her bed covered with bags – clothes for every occasion, with lots of accessories and shoes too. It had taken most of the day, but they had also found time to buy her a laptop and a TV. Reggie thought it important that she could retreat to her room whenever she needed her own space and to have everything she needed.

He sat on the corner of the bed.

'You okay, boss?'

Reggie looked over at Frank, who was trying to get the TV sorted. 'I'm fine, bud, I'm just feeling my age.' In truth, he was thinking that as wonderful as the day had been, tomorrow wouldn't be. He would need to talk to her about the funeral arrangements. Reggie was dreading that. She seemed to be able to forget the bad stuff – at least in their presence – unless they mentioned something, which would trigger a sad face, a still face, a face without emotion, causing them to shut-up, regretting whatever had been said. Reggie admired her strength, her ability to find happy quickly. He assumed that she'd had years of practise trying to move on, trying to find happiness!

CHAPTER FIFTEEN

Richard felt exhausted. Just sitting up had left him worn out. The morning sun was too bright. He much preferred the evening gloom – it seemed to suit his mood better. It was hard not to feel angry. He knew very little about who he was. He imagined that he was quite fit, and that he was quite active – he seemed to be in good shape. He must have been worth knowing. He had a beautiful pregnant wife – at least, he hoped it was his child. However, that didn't mean happy families. It was a gut-driven thought… the need to produce, to father a child.

The one thing that scared him more than anything else, more than the rest put together, that kept him awake at night, was what if he was the sort of monster who would prey on young girls. He knew one thing, if he was, he wouldn't want to live. They could put him down now.

The docs had just left him. They'd talked about the future – his future – and the time it might take to remember. He'd switched off, thinking his future probably included a trial and prison. He had wondered if that might be best, hiding from the past and not confronting it. Why would you want to remember everything? He heard the door open, and he considered feigning sleep, but she had already entered his room and had seen him awake. She had stayed away as he had asked – which he appreciated. He was torn and had been for days. Part of him, probably his heart, wanted her to stay, to hold his hand, to tell him everything would be okay, but another voice shouted louder, and that voice was insistent, saying to send her packing, to get rid of her. That would be best for her, that would be the kind thing to do, he thought.

***

Today she stopped herself from sitting on the bed. She had promised to give him some space. 'Hello, darling.' She uttered the words without thought. He had always been 'darling' or 'my love', but she saw the reaction, the impact, as if she had hit him. She wanted to hug him, to hold him, to tell him everything would be okay, but she didn't believe that. She was tired, and she was the one who needed to be hugged and be told everything would be okay.

She watched him slump back into the pillows. He had always been an active man, a man who did a job as soon as he had thought it, so this was a very different Richard. She didn't know if she could cope with another hour of polite conversation, so she'd brought some photos to show him in the hope they might spark a memory. However, she decided to leave them in her bag. In truth, she was looking forward to leaving, and that thought troubled her more than anything else.

***

Reggie was sitting at the kitchen table, and Frank was sitting opposite, both of them drinking tea. Reggie had just finished telling Frank about his call to the funeral director, who had happily agreed to make lots of changes to Liz's funeral tomorrow and was very, very happy to send him the bill.

'I was thinking about inviting Aarav and his family?'

'Not a bad idea. Otherwise, it's just you and me... poor little love.'

'Thought we could have them back for a bite to eat?'

'Good idea. I'll get some stuff in.' He grabbed a pad and pen to start his list. Without looking up, he asked, 'What about the social worker?'

Reggie pondered. 'That's not a bad shout. Show her who we are.'

'I think she knows who we are.'

They chatted while they waited for Lucy to wake, both of them not looking forward to having to talk about the next day. Once the funeral had passed, they would need to address the question raised by Ms Harper regarding Lucy's future. Reggie knew he wanted to be part of that; he had come to love the girl already. She was a ray of sunshine, which was remarkable when you factored in her upbringing. He could only imagine her potential... where she would be in a year or two and what she would be doing. It was obvious that she had survived, stayed in the background, where it was undoubtedly safer, hidden from the world only because her world hadn't been that nice.

***

Sarah reached in for a kiss, hoping he might delay leaving for the city.

'Got to go, babe.'

'Really? The agents are coming today to value the house.'

'You'll be fine. Best I'm not here for that.'

'Okay,' she agreed, glumly.

James pulled her close, smiling mischievously. 'I might set you a little challenge, a little game to play.'

'I like to play games,' she said laughing, jumping up and wrapping her legs around him. 'What do you have in mind?'

'I'll call you later, babes, I've got to go.' He backed her towards a hardtop, sitting her down and ignoring her protests, her pleas. He turned and left.

***

Reggie and Frank were in the study, Frank sat behind by the window and Reggie pacing back and forth. Both had been busy making arrangements for the funeral to be held the next day. Frank was in the middle of a shopping list – the wake to be held at their home. It would be a small wake, but everything had to be just perfect. Reggie had called to invite Aarav and his family, offering to send a car to collect them. He'd also invited a few old friends – people that he trusted to attend, to behave themselves, and to meet Lucy. Each of the invitees had understood the not-so-subtle request.

'I'll be happier once tomorrow's been and gone.'

'Me too, bud. Me too.'

'Do you think she'll be okay?'

'Do you know, I think she'll be fine. She's an amazing girl. Way stronger than I thought she'd be.'

'Yep. When you think of the screw-up of a mother she had, it's incredible she's survived.'

'I thought we might have tears and tantrums.'

'That would have been understandable.'

'Yes, it would. She's a bit special.'

***

It was the laughter that woke Lucy. For a moment, she lay under the covers, hardly able to breathe. Only her head was visible. She checked her room out as if seeing it for the first time. It was a beautiful room, and it was hers; she couldn't get used to the size of it. It really was as big as her old house.

Getting out of bed, she walked to the window, pulling a curtain to one side. It was a beautiful day. The trees in the distance moved with a gentle wind, and she stood still watching the trees sway for a little while. She could have stayed all day, but she heard the shout of 'breakfast' and quickly headed for the *en suite* to wash and dress ready for whatever the day threw at her.

Soon she was taking the stairs, the smell of bacon frying making her taste buds kick into action. She paused by the door, listening to the banter taking place in the kitchen. She was already very fond of both of them. She would have to show them that she wasn't made of glass, that she wouldn't easily break!

'Here she is, and how are you this morning?'

'I'm doing pretty good thanks, Frank.'

'Come and sit. Breakfast is ready, madam.' All three laughed at the fake solemnity. Lucy sat marvelling at the plate put in front of her, and she sat back happily, trying to ignore the voice telling her that this wouldn't last. *Nothing this good lasts.* She looked at both men, reminding herself that she could trust them, and that these were good men. Her past was in the past. She would quieten the nagging voices. She would!

Lucy tucked into her breakfast, listening to Reggie telling her about the arrangements for the next day – her mother's funeral. The last few days had felt like weeks or even months. She felt confused, and she was struggling to understand why she felt the way she did. She mourned her mother's death, but… but she didn't miss her. In truth, she sometimes found it hard to remember her face or recall a happy memory of her. She felt bad for not feeling what other people felt, but her life wasn't like the TV. She became aware that the room had gone silent, and they were looking at her, their concern showing. She wondered what she'd missed.

Looking down, she was surprised to see that she had finished her plate. She got up, pushing her chair back. 'That was lovely. Thank you, Frank.' She picked up her plate and went to the sink to wash it, returning to the table to collect the other plates and cups.

'I can do that, lovely.'

'I want to help. I'd like you to teach me everything – how to cook, how to bake. I want to pull my weight in this house.'

Reggie smiled at Frank. 'Frank will teach you; my limit is beans on toast.'

'Aye, and he fuc... um, well, he ruins that too,' said Frank, ruefully.

'Don't worry, Frankie Boy, I've heard way worse than that. A lot worse than that.'

With laughter again filling the kitchen, Lucy asked about the day ahead, enquiring if she could go to the shops with Frank to get the necessary shopping for the wake. It was something she wanted to do.

Reggie pushed his chair back, watching the two of them natter. Even Frank had fallen under her spell. It was as if she had been a part of their lives for a long time. He realised he would have to have a word with his son – to update him on the changes, including her arrival. James would have to keep his promised distance awhile – at the very least until she had settled in.

For a moment, his thoughts drifted to the chap in the hospital. He felt bad for him, but long ago he had found a way to separate the things he did from the life he led, so he closed his mind to the crap stuff to focus on the good. Maybe the future could be a good one – a chance to even the score a tad?

Grabbing paper and a pen, he started to scribble a few notes. He liked his lists as they helped organise his thoughts.

- Funeral Tuesday (that's tomorrow!!!)

- Must call Ms Harper, set up a meeting – must try to establish age & guardianship – invite her to the wake???

- Ed's Funeral (I hate funerals) Monday must call on Sarah to offer to help?

- Etc…

Thinking about Ed, he paused. He missed his old friend. He'd never been happier than he had been these last few months. He had been worried that Sarah had been a bad choice, that Ed was suffering from middle-aged male syndrome, but to be fair, she had brought some joy into his life – however short-lived.

Once at the shops they split up. Reggie had wanted to get something for her – a bracelet or a necklace. Something from her mum. Something to remember her by. He would lie, claiming the money was given to him by Liz. He'd had a word with Frank, asking him to take her for a wander – buy a milkshake or a coffee, so he was surprised to see Frank walking towards him alone.

Breathing hard, he said, 'I need to exercise more.'

'Sit down, before you have a fucking heart attack.'

'I've got some news, Reggie. Some great news.' Frank sat slowly, knowing that it would be harder getting up. It always was.

'Spit it out.'

'She's sixteen.'

'Sixteen? How'd you work that out?'

'We were talking about parties – maybe having one here with fireworks and everything – and she said she'd never been to a fireworks party, but then she said her mum had called her a millennium baby, she'd gone out to celebrate – had gotten so pissed she couldn't remember anything – but nine months later…'

'So' – Reggie counted the years off – 'she's sixteen?'

'Yep.'

'That means she can decide…'

'Yep.'

'Does she understand the significance of that?

'Don't think so. I don't think they celebrated birthdays much, to be honest. I don't think they celebrated anything much. I came to find you straight away. I haven't said anything.'

'Let's go and find her.' Reggie hugged Frank. 'This is wonderful news. I'll call Vicky – Ms Harper – once we've spoken to Lucy.'

'Boss.'

'Yeah?'

'Think it best we wait until we get home, don't you?'

'You're probably right. You go find her and get the shopping done. I need to buy something.'

***

Lucy was trying to make sense of the conversation they were having. She could see that Frank looked happy, very happy, but Reggie looked anxious.

They'd talked about birthdays and her age – she didn't know the date, but they usually celebrated sometime in September, and maybe a couple of times in October, but they'd never made a big thing about it. Frank had grabbed her hand after they had talked, wanting to find Reggie straight away. She didn't understand the excitement and why her being a millennium baby would be so important.

'I know it's a lot to take in, but take your time,' said Reggie.

'Yes, it must be very strange for you,' added Frank.

'It's your call. Our home is your home for as long as you want.'

The penny dropped. She knew she didn't need to think this through. Her decision was easy. She hugged Reggie, then beckoned Frank to join the hug. 'I'd love to stay with you guys. Thank you.'

***

Sarah stood in front of the mirror. He'd asked for a selfie, and she felt a little silly but also a little excited, flustered, her heart beating rapidly. To be truthful, she was more than a little turned on. James had told her what to wear, and now her reflection stared back at her. She thought she looked a little slutty – the heels a tad too high, the skirt much too short. She looked ready for a good night out, but she had done as she was told. The picture sent; she heard the doorbell – that would be the estate agent. She walked to the door, feeling incredibly nervous, her senses heightened.

'Good morning,' she greeted. She saw the look on his face. He was younger than she had feared and not bad looking. 'Come in,' she added, feeling strangely empowered, standing a little taller.

***

James opened the message, smiling. 'That's my girl.' She looked good – *sex on legs*. He'd known from the first look that she was going to be fun, but he had been surprised by her passion, her desires, and her commitment. She'd blossomed very quickly.

One of the things he loved about her was her giving way to her needs without pretence, without allusion – accepting a fucking good fuck for what it was… well, it wasn't art. It wasn't anything other than a fucking good orgasm to be enjoyed whenever and wherever, and in time, with whoever. He had wondered, in a rare moment of self-assessment, if this freeing of her body and soul had been for her benefit or his. To be truthful, he needed his own little adventures, without guilt and without consequence.

His cock stirred as he drove, and he smiled again at the question posed. Should he continue driving, hoping for his own little game later, or should he turn around and take her, knowing she would be aroused to the point of madness. He had told her to play, to flirt but to draw the line at that – no touching permitted. Would she have listened? Would she have obeyed, or would he find her in jeans and a baggy T? Swinging the car around, he headed back. He would park out of sight waiting for the estate agent's car to leave, and then he would find out!

***

Richard watched her leave, grateful to be on his own again. He felt torn. Part of him tried very hard to remember, but at the same time, part of him hoped not to. The thought of the truth scared him. He lay back against his pillow. The bed was uncomfortable, and he longed to get out of here, but where would he go? The police seemed pretty confident he was guilty, which meant a prison bed. His wife was convinced of his innocence and that he was a good man. They couldn't both be right!

Closing his eyes, he rolled away from the window, the light still too bright. He prayed to remember. At some instinctive level he knew that to survive, to move forward, he would need to know if he was a good man or not. If guilty, he wanted to be punished, and he would plead guilty, taking his punishment – looking to rebuild his life, to start again, once out. Maybe someday becoming worthy of a second chance. Maybe as a husband, but definitely as a dad. He knew he wanted to be a dad – a good dad. The kid, his kid, hadn't asked for any of this.

If found guilty, his sentence shouldn't be too long. *I can survive a few months… can't I?*

***

Jackie made a decision as she stepped outside, heading for the car park. She would have to come up with a Plan B, no matter how much that broke her, no matter how much that hurt her. She would be there for him, and she would stand by him, but she couldn't ignore the obvious – he might never recover his memory. He might be found guilty and sent to prison. If that happened, the baby would have to come first.

It was a sad thought. If she lost him, she had no one. She had friends but none that would want her borrowing a bedroom for more than a few days. If Richard was jailed, the house would go pretty damn quick, and their savings would be gone within months. This wasn't a good time to sell. The tears came, and she ran to the car, needing the sanctuary it offered.

***

Sarah lay in the bath, eyes closed, enjoying the heat spreading through her body.

'How long have you been there?'

'Me? Not long.'

'So, it wasn't you parked down the lane?'

'Might have been.'

'Was it you hiding in the shrubbery?' she said, laughing.

'You've got me.'

'Yes, I have.'

'So… were you a good girl?

'Yes.'

'Did you think about being a little bad?'

'Yes,' she whispered.

'How did it make you feel?'

'Wet. Needing too – but not him.' She stood, her body covered in soap. 'I'd like to fuck you.'

'Well, you're certainly wet enough.' He grabbed her, lifting her out of the bath, and they kissed. She liked the kiss, her body still warm from the bath, still covered with bubbles.

'Think we need to dry you off, you're soaking my clothes.'

'Take them off.'

Together they removed his clothing, which was tossed to the floor amidst lots of laughter and sloppy kissing.

CHAPTER SIXTEEN

Reggie reluctantly opened his eyes – an admission that he wouldn't be finding sleep again anytime soon. One of the joys of ageing was the ability to fall asleep at any time during the day – just about anywhere, anytime – but try as he might, he sometimes couldn't sleep after a night-time trip to piss, all too often enduring the slow return to bed shuffle in the dark, with eyes closed, desperately trying to cling to sleep.

Today was going to be a hard day for them all but especially for the girl. He'd done the best he could to make it better, to hide the fact that only one person cared about what had happened to her – that her mother had been a whore, a junkie, a shit mother, and if truth be told, a pretty worthless human. He pitied the chap taking the service. What words would he find to tell the story of her life?

Reaching for his phone was the final acceptance of no more sleep. He often used these hours to tick a few boxes, to get a few jobs done or just to catch up with the news. He had an email from Ms Harper confirming their meeting for the morning and her attendance at the funeral. He liked Vicky Harper; they'd spoken briefly the night before about Lucy being sixteen. He had invited her to join them at the funeral and had been strangely pleased that she had accepted. He thought she might be the best to talk to the hospital about the birth, hoping they would confirm that Lucy had, in fact, been born in September 2000.

The world was still dark outside – no hint of sunrise beyond his curtains. His bedroom suite overlooked the front – the long drive and the small lake, all the way back to the woods. He lay back, a smile forming. It was funny how his life had changed in just a few days. The smile soon left his face as he thought about James. His son had been a pain in his proverbial... pretty much from the moment he'd – they'd – lost his wife, his soulmate... the boy's mother. The truth was that he'd failed him. He had realised that way too late, with, it seems, no time to make it better. There was a darkness in James, a different darkness. He'd been a bad man – he had done some truly awful things but never for fun. He'd done those things to make a better life and to protect what he'd done – what he'd had. James was different. He enjoyed the easy life, chasing the next high.

Lucy was his chance of doing something right – maybe even to try and make amends for the past. Thinking she could have been his, he'd spent part of the night trying to remember when he'd met Liz. The girl was sixteen, and he'd met Liz around the millennium, but he couldn't, with hand on heart, recall the date, so he boxed the thought. He would do the best he could by her, to give her the best life possible, subconsciously knowing this would be his best life too!

***

Lucy was also awake, once again surprised by her room. She thought that one day this would feel like home... like... normal. For now, each day felt like the first day, and she had to remind herself why and where. Usually, she would wake happy, grateful. Today, however, was the day she would have to say goodbye to her mum. She wasn't an idiot. She knew she'd had a pretty rotten life. That said, she knew she wasn't the only one, that there were thousands of girls and boys just like her – some having even worse lives than she had. A thought began to grow. She wanted to do something to help some of them. She thought she might try nursing or social work, so she resolved to talk to Reggie sometime soon.

It was funny how one change could cause so many other changes. Today she had dreams, possibilities ... maybe even a life worth living, no longer hiding in the shadows. No longer scared of making bad choices. No longer walking the streets, waiting for her mother's friends to leave the house. The past was beginning to feel like a bad dream. Her new life beckoned her, called to her. She wouldn't question why anymore. Her new life was just starting, and she was determined to enjoy it.

***

James stretched, waking slowly. Sarah was asleep, lying naked beside him, he pushed the covers off her, watching her breathing. She slept deeply, untroubled, and he envied her that. The smell of sex lingered from the night before. They'd fucked whilst he whispered in her ear, whilst he asked her questions about the estate agent, what she would have done to him if she could. She'd come hard!

Rolling over, he kissed her back. She had great skin – skin that needed to be touched, to be kissed, to be licked, and so he did. Once she murmured, he rolled her onto her back.

'Morning, beautiful.'

'What time is it?'

Spreading her legs, he entered her. 'It's time to get up,' he said with a devilish grin.

'You are an incorrigible...' She wouldn't finish, her back arching as she pushed against him.

***

Jackie entered his room, the bed empty, unmade. There was no sign of him, and her heart skipped a beat as she felt a chill run down or maybe up her back. She turned, heading for the nurse's station, grateful to see one of the nice ones on duty.

'Excuse me I'm looking for...'

'Haven't they told you?' Her tone implied frustration.

'Told me?'

'He's been moved to St George's in London.'

'Why?'

'They specialise in head trauma; a bed came free, and they wanted him moved, but they should have told you.'

'Why would they move him? I don't understand.'

'I'm not sure. I can try to find out if you...'

Jackie turned away, her eyes filling with tears. She mumbled her thanks and left; her emotions mixed. She was embarrassed, yes – why wouldn't they tell her? – and angry too. She was angry with Richard and her life. Her life was destroyed, broken, smashed beyond repair. She was walking through a living nightmare. A month ago, she had been the happiest she'd ever been. She'd had everything she'd ever wanted, and she'd been lucky enough to know that, to appreciate that. Shit, she'd known how lucky she was every day as soon as she woke. Which was why everything now hurt.

***

Reggie rose to greet his visitor. 'Good morning, Ms Harper.'

'Please call me Vicky.' She took the proffered seat. 'You have a very beautiful home.'

'Thank you. You found us...'

'It's not hard, Reggie, it's the size of a small hotel.'

'Yeah. I guess we're kinda used to it.'

'What can I do for you, Reggie? Is it okay to call you Reggie?' she asked, her voice questioning.

'I've been called much worse,' he said with a laugh. 'Much worse.' He studied her carefully. She had a nice smile; she should smile more often. He wondered if she was married. No ring and the use of 'Ms' suggested not.

How the hell am I going to get those questions answered?

Telling himself off, he tried to hide a grin. It had been a while since he'd been remotely attracted to anyone. He guessed her age at fifty-something. 'I'm sorry I missed that last bit. I was…'

'Oh, no problem. I was just suggesting that I check the hospital records for that period, hoping to find something that might help. We had a little chat when I arrived, and she seems very happy to be here. She's a different girl already.'

Reggie stood. 'I hope so. She deserves a bit of happiness. Sadly, we have a funeral to go to. Are you still able to join us?'

'Yes, I've cleared my day.'

'That's excellent. We leave in about an hour. Can I get or do anything for you?'

'A coffee would be nice. I'd like to spend a little more time with Lucy too, if that's okay?'

'I don't see why not. She loves to walk the grounds if you're up for a walk?'

'That would be lovely. I keep a pair of sensible shoes in the car.'

Reggie walked her out, quite impressed by Ms Harper. He liked her – he liked her a lot. It was the sensible shoes that had him smiling. Any girl who kept walking shoes in the car was a little bit special.

***

Aarav stood with his wife and son, he and Aryan both holding big umbrellas over their heads, their mood sombre, only Aarav happy to be there. His wife had wanted to keep the shop open, and they'd shared a few words on the subject; his wife, he thought, only agreed to attend so she could inspect the big house and have a story to tell her friends. They had arrived early, now standing in silence, in the drizzle, the cold beginning to seep into their bones, each hoping to hear the funeral cars pulling into the carpark.

They were, he thought, the only people to have arrived. They hadn't wanted to go into the church after Aryan had confirmed it was empty. He wasn't surprised at the lack of people – he doubted she had friends. She had lived a tragic life. He hoped Lucy would now have a better one.

To his surprise, a car pulled up, and he watched two people get out: a very attractive younger woman accompanied by a slightly older, slightly overweight chap. He watched them pull jackets from the back and their hesitation as to what to do next. Slowly, they headed towards them.

'Are you here for the funeral?' the man asked.

Why do I feel the need to laugh? 'Yes, we are. The church is empty, so we thought it best to wait here.' Aarav introduced his family to them, noticing his son was quite captivated by the girl – as was he to be truthful. He imagined most men were. He guessed they weren't family or friends. He couldn't imagine them socialising with Liz, so they had to be social workers. No, too formal, too uptight, to be social. They would be huggy. So, these two had to be cops. He wondered why they had come.

***

Mickey was wondering why they had come. It was Jo who had wanted to be here. She hadn't explained her reasons, she'd just said that she was going with or without him, so he'd reluctantly agreed to accompany her. He'd even ironed his shirt. He hated funerals – always had, always would. The case was pretty much wrapped up, and they were just waiting for CPS to make a decision. He thought it was a no-brainer that they would prosecute, and he was okay with that, he just wished that Jo agreed.

Jo looked pretty damned good in black, he thought. She took the proffered brolly from the young lad, his face a picture.

Don't worry, my lad. She has that effect on all of us, he thought... black boots, tight black pants, and a black T-shirt under a short jacket; she looked stunning.

***

Sarah was preparing a late breakfast for them both: a pot of tea, orange juice, and toast. She'd left James upstairs researching Brazil. Last night they'd talked for hours, they'd fucked twice, and then talked and talked whilst finishing a bottle off. They had talked about their hopes for the future... their bucket lists. Trips to the Inca trail was one of hers, a gangbang on the beach one of his. She'd laughed at that... but hadn't said no.

***

Lucy sat in the back between Reggie and Vicky, each of them holding a hand as she stared straight ahead, seeing the cemetery in the distance. Frank indicated a left turn, and all she could see was the rain and the wipers swishing. The world looked grey and miserable. She was grateful to be with the three of them. She liked Vicky, who had spoken to her about her life, some of the choices she had, and the decisions she'd have to make.

Ahead, she spotted a small group by the church. She recognized each of them, and she felt a little happier, grateful that they had come. With the priest, they'd number ten – not many but better than she'd feared. Frank pulled up behind the hearse, the flowers draping the coffin. She stepped out after Vicky, shivering, unsure as to what to do.

Luckily, Aarav and his family walked towards her, stopping to speak with Reggie briefly before coming to her.

Lucy pulled Aarav in for a hug. 'Thank you for coming,' she said before hugging his wife next. 'Thank you, Saanvi.' Previously, she'd been too shy to call her by her Christian name, but today she recalled it, remembering the times she'd heard them call out to each other from the shop, shouting upstairs for help. Stepping to the son, Aryan, she almost hugged him, but instead, they swapped shy smiles. Lastly, she turned to the cops to find Jo smiling but no sign of her partner – whose name she couldn't remember. She hugged Jo. 'Thank you for coming. It means a lot.'

***

Mickey was muttering as he walked towards a man – a man he knew quite well. 'I fucking hate reporters.'

He heard Reggie behind him. 'Mickey, leave him alone, he's not worth it.' Mickey stopped and turned.

'He shouldn't be here.'

'I know, but leave it. Not today.'

Mickey turned with one last look, the contempt obvious, and headed back to join the rest. 'How's the girl?' Not hearing a reply, he stopped again and looked to Reggie who was speaking to the reporter who handed his camera over, then left.

'What did you say to him?'

'Nothing much. Just that he wasn't invited.'

'The camera?'

'Told him I needed to borrow it, and he could have it back later.'

Mickey laughed. 'Not worth it you said.'

'He's not, but she is,' she replied, indicating Lucy. Now, let's get this done. I want to get her home. Are you coming back to the house?'

'Hadn't planned to, Reggie, but why not. Thanks. I hate funerals.'

'Me too, Mickey, me too. I've got another next week.'

'Ed?'

'Yep. He was a good man… taken too soon.'

'How's Mrs Horton?'

'No idea. I've offered to help, but she seems to be okay. Don't really know her. She came as a bit of a surprise – not his usual type.' Reggie laughed. 'He seemed happy enough, even had a spring in his step, so you can imagine our shock.'

Mickey touched Reggie's shoulder. 'We really never know what goes on behind closed doors, do we?'

'No, I guess we don't. Thanks, Mickey. For a copper, you're a good lad. Any news on you know what?'

'Nope. I think it's a coin toss on whether the CPS will want to go for him.'

'If they don't?'

'If they don't, it will be case closed.'

'What do you think?'

'Me, I'd prosecute the bastard. I always think what would have happened if it hadn't been stopped – if your lad hadn't been there.

'Don't want to think about that.'

'I wish I didn't!'

***

The service was short – the absolute bare minimum. The priest, understandably, seemed to be in a hurry to be gone. Lucy was sat between him and Frank, staring straight ahead, her hand in his. He noticed her other hand was lost in Frank's huge mitts. He was grateful to the ones who had answered his call, a few old mates arriving just in time. He wanted her to be able to picture faces in the chapel, people who had come to pay their respects.

Catching Vicky's eye, he smiled, nodding and mouthing 'thank you'. The chapel felt cold, though it might be an age thing, he thought. He knew one thing: too many bleeding

164

funerals, each one a reminder that he wasn't invincible. His turn would be...

He stopped that thought.

I've got a few good years left in me yet! The golden years.

His laugh turned into a snuffled snort. Pulling out his hanky, he blew his nose. Better they thought he had a cold over early-onset senility. He felt her grip tighten; he pulled her close for a hug, whispering, 'Soon be home, sweetheart. Soon be home.'

CHAPTER SEVENTEEN

Checking her appearance for the umpteenth time, Sarah decided that black was her colour. All week she had worried about what to wear, but her reflection looked good. She smiled, then quickly chastised herself; today wasn't a day to smile, it was a day to be endured. She had a part to play – the grieving wife – and she'd have to do it alone. James had offered to go to hold her hand, and that had been tempting, but even she knew that it would have been very risky… and more than a little inappropriate.

It was the tires crunching on gravel that told her the cars had arrived. She glanced out of the window to see the funeral cars inline, the funeral director exiting the hearse and holding his hat. They made for an impressive sight. She also saw Reggie getting out of the last car. She groaned but was pleasantly surprised he hadn't made himself comfy in her car. She grabbed her coat and bag, telling herself to be nice. *Count to ten and don't smile.*

Once outside, she slammed the front door shut, the bang sending countless birds skywards, screaming their displeasure. She almost bumped into Reggie by the gate, taking his proffered hand to guide her to the cars.

'Thank you, Reggie, I'm fine. I'll take it from here.'

'Do you want some company? I could leave my car here, collect it tomorrow?'

'No, that's very kind of you, but I'm fine. I'll see you there.' *I need the time to compose myself.*

Once sat, a tear ran down her cheek, noticed by the driver who had been watching her in his mirror. She smiled, and he seemed to approve. She took it as a compliment because he must have seen hundreds of grieving widows. She could imagine him thinking *'beautiful and classy'*, and that would do.

All too soon the cars pulled into the car park at St Faith's. It seemed incredibly full, and the thought reminded her that even if she hadn't ever truly loved the man, her husband had been loved and would be missed by all these people.

The weak sunlight did little to improve the view. It was a soulless place. Maybe she should have taken Reggie's advice to use the local church – a far prettier building – but she'd put her foot down, saying that they had married there, and anyway, Ed had told her he wanted to be cremated, not buried. He wanted his ashes to be scattered at home. That had been a lie, but it was one that Reggie had bought into. The truth had been that it was she who wanted him cremated… gone for good… scattered to the four winds, not buried with the ex-wife!

As she stepped out of the car, she stumbled, and it was Reggie who caught her. She smiled and straightened her coat, and with her head held high, she headed for the chapel. As she walked, she noticed there were two groups. The larger group would be for Ed, but to one side there was a smaller group of people, not quite so well dressed, their grief obvious. She noticed a few floral tributes at their feet. This must have been the funeral before. They seemed reluctant to leave. Maybe the reality of life and death started on the road, the journey home? Maybe whilst they stayed and talked quietly, they could put off that horrible moment, that last goodbye. Tears welled in her eyes. It didn't matter that she cried for someone unknown, a family she wouldn't see again. Everyone here would assume she cried for her husband – their friend.

Stepping into the chapel, grateful for the warmth, she let Reggie guide her to the front. Ed's coffin was at rest, covered with flowers and a Norwich City scarf, looking a little incongruous. She acknowledged those who nodded or smiled. Once sat, she bowed her head, hoping for some peace and quiet, not wanting to talk. She wondered how many of his old mates would pop over in the coming weeks, hoping for more than a coffee.

Thankfully, the service was soon concluded. Reggie had spoken fondly of his old friend, and she'd wondered if the son would become the man. She almost hoped he would. Reggie had a strength – an inner strength – that suggested that he would protect those he loved with his last breath. When he spoke, everyone else listened.

James had rarely spoken of his father, and when he had, it wasn't nice. She loved James, but he was a boy in comparison – albeit a troubled boy that excited her, made her think things, sometimes unthinkable things. He definitely turned her on, made her want to live, to get up each morning. She missed him. She would go home avoiding the gathering to be held at Reggie's... if she could.

***

Frank was feeling very much like a fish out of water, walking the city's streets with a beautiful girl on his arm, several bags in his other hand. She was unaware of the looks she was attracting, chatting happily as they headed to the car park having just left McDonald's. To his surprise, he'd quite enjoyed the burger and banana milkshake.

It had been Reggie's idea to take her out. She needed more clothes to be sure, but more than that, she'd needed to be somewhere else – anywhere other than another wake. Reggie had said: 'She won't ask for much, so spoil her, buy the stuff she likes but puts down.'

She'd done that a lot, and now the bags were full. There was stuff for her but also a present for Reggie. Lucy had spotted a bright cardigan, and Frank was sure about two things: one, he would hate it, and two, he'd wear it every day until he'd worn it out.

'You're not listening to me, are you?' she said with a laugh.

'Sorry, lovely, did you say something?'

She poked him in the ribs. 'I was saying...'

'That you've had the most wonderful of days, and you wouldn't complain if every day was like this, oh, and that I'm the best personal shopper a girl could have.'

She stopped and looked at him. 'I *have* had a wonderful day, I really have, but I was asking you if we should get a couple of dogs? I think two would be better. They could keep each other company?'

He laughed. 'I think you'd better ask the boss.' He'd been surprised when Reggie had agreed the night before to them getting a dog – a rescue dog at that.

'I will.'

They continued walking to the car. He realised that days like these shouldn't be hurried and shouldn't be taken for granted. He'd had a funny old life – a good life – devoted to Reggie. They'd shared the good and the bad. He'd done things, terrible things, things he wished he could forget – images that sometimes appeared in the brightest part of the day or the darkest of nights – but if a life could be redeemed, he hoped they had time to balance the books a little more. *You're going to have to live a long life, old man.*

***

Sarah stood alone, although she was surrounded by people, but they were his people, his friends, his acquaintances, she recognised a few, but this was very much his world, not hers. She checked her phone, having felt it vibrate. She had a text from James.

Come upstairs I need u x

Where r u???

Upstairs :)

What? Here upstairs?

Yep :)

What r u doing here???

I've come to fuck u :)

Which room?

Second floor (top floor) I'm in my old bedroom

Ok r u sure

The doors open – be quick

She took the stairs, trying not to run. At the top, she paused. There were hallways to the left and the right. She took the left.

'James?' she said quietly.

'In here.'

She entered a huge bedroom with windows on two sides and a massive bed in the middle. He lay on the bed naked, wearing nothing but a big grin, his happiness to see her obvious. She undid her trousers, letting them drop to the floor. She stepped out and removed her underwear, throwing it behind her, not once taking her eyes off his. Then she climbed up onto the bed, crawling up his legs to kiss him.

'I haven't got long.'

Feeling his cock already pushing into her, she leant back, arching, before feeling him enter her completely. Falling forward, her hands on his chest, she huskily whispered, 'You're a bad boy. A very bad boy.'

'Do you love me?'

'Yes.'

He started to fuck her slowly. Very slowly. 'Do you love me?'

She paused, sitting up. 'Um… let me see.'

He pulled out, throwing her to one side, then smacked her arse.

'Ow! Owwww, that hurt!'

'It was meant to. Now, answer me.'

She kissed him, 'I love you – only you, forever, until death do us –' She kissed a wet trail down his chest to his cock, which throbbed. 'And I love *you*.' She took him into her mouth and the talking stopped.

***

At last, Reggie heard the car arrive. He went to the door to welcome them home, pleased to see so many bags. The house was empty. The last of the guests had gone, including a very flushed Sarah. His heart had gone out to her. She was obviously struggling with this more than he'd thought. He had resolved to pop in to see her during the next few days.

The three of them made their way to the kitchen, Frank doing the heavy lifting and Lucy chatting away, describing their day. Reggie once again couldn't believe the change in her; she had adapted so well. He imagined that over the years she must have developed a natural survival strategy – one that allowed her to cope with a miserable, lonely, and sometimes very unpleasant life. For sure, she had issues, but they were nothing she or they couldn't deal with. He had talked to Vicky about what help to get her. She needed some tutoring. She'd pretty much taught herself to read, so he knew she was a bright kid, but they had to get her the tools she needed, and they had to surround her with love and support.

Frank was preparing tea as he sat watching the fashion parade. They'd done well, the pair of them. She looked like any other teenager. Once everything was worn and then folded again, they sat and chatted. It didn't take long before they returned to the subject of a dog.

'So, can we go and look tomorrow?'

'I don't see why not. There's a rescue place over at Snetterton.'

'Yes. YES!' She stood and ran to him, almost knocking him over with the hug.

'You like that idea, rehoming a dog rather than a puppy?'

'Yes, I've been rehomed, and I think our first dog should be a rehomer too.'

Frank turned, laughing. 'First dog? How many do you think...'

'At least two. Maybe more. We have a huge house and an even huger garden, so I think we can cope with lots!'

'Frank, I think we'll need the Range Rover tomorrow.'

'Might need two.'

***

Jackie lay on the couch, gently sobbing. Her world had truly crashed. She couldn't see a future, and she felt very sorry for herself, which was a double whammy as she hated that feeling of feeling sorry for herself. Richard had asked that she not visit him in London. If that hadn't been bad enough, he had asked for her name to be removed from the approved visitor list. She had protested, begged even, but it had been no good. She wouldn't see him until the arraignment scheduled for the following week, for which he had been passed fit to attend.

***

James sat outside in the car on the drive approaching Sarah's house. He'd been sat there an hour or so. It wasn't that he didn't want to get out of the car to go into the house. He sat there coming to terms with the fact that his home was no longer home. Before leaving for what might be the last time, he had wandered the house, careful to stay out of his father's way. He had no problem with the bricks. It was a good house, a little out of the way, but he'd made friends in the village. He could recall wonderful days at the local beaches, girls and balls, and as they had become teenagers, bottles of booze and pinched cigarettes. They had been good days.

The problem had been his dad.

So, he sat in the drive, his mother's pearls in a pocket. Taking them had been an impulse, but he had wanted something of her to make the journey with him. He knew he had to get out to go in. Sarah had plans. They were going out and meeting her friends at a party, and the thought filled him with dread. He'd rather stay in, watch some telly, and have a beer. He just wasn't in the mood to be nice, and tonight she had said she wanted nice James.

***

Sarah breathed a sigh of relief once they had parked. They'd driven to Cambridge in virtual silence. She had asked him a couple of times if he had wanted to turn back, to return home, but he'd shaken his head. This was a night she had been looking forward to, a chance to meet some old uni' friends – friends she hadn't seen for years. It was a chance to show him off, to revel in their admiring glances and secret – but guessable – thoughts.

'Are you sure?'

'Yes.' He sounded dark, almost angry. *I like you angry,* she thought. *It's hot as fuck.*

'Do I look okay?'

He studied the powder-blue wraparound dress that showed off her incredible legs and wonderful breasts. 'Almost perfect... almost.'

'What?' she almost shouted, checking her appearance – mentally ticking off shoes, dress and... 'Do you want me to take them off?'

'Yes,' he said smiling and trying not to laugh, watching as she pulled her underwear off. Once removed, she threw them behind the seat. 'Better?' she asked.

'Almost.' He watched her frown, then smile as she reached behind to undo her bra, soon joining the panties in the back.

'Is that better?'

'Much, much better.' He smiled. 'Just...'

'WHAT?' she almost screamed in frustration. 'I can't go in naked – I won't.'

'Close your eyes.' He removed the pearls, reaching behind her neck to fasten them. 'Now, open them.' He watched as she looked at them.

'Oh, James, you complete and utter bastard, they are beautiful. Thank you.'

'They were my mother's, and now, they're yours.'

She leant over, hugging him, kissing him, planting lots of tiny kisses all over his face, his neck, each one with an 'I love you.' She pulled back, staring into his eyes. 'Does that mean I can put my underwear back on?'

'Nope.'

They got out of the car laughing, walking down the path to the cottage, hand in hand. They could hear party noise spilling from the back garden, and there was a sign pointing to a side gate. They opened it and stepped into a beautiful garden festooned with lights and maybe as many as a hundred people who seemed intent on having a good time.

'This looks better than I feared,' he whispered into her ear, his hand on her arse.

'Behave, mister.' Her laugh betrayed her true feelings on his behaviour. 'You'd better be good.'

'Me? I'm always good.'

They stood, Sarah trying to spot the hostess whilst James scanned the guests. 'Who's the girl in the gold dress?'

'Which girl?'

James pointed.

'No idea. Why? Do you fancy her?'

'I'd like to fuck her,' he whispered.

She dug him in the ribs. 'James, behave. I mean it. These are my friends! Just be a good boy please, just for tonight please. PLEASE!'

They walked towards the hostess, James catching the eye of the blonde in the gold dress. He smiled, knowing she was thinking the same as him. He didn't need to turn; he knew she was still looking. He could feel her eyes on him as he walked away.

The evening proved to be more enjoyable than he had feared. They were sitting at a table towards the edge of the garden, with Sarah's old uni' mates, who were all pretty tipsy and quite loud. He had kept his promise. So far, he'd been a good boy, honouring her extracted promise of good behaviour. Needing a piss, he got up and walked to the house. Out of nowhere, the blonde grabbed him, pulling him to one side.

'I've been waiting for you all night.'

'You might have to wait a while longer,' he said quietly.

'I don't think so' – she grabbed his groin – 'I think you want me.'

'I'm afraid my cock is not terribly choosy.'

Throwing the last of her drink in his face, she shouted, 'You bastard! You fucking bastard!'

The commotion soon drew a crowd, parting for an angry young man who approached them, yelling, 'Get your hands off my fucking wife.'

James turned just in time to see a punch coming his way. He ducked, then threw a short jab into the man's gut, causing him to double over.

James bent over him, whispering, 'Stay down, mate. This isn't what you think.'

'Don't just stand there, hit him!' screamed the blonde.

James turned. 'Be a good girl and just shut the fuck up. Look, mate, we can sort this out, or you can take the *lady* home. Personally, I wouldn't touch her with yours.'

'He's telling the truth, Bob,' said another chap, coming to his rescue. 'I heard the whole conversation. He turned her down, and she didn't like it.'

Bob stood hesitantly, both hands holding his gut. 'Is this true?' he asked, watching as his tear-stained wife turned and ran, sobbing as she went.

James spotted Sarah and gladly joined her. 'Time for home don't you think?'

Sarah smiled 'So soon? Can't we stay until the fireworks? Please?' She poked him playfully in the ribs. 'We haven't danced yet, and you promised me a slow dance.' They walked slowly to the patch of grass where people swayed.

James pulled her to him. 'One dance, and then tomorrow we pack. Day after we fly somewhere… anywhere. Tomorrow, we start the longest holiday ever. Agreed?'

Sarah smiled, kissing him gently and enjoying the feeling of his lips on hers. 'Agreed.'

PART THREE

CHAPTER EIGHTEEN

Three years later…

The coffee tasted wonderful, smelt wonderful. Richard was determined to savour it, to drink it slowly. It was, after all, the first cup he'd bought in three years. Every mouthful was to be enjoyed. The waitress delivered his breakfast – a full English. It was, without question, the best meal he'd seen in three years. Whilst doing his time he had enjoyed many so-called fry ups, but none had looked like this, smelt like this. The plate in front of him had thick bacon with crispy fat, big proper butcher's sausages, tomatoes, mushrooms, black pudding with beans, and on the side, there were two big, hand-cut pieces of golden fried bread.

The food tasted even better than it looked. He hadn't realised how hungry he was, soon clearing the plate. He sat back, accepting a coffee refill just because he could.

He'd walked out of Wayland Prison that morning ready to start again. They'd given him the princely sum of £46, and that was meant to see him through to the benefit payments hitting his bank. He knew he didn't want to live off benefits – that would be a last resort – so he had to find a job, pay his own way. He wanted to feel like a man again.

Like every other con, he had thought about little else, other than the day he could walk out a free man. He should have walked out some thirty months previously – he could have qualified for an early Home Detention release – if he hadn't gone and got himself a hefty extension! That had been Benny's fault. Benny was the only real friend he had made inside. He was a good lad, but even he would admit that he had a few problems, the biggest of which was his big gob. He had a bad habit of his mouth writing cheques that the rest of him couldn't cash, which got him into trouble with both the lads and the screws.

One day he'd got into a brawl with some of the lads, getting, it has to be said, a thoroughly deserved hiding. Richard had known he should have stepped away, that he was a month away from leaving, but that hadn't stopped him. So, he had jumped in, putting one of the attackers down, only to be grabbed from behind. He'd turned, punching his assailant, unknowingly breaking his jaw. He had watched, thinking, *Fucking hell.* The screw had hit the floor like a bag of spuds.

It was sod's law that the officer had been the one in his face from the day that he'd arrived. For some reason, he had seemed to hate the very sight of him. The bastard was almost smiling when he'd finally stood; he'd known in that moment that he would pay the price – the full price. Protecting Benny had cost him another four years, and now, released two-thirds through, he was finally a free man. Well, free as long as he stayed out of trouble and kept his probation officer happy.

He looked around him, a full circle, checking everyone in the room – *old habits die hard* – but he saw nothing to worry him. No one was paying any attention to him. Well, apart from the waitress who nodded and smiled as she worked.

Breakfast had cost him £12, leaving him with just £34 of his discharge monies remaining. It was no wonder so many couldn't break the cycle. Accepting another refill, he had offered to pay, but she had refused, smiling again – her smiling recharging his 'goodwill to all men' battery. He wouldn't be able to put into words how wonderful it was to be able to just smile at strangers without fear of the reply.

He went through the list of jobs in his head; he had a few things to do. He would have written them down if he had pen and paper. First-up he had to go to the bank. Jackie had sent a short note to him. It had been the only contact he'd had with her. He'd kept the note.

Richard

I'm going to have to sell the house. The agents tell me that we will have a little

equity after costs.

I will leave 1/2 in your account.

It won't be much but enough for you to make a fresh start.

I don't know what else to say other than that I wish you good luck, and I hope

that you find your truth. You are not that man. I know that deep in my heart.

You are a good man; you've always been a good man.

I wouldn't have loved you if you hadn't been a good man!

Jackie x

That note had kept him going, had seen him through some dark times. He'd read it many times, sometimes searching for the unwritten word, seeking the nuance. Had she written him off, or was there a hint of hope? He had to try and find her and find the girl. He wanted to speak to both. He needed to have the chance to say sorry. He couldn't recall anything from that night, and he had stopped trying to remember. The doc had told him that he couldn't force it; if he was lucky, something might come back to him. Sometimes he even thought his memories were not his but stuff he'd read or had been told. He struggled with how he felt inside compared to the man he must be. He felt better than that, trusting his instinct to help others, to support others. He couldn't be that man.

Lucy would be easy to find. He'd read about her in an old copy of the local paper whilst in Wayland. She seemed to be having a wonderful life with the old man; he was pleased for her. Genuinely pleased. Jackie would be way harder. She had literally disappeared from his life, which was what he had wanted. Sometimes he regretted his choices, wondering how she would be living her new life.

So, bank first, to find out how much Jackie had left him, and then he needed somewhere to sleep. He needed to have that sorted before his first probation meeting, and then there was the matter of a job. He wanted to find a job ASAP… and clothes, toiletries… He had a lot to do.

Having finished his meal, he stood and thanked the waitress who had appeared out of nowhere to clear his plate and cup away. He thanked her profusely and left the café, leaving her a £2 tip. He now had £32. Once outside, he stood for a moment, just watching the madness outside – so many people, so many vehicles, the cacophony of sound, was almost overbearing.

It was wonderful to be back in his adopted city. He walked slowly up Prince of Wales Road, heading for the bank. Not much had changed. The road was still full of clubs, bars, and cheap takeaways. At the top, he would turn right, then left into London Street – a much nicer part of the city. It would only take him a short while to get there, and to be frank, he didn't care if he bumped into old colleagues – prison had hardened him that much. As he walked, he confirmed the decision to not think about the last three years. He would start again. He was getting quite good at boxing things up… drawing lines.

***

James sat slumped in his seat; his re-heated meal barely touched. He could almost sense the question on his neighbour's mind – a woman he had just about ignored for the last eight hours. He had no answer for 'are you okay?' He had hoped for empty adjoining seats when boarding, but the plane was full, so he had sat in almost complete silence, only speaking to order something. The drop down was covered in empty whisky bottles; he'd emptied quite a few of the way-too-small-to-make-a-difference bottles. Nothing could dull the pain. Awful images were still playing in his head.

Finally, he was heading home; home would be his salvation. A tear ran down his face, understanding that he was desperate to get back to the man that he'd once been desperate to leave. *The irony*. The old man, his dad, would make it better. He would hold his hand until he no longer needed to.

He groaned, his watch telling him that he had another two to three hours in the air. He closed his eyes, aware that his neighbour was again checking him out. He knew he looked rough, but he stifled a laugh. *You should have seen me a month ago, darling.*

He needed to sleep, to stop thinking.

He needed a sleep free from the images of the drug-addled Sarah dying in front of his eyes at the hands of a backstreet abortionist, completely unrecognisable from the girl he'd met just three years before.

Their adventure had started so well. They'd travelled the world together, partying hard – sometimes too hard – especially Sarah, who in the end had played the game harder than him. He would have laughed out loud if someone had told him that he would be the one begging her to stop, begging for a time-out. Stopping had almost killed him. It had been a nightmare coming off his various addictions. He still drank and smoked, but they weren't going to kill him – that would have been the drugs.

Many mornings he'd woken in their fleapit of a flat, alone, aching with everything that could hurt hurting. He'd lay drenched in his own sweat, sometimes his own piss, trying to find the inclination, the energy, to crawl to the bathroom to shit. More often than not he woke alone to find himself lying there, curled around the toilet. He never gave in, even when she'd returned triumphantly with her purchases. He'd watch her, plead with her – it had taken every ounce of his stubborn bastard streak to not give in. He'd wanted to countless times, but the voice in his head drove him on. *You really don't want to fucking die here, do you?*

They'd arrived in Brazil in pretty good shape a year before, the money holding out well. Copacabana Beach had become their playground. It had been on that beach that they had decided to stay, agreeing to leave their expensive hotel to rent a nice apartment within walking distance of the Lapa – home of the party.

The first three months had been incredible, and they'd both enjoyed the hedonistic life: eating, drinking, smoking, and fucking. It had been Sarah who'd started the heavy stuff, chasing increasingly hard to find moments of joy. They had both graduated from smoking lots to anything that could dull the ache.

Towards the end, Sarah had whored herself out when the money ran out, fucking for drugs, but even she had dulled, so the hits were harder to come by. At the end, she'd been taking anything, any pill she could find or steal. He'd gone to the abortionist with her. He'd argued against it, he'd begged her to not go. He'd begged her to go to the embassy with him.

The ticket home was paid for by the only thing of value he had left – his watch. He'd hidden it from her a couple of months before. He'd let it go cheap, too cheap, but he needed to get home quickly, so the watch went, the car abandoned at the airport. He felt bad; it had been a brutal wake-up call seeing her self-destruct in front of him. He would cry for her another day. For now, he would need all that he could muster just to get home, grateful that he had a place called home, a place where he could hope to start again. Closing his eyes, he found some comfort believing the worst was behind him... that he would find a better life, that he would be a better man this time round. That thought, that hope, had seen him through some dark times!

***

Lucy sat lost in thought on the window seat in Reggie's bedroom. It was a truly beautiful day. She had known that this would be the hardest of days. Flint and Stone lay at her feet. Flint, a 95% collie mixed with something else – maybe a German Shepherd, maybe a Husky – and Stone, their golden lab, were both rescued from the rehoming centre at Snetterton. She loved this room; it had the best views and some of the best memories.

Beyond the hedging, she could see the timber lodges. She knew there were nine dotted through the woods and the meadows, with more planned. Their dream was coming true. Just two years ago they had started their own sanctuary, offering respite care and breaks for young carers. They had started small, converting the coach house, but once the word spread, they had been overwhelmed with enquiries; they had expanded quickly.

Reggie had embraced the idea almost immediately. They had been shocked to find that a quarter of a million children in England were looking after adult family members. Reggie had shaken his head saying, 'That's Carrow Road filled 10 times – 250,000 kids looking after adults.' They had found partners to work with, including the local councils, but most of the funding costs had been covered by Reggie, who had set up a foundation in her name, transferring just about everything into it. She could live here, but the foundation owned the place, which was just as she had wanted.

They could now offer weekend breaks to twenty young carers at a time – that was a thousand each year. Their next step was to offer week-long breaks, initially during school holidays, but in time, throughout the year, accepting they would need teaching volunteers. That prospect didn't worry her – they had a waiting list of nursing staff and others to house sit the kids in the cabins and keep them entertained. It seemed the volunteers loved the place as much as the kids did. The big challenge was the one Reggie had been working on – finding funding to cover respite care for those that needed it, respite care in a home whilst their sons or daughters were with them.

It had become their special place, and everyone who came fell in love with the cabins, the pathways through the woods, and the gentle streams often walked in the summer. Some hadn't seen a wood filled with deer and rabbits before. The 'hub' had only been up a year with playrooms, a pool, and a cinema room. The memories they'd created, shared in such a short time, and the difference they'd made to so many lives… She felt the tears form as she heard Frank enter the room.

'Are you okay, poppet?'

'No, not really.'

'Come here, sweetheart.' He opened his arms for a hug, holding her as she sobbed.

'He wouldn't want this, would he?'

'Of course, he would. He'll be sitting up there, laughing at the pair of us.'

Lucy kissed his cheek, wiping away a tear. 'Right. We have lots to do, don't we?'

'Aye, lass, I think we do. The funeral director will be here shortly, and the caterers are here already.'

'Already?'

'Yes, lass. We don't know how many are coming – could be dozens, could be more.'

'More?'

'Could be…'

'Oh my God. Frank, you might want to revise that figure; you might want to speak to the caterers.' Her voice was breaking with every word. 'We might have hundreds.'

'What do you mean, poppet?'

Lucy turned Frank around so he could see. Neither said a word as they watched the cars coming down the drive – a line of cars as far as the eye could see, all the way to the gates. It was a multi-coloured line of sparkling metal, nearly a mile long. Some of the cars had balloons tied to them, and some had kids standing up and poking through sunroofs, waving to each other.

'Oh my God. They've come. All of them. They've all come…'

'I think they have, sweetheart.'

Lucy turned to him, laughing. 'He would love this. We'll have a party in the park.' The cars kept coming.

'I'd better sort out some overflow parking and quick. Are you going to be okay?'

'I'm fine. Actually, I'm better than fine. Let's go. We have a thousand and one things to do, but it's going to be a good day. A better day than I feared, at least.'

'I'll warn the caterers on the way out,' he said, laughing. They hadn't laughed much the past few days. It sounded wonderful to them both. 'We're going to need more, a lot more – more of everything.'

Lucy ran through the house and out through the front door, not pausing until she arrived to find the first few exiting their cars. Some faces she recognized instantly, and some took a few seconds, but they were all friends, all members of her extended family. Today was going to be a wonderful send off – one he truly deserved!

Later she would find out that one of the kids had started this. He'd contacted friends made here via Facebook, and each had spread the word, with the help of a few parents and the charity partners they had managed to reach. She spotted one of her favourites, amongst a group of volunteer nurses walking towards her, and she ran to them, sobbing and laughing.

***

Richard took the stairs to his room, which was on the second floor. He'd picked this hotel on a whim. Whilst inside he'd read a wonderful book about the Kett's rebellion, which had featured the Maids Head, and now he had the money to cover a couple of nights. In truth, he could stay a few weeks, but he knew he would need to find somewhere cheaper. Finding a job might take a while, given his CV.

Once showered and shaved he would sit in the yard bar to enjoy a very special pint. Tomorrow he would need to do some more shopping. He'd bought a few essentials on the way through the city, but he needed a change of clothing quickly. If he could smell himself, he knew others could.

Stepping into the room, he had to suppress a chuckle. The room was beamed – so many beams – and the roof was slanted, with a picture window and a bath in the actual room. He thought some might find it a tad claustrophobic, but to him, it was a palace fit for a king. From somewhere, he recalled that a certain Horatio Nelson had been rumoured to have stayed here. He might have slept in this very room. It was still troubling that he could remember many things, almost everything, apart from him. Apart from his previous life. His life was built on what a few people had told him of the man that he was. Throwing his bags onto the bed, he went to the window. He opened it, and the noise from the street below caused him to smile. He didn't know what the future held, but he was ready for it. He would be a better man this time around.

***

For a moment, Lucy didn't know what to say. They'd returned from the crematorium in Cromer – which had been packed. The service had been beautiful with some wonderful photos of Reggie displayed. After Reggie had been reunited with his beloved Nancy, everyone had returned to the house with her, some surprised to see the lawns filled with people, picnics on car boots, and kids playing, with some having erected tents – looking to stop overnight.

She stood holding Frank's hand and looking at them all. 'I just want to… to say thank you to you all. To each and every one of you. I know he is looking over us right now, thinking it's time to stop the talking. It's time to raise a glass, to eat, to hug, and to talk about the past and what will happen tomorrow. It's time to have a g-good t-time…' Her voice was breaking. She found new strength as she felt Frank tighten his grip at the same time as her other hand heated up… as if once more she had both men holding her hands.

The tears flowed. She looked to her left as if expecting to see him there beside her smiling down, whispering words of encouragement. 'He loved us, as we loved him. Without condition, and without compromise. He saw the best in each of us; he made us see the best in ourselves. He made us want to be the best version of us that we could be, and so we started this place. His place. This very special place. In doing that, we helped him be a better man – the man he wanted to be.' Her voice broke, and the tears flowed as she looked left and right, squeezing Frank's hand even harder.

'We love you!' someone shouted, and another started to sing: 'I'll be seeing you' – one of the songs they'd sung earlier. Others joined in, and soon just about everybody was singing it.

Lucy looked at the crowd through tear-filled eyes. She didn't need words. She stepped towards the closest family to hug them, each of them, before moving to the next group. She had a lot of hugging to do.

***

Frank stood watching Lucy make her way through the crowds, stopping to speak to everyone, even dropping to her knees to talk to the little ones. He felt incredibly proud of her. Once she'd disappeared from view, he turned to scan the crowds, checking to see that everyone looked happy, that everyone had a drink.

Think I need –

He didn't finish the thought, spotting a taxi coming down the drive slowly. He watched as a man emerged from the back, immediately knowing who it was.

***

The hairs on his back pricked, and he looked at Frank as he walked towards him. Then he looked at the gathering, the song being sung. Tomorrow and the day after he would convince himself that he knew what Frank would say. Today, however, his world stopped as Frank spoke. He'd come home to seek forgiveness, to make amends, to hope for a second chance… and that was gone. Long gone. He felt crushed and disappointed, the hoped-for reunion not to be.

'How? When?'

'In his sleep last Tuesday. We tried calling you… several times.'

'Yeah, I'm sorry. No phone. Haven't had one for a while, and I've moved around quite a bit. Look I'll go. I'll come back another time.'

'No, lad, he'd want you to stay.' Frank's tone was soft, his concern obvious.

I must look as fucked as I feel.

'I'll find you a room – one of the new cabins. Might be best to leave the… um… introductions until the morning.'

James followed Frank away from the house, wondering where they were headed. They seemed to be heading towards the woods. As he spotted the first log cabin, his bemusement was obvious.

'Frank?'

They passed a bench, and Frank indicated they should sit, so James sat. Neither spoke for a time, the noise in the distance now a whisper.

'Look, son, I'll fill you in on all this later, once you've showered and freshened yourself up, but I've got to tell you something now so it can sink in. There's no easy way to say this.'

'I'm a big boy, Frank.'

'You broke his heart, and before you say anything, I know he broke yours first. It used to cut me up, seeing you two at it. He loved you. He loved you even more than he would admit, and I know he hoped that you would return. He hoped you'd come home, that you'd have a second chance.'

James had never heard Frank speak so much; he was usually the silent type. 'Thanks, Frank. That means a lot. I can't really think – too much jet lag. Can we talk later?'

'Sure, but I need to tell you one more thing first, and it's a biggie. Do you remember the girl? Lucy?'

As Frank told him his head spun, feeling like he was in a bad movie. Nothing made sense. His dad was dead and buried, he was going to be spending a night in a glorified shed, and the girl owned the house. He knew that wasn't what Frank had told him, but that was how it sounded to him. How was he going to make sense of this? He hadn't come home for the money; he'd come home to be saved, and that was the truth. He hadn't thought beyond the first day back. He'd assumed that the old man would make everything alright, that he'd find a life worth living, worth the pain of waking up each day.

'So, you see, most of the money is tied up in this place. She's not poor by any stretch of the imagination, but this is where the money is, tied up in trusts to cover the running costs going forward. This is – was – everything to them. To us really.'

He stood. 'Right, I think I need to sleep and eat... or the other way around.'

'I'll show you to your cabin and I'll get some food for you.'

Nodding, he followed Frank along the pathway, lost in thought and too tired to make sense of anything. Tomorrow will come soon enough.

CHAPTER NINETEEN

It was the noise from the street that woke him. He lay still, just listening to how wonderful the world sounded. It was the little things that mattered. This was the first morning in three years that he could stay in bed for as long as he wanted. Last night, when struggling to sleep, he had decided three things. First, he would treat himself to a full English downstairs. Secondly, he needed to buy some clothing, and then, he had to sort some transport – a cheap car most likely. Once those jobs were ticked off, he would need to suck it up and go and find Lucy. Finding Lucy troubled him, but he wanted to stand in front of her and apologise… explain. He knew it had to be done. He had to find some closure in his old life before he could start this new one.

The city was busy, everyone enjoying the sunshine, focusing on the important things in their lives – which was probably how it should be. He'd always loved people watching but had forgotten how wonderful it could be – the young, the old, walking the streets laden with bags. He had a few at his feet, enjoying a coffee outside a coffee shop on the Haymarket. He'd been busy, his wardrobe greatly enhanced. He'd walked through the men's section, grabbing anything in a large that wasn't too mad, too colourful. He'd also treated himself to a couple of books from Jarrolds, instinctively knowing that he liked to read. He'd also bought a phone – a necessity these days – and was now scrolling through cars for sale. His budget was tight, but he had about fifteen hundred pounds to spend on a car, which would leave him about five grand. He was looking at cars within walking distance. He found a couple of possibilities at two dealers, both just a short walk away. One was on Kett's Hill and the other on Oak Street – both about two miles as the crow flies.

It's a good job I like a walk.

***

Frank was up and about early. He loved days like this. The estate was beautiful all year, but it was never bettered than when bathed in the early morning sun. He'd made a coffee in a to-go mug and was walking the woods, slowly making his way to the far side where the new cabins had been installed, one of which was occupied by James.

Having slept on it, he had decided that he couldn't hide him past today – that wouldn't be fair to Lucy – so he needed to have a serious chat with him, then decide what to do. It was a mess however you looked at it, but he knew she would find him a home. She collected strays regardless of why or how. She saw only potential. It was part of why they and everyone who knew her loved her. That was why he had to know if the lad deserved that chance – *wanted* that chance – and would make good use of a fresh start. He couldn't risk an unhappy ending if he didn't. He wouldn't.

Must be sound asleep, he thought. The hard knocking had not woken him. He walked around the cabin, peering in through the windows. As he turned the corner, he found him on the little back patio, sat on the steps, lost in thought, staring into the woods beyond with a smoke on the go.

'Morning, lad… you're up early.'

'Couldn't sleep.'

'Jet lag?'

'Maybe… but mostly regrets.'

'Dad?'

'Yep, and everything else.'

193

Frank sat beside him, passing him his coffee. 'I think you probably need this more than me. I hadn't thought about coffee and stuff. We usually have a little welcome pack in the kitchen.'

'Cheers. So, tell me everything, Frank.'

'That's why I'm here, lad.'

***

It was a piece of shit really, thought Richard, but his budget was stretched with the agreed fifteen hundred in cash for the 'mostly red' Ford Focus. He'd walked the two miles from the city via the hotel to the dealers, and he hoped to drive back. It had driven okay to be fair, and the MOT had 4 months left. He knew nothing about cars, so he had to trust the short drive. He was now sat in the portacabin wearing Primark's finest, in a chair that probably needed a deep clean, staring across a battered desk at the salesman who had asked if he wanted to borrow the laptop to tax and insure it?

Fuck… shit… bollocks! he thought. *Insure it! You twat.* 'Bugger. I'll need an address for that, won't I?'

'Yep. None of them will touch you without an address that you can prove.'

'Any ideas?' The question hung in the air. Richard was kicking himself. If he needed to sort an address first, that meant buses as he trawled the city.

'Look, chap, I shouldn't do this, but I'll leave you on my trader's policy for two days. That should be time for you to sort an address. However, in two days I will take it off. We'll call it a test drive. A *long* test drive.'

'Thank you. I don't know what to say.'

'Wait up, bud. That's going to cost you another hundred in cash. I'm not a pissing charity.'

Richard had to bite back his first thought, but he managed, 'Done.' At least, now he could find the girl, improve his job prospects, and find a cheaper place to live.

***

For a moment she didn't know what to say, how to react. James was home. He had been home since yesterday. She understood why Frank hadn't told her yesterday, but she wished he had. It was true that she knew very little about why Reggie had in effect virtually disinherited him, but he was his son, and yesterday, they'd buried his father.

'He arrived after the funeral, sweetheart. He didn't know.'

'Did you tell him we tried to get him? We tried so very hard.'

'I did.'

'How is he?'

'Not good. He's had a bad time of it.'

'What does he want?'

'I think a fresh start. He's – he's been doing drugs – hard drugs – but he's clean enough. He's a fighter, that's for sure. He got himself clean in Brazil. He had to get clean before he could come home… before he could face his dad.'

'That can't have been easy.'

'Nope. I can't imagine how tough that was. He's got a long way to go, but he wants to make the changes.'

'Sarah?'

Frank glanced away before answering, 'She's dead.'

'Dead! How?'

As Frank explained, she made her mind up that she would offer him a home here and find work for him. There was always something that needing doing, and Frank wasn't getting any younger. She'd sensed a warmer relationship between Frank and James than that between father and son.

'Right, let's go and talk to him.'

'Do you want me to tag along?'

'Yes, please.'

They continued to chat as they walked, with the dogs in close attendance, but she was thinking – wishing – that he had made it home a month earlier. Then they'd have had time to talk to sort things out, to mend broken hearts before...

They paused in front of the cabin. 'Actually, Frank, do you mind if I go in alone?'

'No worries. I'll wait here for you. Shout if you need me.'

She turned to kiss his cheek. 'Thank you, but I'll be fine. You get home and I'll be there shortly.'

***

It had been a fun trip. He'd stalled it a couple of times, but he had blamed the clutch rather than his driving ability. He'd also had to fill up soon after leaving the dealers as the car had been running on fumes. Whilst paying for fuel, he'd grabbed a hot pie and a coffee *to go*. Once back in the car, he drove to the top of Mousehold to enjoy the wonderful views.

They hadn't lied – the signs proclaiming Norwich to be a beautiful city. It was. He wondered if Jackie was out there somewhere, down below, living a new life – a life without him. He hoped she was and that she was happy. It still troubled him that he had sent her away, but it had been about self-preservation; he couldn't face her upset, her disappointment, or her disbelief. He'd had time to think lying in that bed, and his one inescapable conclusion was that she was better off without him in her life.

Whilst being moved from Leicester, following his extended sentence, to Pentonville, his prison escort had goaded him about the transfer. 'You're in for a shock, mate. I wouldn't want to spend one night there.'

Whilst inside he had tried to forget about her and the baby. It had been the only way he could survive the place. He hadn't felt pain or angst; one of the many lessons he'd learnt the last three years was to worry about the day, about protecting your back, the next meal. It was pointless to think too far ahead or worry about the things you couldn't control.

The pie tasted good, the coffee even better. He decided that he was feeling happy, which made him smile. Once he finished, he knew he had a decision to make. He needed to find digs or go and find the girl. He knew it should be the girl. Knowing he had to man-up if he was going to be able to look at himself in the mirror, he turned the key and headed off.

***

James opened the door, the sunlight pouring through the trees behind her, almost blinding him momentarily. Bit by bit he saw her, a beautiful woman standing before him, smiling. He knew that if she knew the truth about that night she wouldn't be smiling. She'd probably slap him and walk away – which is probably what he deserved. He had to remind himself that all he had wanted that night had been a date, just a fucking date, but he'd been happy to pay for the privilege if needed. It had been the white knight arriving who had screwed things up. The white fucking knight who'd turned a misunderstanding into something else, something bigger, something ugly. True it was him that had paid the price. He often wondered how his life would have been if he hadn't succumbed to temptation as often as he had, if he had lived a different less impulsive life, a life where he asked himself, just occasionally, if what he was about to do was a good idea. Going forward he had to ask that question.

His rehearsed speech deserted him, and he stood silently, lost, with no clue as to what he might say. He thought '*I'm back*' might do, but he had to stifle a nervous laugh. That would be somewhat inappropriate but so like him… to seek humour when emotionally under pressure.

'Can I come in?' she asked.

'Sure.'

He stood to one side, allowing her enough space to enter, her scent wafting over him. She smelt as good as she looked. He sensed a very different girl. She had an aura, a presence that belied her age. She was quite incredible. Instinctively, he knew that she would be very much loved by anyone coming into her life. He felt a compulsion to come clean, to explain, to throw himself at her feet and beg for a second chance. It's what every sinner wanted – a clean start – but, in truth, he didn't have the balls to do that just yet. *Maybe once I've settled, I'll tell her the truth of that night, but not yet, not yet.*

That thought surprised him. So, he wanted to stay and become part of this – whatever this was.

'Thanks.'

James sat on the small sofa opposite her and listened to her talk about his dad, the short illness, the house… After a while, the words blurred, becoming noise – a beautiful noise – but he was regretting how he had lived the last three years. If he was honest, the truth was that he regretted much of the last ten. He became aware of the silence and looked at her. It was obvious that she'd asked a question that needed an answer. In the past, he'd had a knack for replaying conversations in his head when faced with silence.

'I'd quite like to stay here if that's okay?'

'I think we can find you a bedroom in the house,' she said, laughing, 'and we can definitely do with more help around here!'

She appeared completely genuine, the warmth of her words convincing him. 'Are you sure? I'd love to.'

She stood as he did, thinking it was time to leave when she hugged him.

'Come on, let's get you moved into your old room.'

'That won't take long. I'm travelling light.'

***

Frank heard the door opening, quickly extinguishing a crafty rollup. He'd started smoking again following Reggie's passing. He was pretty sure she knew, but like many a relapsed smoker, he liked to hide it, deluding himself rather than anyone else. His pockets were full of mints and gum.

They looked happy enough, Lucy introducing Flint and Stone as they left the cabin, the dogs happy to make a new best friend. He followed them up the path to the house, happy to hear them chatting. Maybe things would be alright – he hoped so, for all their sakes. The family had had a bad time one way or another.

Reggie had often expressed remorse for both the loss of his son and also the price paid by the other chap. Shortly before he passed, he'd spoken of his regrets regarding both men, whilst working their way through a bottle of the good stuff. His anguish was real but balanced knowing that they wouldn't have had Lucy in their lives without that night. That they wouldn't be living their best lives without that night. That they wouldn't be changing thousands of lives without that night. Reggie had said just before he slept that 'life has a balance...'

***

Lucy was worried about James. He looked gaunt as if he'd had the life beaten out of him. She knew very little about him; he wasn't a subject that Reggie had wanted to talk about. She knew he'd saved her; her mum had told her more than once how

199

lucky she'd been that night. She didn't think about her old life much. There wasn't much to think about. Every morning, she woke up grateful for the life she had. The joy that she experienced every day mixed in with the hard work too. This place didn't run itself. James, she hoped, would be a huge asset in time, maybe helping in the office, freeing up her time – time to be spent in the park. That was her favourite thing. Time with their guests.

'I'll let you go up; I think your room is pretty much as you left it.'

'Thank you.'

'Flint, Stone, here,' she said and chuckled. She'd never called them in reverse order – it never got old.

Both dogs had followed him up the stairs.

'Are they allowed up?'

'Yep, just thought you might want to settle in, have a bath?'

'If you're happy, they can help me unpack,' he said, laughing. 'I'm happy to have the help and the company to be truthful.'

'Sure. You hungry?'

'Starving.'

'I'll get Frank to get something on. See you later.'

He turned. 'Thank you again. I mean it. Thank you!'

***

Richard pulled to a stop, checking his phone to confirm this was indeed the right place. The huge gates opened, revealing another world – the long drive, and in the distance, a huge house, evident beyond the woods. Google had *painted* a picture, but the reality was way more impressive.

For a moment he questioned why he was here. He considered turning back, but something, maybe it was pride, stopped him from retreating. Maybe it was something else? Moving forward, he proceeded slowly down the drive. As he neared the house, he saw her exit the front door, walking towards him. He had hoped that it might be someone else, a chance to get a feel for, but... *it's probably best that it's her,* he thought. Parking his car, he took a deep breath and got out.

'Hello.'

'Hi, how can I help you?'

'I'm Richard.'

'I know who you are.'

He stood quite still. Her tone wasn't hostile, and her face betrayed nothing of her feelings, so he continued, 'Can we please sit down and chat. I'd like to talk to you – if that's okay?'

'Sure.'

She heard Frank shouting from the house.

'There's a bench over there. I'll join you in a moment.'

He found the bench and sat, then stood, and then sat again, thinking he shouldn't have come, but... He couldn't hear the conversation between her and the old boy, but she must have reassured him as she re-joined him shortly after.

'Please sit.'

'Thank you. You don't seem very surprised to see me?'

'No, I was expecting you.'

'What, really? How? Why?'

'Jo called to tell me you... that you were out.'

'Jo?'

'She's a friend. A policewoman. She thought I should know.'

'What did she say? Did she warn you?'

'Warn me? No. No, she said she didn't think you were a problem – she was pretty confident you wouldn't be.'

'I'm not. I promise you I'm not. I wanted to see you to say how sorry I am.'

'But you have no memory?'

'No. I get what they call flashbacks, but it's true that I can't remember much.'

'So how can you apologise for something that you can't recall?'

'I read the papers; people have told me.' He stopped as she stood before him, scanning her face, trying to read it. 'I needed to explain, sorry, I'm doing a shit job. I wanted to stand in front of you to say sorry, that I… that I'm not a risk to anyone, that I think I'm a good man – that's what I'm told anyways.'

***

Her thoughts were conflicted. She wondered why she was even thinking such thoughts, but something drove her on. If she trusted this man enough to do this, what would Frank and James have to say? She wanted to help if she could – it was obvious that he had nothing to come out to. Jo had filled her in regarding his wife's disappearance; she'd heard that she'd miscarried.

She had a wonderful life thanks to that night, which now seemed so long ago, and he'd paid a big price. However, hand on heart, she couldn't recall much either. She would have to sit down with Frank and James.

They had both had second chances – maybe more than two. She'd had a second chance, so why shouldn't he? She could still remember what bad men looked like, and he didn't look much like a bad man.

'Do you have somewhere to live?'

'Nope. I'm looking at some bedsits tomorrow. I'm in a hotel for one more night.'

'Do you have a job?'

He looked away. 'No, but I'm looking. I'll find something.'

'Look, I can't pay you much.'

He stood. 'No, I couldn't. That wouldn't be...' He stopped when she stood and put her hand on his arm.

'You'll have a bed in the staff section, three meals a day, and a modest income. Take it. Quite frankly, you'd be daft if you didn't. It will get you back on your feet, and I promise you we need the help.'

'Thank you. I don't know what to say. Are you sure?'

'Yes.' *That's the easy part*, she thought. 'Meet me here tomorrow, say ten o'clock in the back car park, and I'll introduce you to the team. There's not many of us. Does that work for you?'

'I can't begin to find the words.' He looked her in the eye. 'I promise you that you won't regret this day.' She could feel a tear forming; he'd obviously come expecting a hard time – the hardest of times – but he would be leaving with something much better, something very precious. Hope and the chance to find some pride. She liked how it felt inside, making other people's lives better. *Helping people fly was so much better than kicking them.*

***

Frank watched her wave goodbye, standing quite still until he'd left the grounds. Still, she stood. He could imagine her thoughts – confused, wanting to help, to make everything better. Sighing, he walked towards her, the gravel crunching under his feet announcing his arrival. He stood behind her, hands on her shoulder, and she turned, her apprehension obvious, for a hug.

Without speaking, they walked slowly back to the house. Once through the door, he asked, already knowing the answer.

'Let me guess. You've invited him to join us?'

'I have. Is that okay?'

He pulled her close. 'This is your house – my home, for as long as you want me here.'

'Forever. You know that.'

'I do, sweetheart, I do. And I love that you… that you take in the waifs and strays, and I do understand why.'

'You do?'

'Yep, I just hope James...'

'I wasn't worried about your reaction. Strangely. I knew you'd be fine about it. James does worry me, but he'll have to accept this. If not, I'm ready for a fight!'

'Let's hope he's going to be okay; I hope he might surprise us,' he said, thinking, *the lies we tell ourselves are sometimes worse than the lies we tell each other.*

'Right, my love, where are we going to put him? Do I make another room up?'

'What? No… No, I'll put him up in the staff quarters. That way we can keep them apart for as long as possible; I'm hoping James will help me in the office, and we'll keep Richard busy outside. There's always something needs doing. Right, wish me luck.'

'You going to talk to him now?'

'Yep.'

Frank watched her take the stairs. She was a bit special. They'd had no idea of the impact she would have on their lives. He hoped James would accept the situation for what it was. As he headed for the kitchen, he laughed. They made an odd bunch: the reformed gangster's chauffeur, the abandoned and neglected runaway, the innocent ex-con with no memory, and a recovering druggie of a disinherited son. All four of them could have had different stories, different endings – just being alive was a miracle – but to find all four calling this place home… *this place must be special; you couldn't have made it up*!

***

James heard the knock. 'Come in.'

He was sitting on his bed, and his old laptop lay beside him. He'd been Googling, looking for any news on Sarah but finding nothing. Apparently, druggies dying at backstreet abortionists didn't matter, didn't count. He closed the laptop.

'Sit down.' He indicated a chair by the window.

'That's okay… I need to talk to you.'

Shit, he thought, *what have I done; what haven't I done?* He couldn't think of anything, to be fair. He hadn't done much except eat and sleep. The room looked tidy enough – it was pretty much as he had left it three years before.

'Okay… look if I...'

'No, it's nothing you've done. I had a visitor.'

'Who?'

'Richard.'

'Richard?'

'He's out of prison.'

'Oh… that Richard.' His heart seemed to stop, and his breathing shallowed. He knew he had to think before he spoke. This could impact what happened next, what would happen tomorrow, and what would happen next week!

'How is he?'

'Well, he still has no memory… nothing.'

James came close to uttering a contemptuous 'That's convenient', but he managed to cover it with a cough.

'No. No, he has… Do you remember the policeman? Jo? She called to let me know that Richard was being released. She told me quite a bit.'

Here it comes. He'd almost managed to forget that night. He'd almost managed to forgive himself once freed from the past. That was why he could come home. He couldn't ask for forgiveness until he'd forgiven himself… until he had been ready to face the music… until he had sat down with his dad. That wasn't going to happen now. Things had changed; his life had changed. Did he need her forgiveness? He thought not, but he might need it in a few seconds. It all depended on what came out of her mouth next.

'It's quite sad really. His wife left him, and he has no idea where she is.'

He heard the catch in her voice.

'He thinks she lost the baby. No home, no job, and he can't remember a thing. He was a banker before… before that night. Apparently, he was a very nice bloke. It's strange really.'

He weighed every word, looking for something sinister, but he found nothing. He relaxed a little. As he saw it, he had two options. The first was easy – to try to get her to change her mind. The second was to accept and make the best of it. His life had come to this. He'd found some peace being back, but it was brittle, built on nothing more than hope. However, it offered something better than he'd had for a long time, so he took it. He walked over to her and took her hands.

'You've made the right call; everyone deserves a second chance – a chance to make something of their lives.' As he said it, his inner voice accused him of speaking on his behalf, not Richard's.

Another thought crossed his mind as he thought ahead to meeting Richard for the first time. Would he see something in him that could be trusted? Would he see his truth? Even if he did, memory was a funny thing. What if it returned?

He now understood why some of the married women he'd shagged beyond a month felt the need to confess. He had always counselled no, but now he could see the attraction. Maybe it was better to live one day free than a lifetime of hiding secrets. If he confessed, she might kick him out, but she might not. One thing was true, though. Richard deserved a better life – more than he. *This could be interesting*, he thought. *Have I just become a better man?*

CHAPTER TWENTY

The room looked tidy. He'd made the bed – stupidly really as sometime soon a maid would strip it – but he liked to look back when leaving a room to see the first impression he or she would have of him when entering. The used towel lay in the bath. He'd only used the one. Grabbing his stuff, he headed for the door. He had enjoyed the last two nights. The comparison between his old room and this could not be made quickly. He had tasted two very different worlds since his release. One he wanted to enjoy, and one he wanted to forget.

After checking out, he walked to the car park to collect his car. The early morning sunlight was beautiful, the air cool. Early autumn had always been his favourite time of the year. It had been two days of happiness, and he hadn't been truly happy for three years. He had experienced happy moments inside, but they had been fleeting, a reaction to something that had happened. This was happy, an internal hopefully sustainable happy, and it felt good.

The car started first time – he thanked the *car gods* – and he pulled out, driving towards a new life. He was both excited and nervous. Nervous at the thought of meeting everyone for the first time – especially James. That was understandable, he realised, but it didn't change the fact that sometime soon he would be face to face with the man who'd saved her, and now she was saving him. The irony was not missed by him. They hadn't discussed anything like pay or the work. He hadn't felt the need. He knew his options were limited, and the chance to live somewhere decent, working with decent people, working outside, appealed to him. He was grateful, and he would move heaven and earth to make this work.

All too soon he arrived, parking in the staff car park beside the coach house, wondering if he should go there or the house. For a few moments he sat in the car recalling that she had said 'meet me here' when at the front of the house. He'd remembered to enter the estate via the *tradesmen's* entrance behind the coach house. Exiting the car, he was still torn... should he walk to the house or the coach house? Feeling a tad daft, he looked around, very relieved to see her come around the corner.

'Hello.'

'Hi. Do I need my bag now, or should I leave it for later?'

'You might as well bring it; I'll show you to your room whilst we're here.'

Collecting his bags from the back seat, he followed her to the coach house. 'That's a lovely building.'

'It is, isn't it. It's as old as the house – built around three hundred years ago.'

'It's a lovely place.'

Following her into the reception area, he noticed the usual board on the wall filled with happy smiley faces – the staff and volunteers. The walls were covered with drawings and paintings completed by the kids. It felt good. It was a happy building.

'Right, let's get you settled in. Take a seat. There are some forms to fill in, I'm afraid. Everyone has to complete them. Then we need to have a little chat.'

'That sounds ominous?'

'Sorry, you're right. Let's do that bit first. We'll go into the office.'

He followed her into a basic admin room with three desks, taking the offered seat.

'There's been a little change of plan just for now. You will be living in the staff quarters, as we planned, and I'll take you there now, but until we get clearance on your DBS check, we'll have you working in the house. This office is mostly used on changeovers. The business is done up at the house, and you'll be a huge help, you'll probably improve the whole system. God knows it needs improving.

'I thought you said...' *What's his name?* Whilst he considered this change, it was true he'd probably be better suited to an office, but the thought of working outside had appealed. That said, he understood completely the need for her to be careful. His check would reveal what she knew already. 'James would be working up at the house?'

'He's going to be our new maintenance man for a while.'

'Is he happy with that?'

'It was his idea. He thought your skill set would be best used in the office, rather than banging in nails.'

She seemed happy enough, and he couldn't sense anything untoward, so he nodded, thanking her. He assumed James wanted to keep understandable distance between them, but why hadn't he taken the opportunity to stop this? If the boot had been on the other foot, he thought he would have kicked him firmly into touch. *Maybe James is a better man.*

***

She breathed a sigh of relief. This had gone better than feared. He'd adjusted well, she thought, thinking on his feet. It had been Frank who had raised the security check question, to have him CRB'd. She'd talked to Mickey in Jo's absence – who said he wasn't surprised by her decision to offer him a home, and he knew where to come if his current girlfriend kicked him out.' He'd said that laughing, but he added, 'You should probably have him work away from the kids for now, but it is very important to get the DBS check sent ASAP.' Apparently, the CRB had been replaced by a DBS. It would be her call on what happened after, but she should check to see any other history. He had also added that she should check her public liability small print regarding staff, etc.

Feeling happier, she showed him around the place. He seemed genuinely interested in what they did and why they did it. He drew a couple of interested glances from a couple of volunteers as they walked with one of the mums, turning a hello into a ten-minute chat. It was, she thought, going to be interesting once James and he were unleashed on the female population. She wasn't interested in either, obviously: one felt like a brother, and one, well, he was definitely out of bounds. It wouldn't have mattered anyway. Her life was this place. She had no time for romance. However, even as she voiced it, she knew she wanted to be loved, to love, one day… sooner than later.

'This is your room.' She stood to one side, allowing him space to enter. She watched him cast an appreciative eye around the room: single bed, a desk in the corner, a small sofa with coffee table, and a small TV on the wall, with French doors out to a small patio facing the woods beyond.

'This will do nicely.'

'There's an *en suite* behind you and a communal kitchen down the hall, although I don't think there's much cooking done there as most of the volunteers come here for a couple of weeks at a time, and the full-timers live close by.'

'Thank you. I can't express how much this means…'

'You don't need to. I'll let you settle. I've started you off with some basics, so at least you can make yourself a cuppa in your room, and I've put some stuff in the big fridge in the kitchen with your name on.' She laughed. 'Not that that would stop a hungry nurse!'

'Thanks.'

'So, make yourself a cuppa, and come and find me up at the house when you're ready.'

Turning to go, she paused by the door. 'I meant to say that you shouldn't worry about Frank. He's a gentle giant – a big softie really. He's just very protective of me.'

***

As she left, he sat thinking, *it's not Frank that troubles me, it's the other one.* He popped the kettle on and opened the doors to his patio. He had two plastic chairs. This really was a beautiful place. He knew how lucky he was and renewed his determination to pay her back for her trust. Just then, a door opened next door, and a pretty girl stepped out.

'Hi.'

'Oh, hello.'

'Lucy told me I'd have a neighbour. I'm Rachel.'

He took the offered hand to shake.

'Nice to meet you. How long are you here for?'

'I'm permanent. Like you. I'm a nurse. It's good to have one full-time. I work Thursday to Monday – long days, but it's a good place to work. I help out with the kids. I do anything really.'

'Love your accent.'

'You do?' She laughed. 'I'm from Cornwall – lived there all my life.'

'It's lovely.'

'Well, I'm glad you like it.'

'Right, I need to get myself up to the house. It's time to earn my keep. It was nice to meet you.'

'You too. If you need anything just shout.'

'Thank you,' he said and turned to leave. *She was nice,* he thought, but was she too nice? Had she been flirting? He was going to have to relearn social niceties or he could offend or embarrass way too easily!

***

This was still the best room in the house, thought James. He'd popped back for a late breakfast – one of Frank's bacon sandwiches and at the very least two cups of tea. The bread was hand-cut and thick – as he liked it – with loads of crispy bacon, smothered in tomato sauce. He listened to Lucy updating them both on Richard's arrival, impulsively saying, 'I thought I'd catch him before he starts to say hi and let him know that all I care about is today and tomorrow. The past is gone… forgotten. If you can forgive him, if you can give him a second chance, then so can I.'

'That's so sweet of you. Thank you.'

He caught Frank's eye and smiled, seeing a strange look pass Frank's face, though it was quickly replaced with a non-committal expression. He made a mental note to speak to Frank ASAP as he was the only person alive who knew the truth about that night. He'd hoped that Frank had known his intentions that night; he might have been an idiot, but he'd never attack a woman, Frank needed to understand that. It was important to him that Frank knew the whole truth; they'd have to have a serious conversation. He needed this to work. He knew it – as did the voice not verbalised. The voice that said, *you need this to work just as much as he does – maybe more. Screw this up and you have nothing. Keep it simple, and earn her trust. Be a better man. Be a nicer man.* Standing, he grabbed the last sandwich. 'I'll go find him.' As he left, he kissed her cheek. 'See you for supper.'

They found each other on the path, a short distance from the house, stopping about five feet from each other.

'I'm glad I found you.'

'Me too, I wanted to… I wanted a chance to talk, sooner rather than later.'

'Me too. Look, mate, as I just said to Lucy, all I'm interested in is going forward. She's happy to have you here, which means so am I.'

He held his hand out, and Richard shook it. 'That means a lot. Thank you.'

'We don't need to talk about the past ever again. What happened happened…'

'That works for me. I just want to repay her trust.'

As do I, he thought. 'See you later then.'

Walking away, he breathed a sigh of relief. The past could stay buried. He whistled as he walked. Today was a good day, and tomorrow would be a good day. He was alive.

His thoughts turned to Sarah. He couldn't go there. She'd died on the table in front of him, but it hadn't really been his fault. God knows it probably wasn't even his kid, but it was hard to not picture her laid out on a table in a kitchen covered in blood. He shivered and walked on.

***

Richard stood at the door having knocked, still thinking about his encounter with James. He had seemed okay, friendly even, but something stirred in his gut. Had it been too easy? Too quick? Was there something slightly off about him? In prison, he'd learnt how to read people, to get a feel about them. It had been a good skill, and it had saved many an argument or worse. James worried him a little. He decided he would keep an eye on him.

Finally, the door opened to reveal Frank still drying his hands. He was a big man – bigger than he recalled – so he stepped back.

'You don't need to knock, come in. I'll take you up to the office.'

Following the big man up the stairs, he glanced into open rooms and down hallways, impressed by everything he saw. Finally, they stepped into a room – a big room with many windows, making for great light and wonderful views. He turned to thank Frank, only to find he had already left the room. He walked to the windows to check the views, which he knew would be spectacular.

'You settling in okay?'

He turned to see Lucy entering the room. 'Yes, thank you.'

'So, it's just you, me, and Freda in here.'

'Freda?'

'She works part-time. She's retired, and she comes in twice a week, thank God. She keeps this place running, which is how I get to spend more time out there.'

'So, can I ask a question?'

'Sure.'

'Why do you need me?'

'I need you – *we* need you – for the big stuff. I want to create an interactive website where the kids can talk to us and each other for the fifty weeks of the year that they're not here. I want to raise more funds, so we can do more. The list is long. We need to be able to have the carers stay here for a week, and that means sometimes, if they have no other carers available, placing the family member that they care for in a care home. That costs money – lots of money.'

She'd said that in one breath with passion. He'd been impressed. 'Wooo, I'd better get started, but it's not something I've done before. At least, I don't think so.'

'Welcome to our world. None of us had done this before. We either Google or make it up as we go.'

'Well, you've done a wonderful job so far.'

'Thank you, but I've got way more out of this than I've put in.'

'I guess we need to talk about budgets and...'

'Anything you need just ask, but we'll need sponsors to fund the big stuff. However, to date, we've been pleasantly surprised how big businesses want to be involved with us. The secret is to get them to come to us on a weekend. If they come to look around, you can see quite quickly that they want to make something happen. It's the kids who do all the selling.'

'I imagine some of them are' – he was trying to find the words – 'in a bad place?'

'They are, but something happens here. There's something special in the air. The kids who do the caring at home get to be kids again – or maybe for the first time – and kids don't judge. Kids just want to be kids.'

'I'll do my very best.'

'I know you will.'

***

Leaving him to settle in, she went to find Frank. She felt good about Richard. Something told her he would make a difference. She'd done some digging, with Jo's help, to find out that he'd been very well thought of by the bank and those that worked there.

This morning she had shed a tear for Reggie. It could be the littlest of reasons, an empty chair, hearing the echo of his voice over breakfast, taking an early morning walk with the dogs. She'd come to love him. If he had been her salvation, she liked to think she had been his. He and Frank were the best of men, restoring her faith not just in men but in humanity. She knew that her grief would be with her for a long time, but she felt good about adding James and Richard to their little merged family. She hoped Frank really did approve. She needed to know, so headed to the kitchen expecting to find him in his happy place.

'Hi, you, I thought I might find you here.'

'Heh. Do you want a coffee?'

'Yes, please.'

'How'd it go?'

They chatted over a coffee. She thought Frank was happy enough, but something troubled him, something unsaid. When asked, he always responded happily enough, but something hung in the air. She assumed he was just uneasy about her being this close to Richard.

CHAPTER TWENTY-ONE

James was finishing up for the day, his white T-shirt evidencing how hard he'd been working. On the way back, he decided to pop in on Richard. It would be good to keep up appearances. That said he was looking forward to the day when everything felt normal, when he wouldn't need to do things because he should. He walked through the woods to the back of the coach house, surprised to see a pretty young thing on the patio next door, still in uniform – blue scrubs. So, a nurse.

'Hi.'

·'Hello.'

'Hope I didn't surprise you?'

'Are you looking for Richard?'

Richard already, he thought. *He's only been here a day, and already he's making an impression.* 'Yes, I was.'

'He's still working, I think, up at the big house.'

'Yes, I know the big house. It's a place I call home.' He smiled but inwardly groaned. *That sounded just a little pretentious.* He offered his hand. 'Sorry, I'm James – James Taylor.'

'For a minute there I thought you were going to say Bond,' she said, laughing.

He liked her laugh, it was warm and throaty, so he joined in. It was at that moment that Richard opened the doors to join them. He liked the look on his face, slightly territorial he thought. Oh well. If you don't ask you don't get had been his creed before, and it would be again when he was ready to face the world.

'Hi, bud,' he said, without taking his eyes off the girl.

'Hi.'

'I thought I'd pop in to check you were settling in okay?'

'I'm good thanks.'

'Do you guys want a beer? I've got some in the fridge,' asked Rachel.

'I could murder one, thanks,' said Richard.

'I'd love to, but I need to get home – big night ahead,' said James.

'Something good?' asked Rachel.

'Yeah, I found out the old man recovered my Porsche whilst I was… um… travelling. It's been parked up a while, only going out for servicing. It's time to take her out and blow the cobwebs off. Fancy a drive?'

'I'd love to, but I promised Richard a meal.'

'No probs. Catch you both later.'

***

Richard watched him leave.

'Did I miss something?'

'Sorry' – she laughed – 'I couldn't think of anything else to say.'

'So, our big night in?'

'What do you fancy?'

'I'm easy.' He watched her blush; she really was quite pretty… for a blonde – *where did that come from?*

'Right, you go shower, and I'll get something cooking. See you in the kitchen in a bit.'

Going back inside he realised he was looking forward to spending some time with her, but he really did need to buy some decent clothes. His world had changed – and for the better. He stripped and stepped into the shower – a very hot shower – washing quickly and thinking about her, his cock hardening at the thought. He didn't know if sex was even a possibility, but just the thought was enough. He hadn't so much as kissed a girl in three years.

Rachel was very different to Jackie. She was quite tall – a good few inches taller than Jackie. He guessed her to be around 5 feet 10 inches. She looked like she worked out, she was slim, and he thought her to be a natural blonde. Maybe he'd find out later.

She'll have to make the first move.

***

Rachel had slipped into jeans and a T-shirt, having chucked the uniform into a wash, thanking God that she'd shopped a couple of days before as she opened the fridge. At least, she had a few options. She wasn't a great cook, but she could throw a spag bol together with the best, and she even had a few beers in the fridge. She felt excited. She hadn't made many friends since taking the job – partly because they were in the middle of nowhere, and partly because most of the staff were weekend temps.

Singing along with the radio, she didn't hear the knock on the door, so when Richard laughingly shouted, 'Hello!' over her singing, she jumped out of her skin.

'Oh my God, you made me…'

'Sorry about that.' He grinned. 'You sounded quite good.'

'You lie like a rug then.'

'Smells good.'

'I'm a dab hand with spaghetti. Just don't ask me to bake a cake.'

'No dessert then?'

'Nope. Not unless you want to pinch from the fridge. We've all done it at least once.'

'I'm good with the Bolognese thanks. It's nice to have some.' He'd been about to say 'someone', but that might require a fuller explanation than he wanted to give. He wasn't ready to tell her his life story. 'I haven't had a decent spag bol in a while.'

'There are some beers in the fridge if you want to get a couple?'

'Are they marked?'

'No, I have my own little booze and milk fridge by the bed. You'll want to get one too if you want to hang onto your stuff. Some of the part-timers would steal your last drop of milk.'

***

Richard had enjoyed the supper, and they were now sitting on the small sofa watching TV, chatting away like old friends. He was enjoying himself, becoming aware that he had actually switched off. He wasn't thinking about anything, and that feeling was pretty damned good.

'Another beer?' she asked.

'If I have another one, I might need a lift home.'

She laughed as if he was the funniest man alive, and he watched her walk to the fridge. She had a nice arse.

'Here you go.'

He took her hand, pulling her to him, and kissed her. Her lips were soft, and he kissed her harder, her tongue finding his.

She was almost whimpering. He knew they would fuck; they were already trying to find skin. She fell over him, lying on the sofa. Conflicting thoughts fired across his brain: the need to feel human again, the physical need to fuck, to connect, but also thinking about the conversation tomorrow. He could imagine her saying, 'Last night was lovely but…' As she started to force her jeans down, lifting her bum to help, he told his brain to *shut the fuck up*.

He stood to remove the last of his clothing, his socks and boxers, grateful that he had kept in shape whilst inside. She sat up on the sofa, and he knelt at her feet so he could kiss her. He had forgotten just how good this was. Her hands were driving him nuts; he was seconds away from… he didn't want to. Not yet. He wanted to lay her down, feel her under him.

Seeing his desire turned her on. She reached behind to unclasp her bra, hearing him groan once her tits were freed. He pulled her up until she stood, then she felt herself being carried to the bed. She reached into a bedside drawer to find a condom, which she gave to him. She watched him struggling. 'Give it here,' she had almost growled. She rolled it over and down his now-hard cock very quickly.

He gently parted her legs, then entered her, kissing her, fucking her slowly. She was enjoying the sensation as she felt her own orgasm building. She didn't usually come quickly, but this was an unexpected sensory overload.

She flipped him onto his back. Feeling him enter her again, she moved slowly, then started to ride him harder, his voice in her ear whispering: All too soon she came. It was a hard explosion between her legs and in her head, and she collapsed on him, panting. 'Have you?'

'No, not yet.'

He rolled her onto her back, and on raised arms, he began to fuck her hard, very hard. She liked the rolling tumbling gentle waves now washing through her, the remnants of her first orgasm. She tried to kiss him but couldn't reach him. 'Harder!' she implored, and so he did, taking her to another delicious orgasm. She collapsed onto her back with him on top, both breathing hard, both laughing, both happy. *What could go wrong?* she thought.

They lay bathed in each other's sweat for a while, not talking, breathing hard. She liked the intimacy, grateful he wasn't one of those that disappeared, from the room or the moment, which was worse, immediately after. Sitting up, she wiped her mouth on the back of her hand… thinking *classy*, then she sought his eyes. She wanted to see, to stare into his eyes and try and measure what they had? Was it a one-off shag or something more? Would they repeat this tomorrow or avoid each other for days? She'd had both one-night stands and a few boyfriends, each relationship fizzling out. She'd blamed the job. Being a nurse was rewarding, but a price was paid. Family, friends, and boyfriends were hard to juggle when working shifts. In fact, she'd taken this job to escape a truly miserable relationship.

***

The streets were pretty empty as he made his way to meet the boys. Only Jack and Tom had been up for a last-minute night out. They were probably already at the bar waiting for him. He'd missed the boys, but he knew that he couldn't slip back into old habits. He wasn't strong enough to run that risk, so he'd have a couple of beers, but that would be it.

Jack and Tom were okay. It was the other two that could lead him into temptation. Tom had made the first team the season before, and now he couldn't walk into a pub without being mobbed. It could be a good night; the last time they'd met, he'd been the catch. Now, he was anything but. He smiled walking into Bar11 to find his mates waiting. They hugged as men do, the years apart irrelevant. They were mates, and very quickly they made up for lost time. *The car might have to stay the night.* It was going to be a long one. *I deserve a decent night out!*

They drifted from pub to pub. Tom had left them after the last pub with a mini-skirted blonde on his arm, apologetic but unabashed as he headed home to his penthouse by the river, leaving the two of them to continue.

'Think I'm ready for bed too,' said Jack.

'Lightweight.'

'Yep… I am, and I'm not ashamed to admit it. It's a wise man who knows when it's time to call it a night.'

'It's been a good night. Same again next week?'

'Sure, I'll need to check with the others, but I think Tom has a mid-weeker.'

'No probs. Where are you parked?'

'Duke Street.'

'I'll say good night then. Taxis are the other way.'

They hugged, and he watched Jack walk into the distance. *They're good mates, probably looking out for me.* He had a choice, grab a taxi or make his way to his favourite titty bar. The bar won the argument. The stairs were dark, the music throbbing. He loved the darkness, the low lights, the tension, and the energy. He could tell immediately who were the virgins, the first-timers – their excitement was tangible, their wallets ready to be emptied, and they would be emptied. *Poor bastards,* he thought, *Poor me, I've got barely enough to buy a couple of beers!* He sat at the bar, his back to the dance areas. He wasn't playing hard to get, just setting himself apart from the madness behind him.

Soon an attractive brunette joined him, and he smiled. She was very well put together, and as she laid her hands on him, he could feel her body against his. The old James would have taken her into a private room without asking the price – so would the new James if he had the money, he admitted.

'Do you want to…'

'No, my lovely, not tonight.'

Her hand slid onto his thigh. 'Are you sure? I'm very good.'

'I bet you are… but not tonight.'

She left as quickly as she'd arrived, already whispering into a new arrival's ear.

'James!'

He turned to see who could be that excited about his return to find an old friend about to hug him, kissing him twice on both cheeks.

'How long have you been back?'

He knew the face, knew the body – they'd fucked from time to time in the past – but he couldn't for the life of him remember her name.

'A few days.'

'I heard you'd gone travelling.'

'Did you miss me?'

'Always.'

'You missed my tips. The more pissed I was, the richer you got,' he said, smiling.

She leaned in. 'You could afford it.'

'Not any more, my love.'

'Are you poor?' She said it with such disgust that he laughed.

'Not poor poor. Not like *normal* poor; I've still got the Porsche and still live at home, but everything is pretty much tied up in the…'

'I love that place. It's often on the telly and in the local papers. Your dad and what's her name – that girl – have done a brilliant job.'

'You think so?'

'Absolutely.'

'Well, tomorrow I will find out what the old man left me.'

She laid a hand on his arm. 'I was so sorry to hear about your dad.'

'Thanks.'

'You'll be back on your feet before you know it.'

'I'd rather be on my back with you riding me.'

'I finish at twelve. Can you wait?'

'I'll have to.'

She laughed.

Poor cow. Another one hoping to be the one!

***

Lucy was completing her wander through the park. The night air was cool, and she could see the lights from the house through the trees. She walked past the coach house, hearing laughter from the back patio. She was about to pop over to say hello, when she heard a girl joining in. They sounded happy, very happy, so she smiled and turned to go back to the house.

Frank was sat in the lounge watching the news. He loved the news and loved to discuss the big stories, but they had agreed to disagree about BREXIT – him being a leaver and her a remainer.

'Hello, old man.'

'Old man? I'd still catch you, youngster.'

'Only if I let you.'

'Come and sit down by me, lovely. I've not seen much of you.'

'I know, I've been settling in Richard and James.'

'How are they?'

'Okay, I think. I think Richard is doing better than James.'

'I'll keep an eye on him; he's off to the solicitor tomorrow.'

'How do you think he'll react?'

'Hopefully, he will think it's enough.'

'Do you know how much?'

'Reggie asked me at the time. I suggested he needed enough to keep him out of trouble, but he scoffed. He said he needed enough to have a last opportunity to make a positive change in his life – no more, no less.'

'Fancy a nightcap?'

'Sure, make mine a double.'

'I'm taking mine to bed.'

'I'll stay a while, give the lad time to get home.'

She poured two glasses watching the news. Handing him his, she kissed the top of his head. 'Good night, old man.'

'Goodnight, my love. Sleep well.'

***

The taxi stopped, and he thought they were somewhere on the Heartsease Estate – a former council house by the look of it. He followed her in. It was furnished okay and was probably the cleanest and tidiest on the road, with everything polished. He was both a little surprised and impressed.

Away from the club, she had changed. No longer did she appear the most fuckable girl he'd seen since he'd left Brazil. Now, she looked tired as if the only thing she really wanted to do in bed was sleep. To be brutally honest, he felt the same. He was going to either make his excuses or fuck her as quickly as decency allowed. Would it be so bad if he left right now? he asked himself.

***

Richard lay in bed. It had been a good night. Decent food and even better company. He felt content, almost restored as a man, as a member of the human race. He hadn't felt like one for some time! He recalled Jackie's words: 'You wouldn't have done this; you couldn't have done this. This is not you.' Just maybe she was right. He had spent many hours analysing his instinct, his gut reaction to situations and thoughts, how he approached his life, and nothing suggested that he was a menace or dangerous.

If he listened carefully, he could hear Rachel next door singing. She sounded happy. He hoped that she wasn't one of those girls who fell in love on the first date – not that they'd had a date. Did a spag bol, a couple of beers, and a shag make a date? He was out of touch, but who could he ask?

***

It had been a disappointing end to the night. He wished that he had gone home once the boys had left, but he had listened to the wrong voice. He had to learn to listen to the good voice – the one that said you will regret this. He needed to do the sensible thing sometimes.

They'd arrived tired, and he'd ignored the offer of a drink or coffee before she'd taken him upstairs to her bedroom. The bed had been unmade, clothes lay where dropped, and a half-full cup of coffee was on the bedside cupboard. She had quickly dimmed the lights, but the impression lingered. Her bedroom was very different to the rest of the house.

Maybe she only uses the bedroom?

Stacey did her best, but still, he'd almost given up – which would have been a first. He had almost faked his orgasm, and that would have been another first. Instead, he had imagined it had been Sarah – the young Sarah – lying under him. He'd fucked her without seeing her. Afterwards, he had dressed whilst she used the bathroom. He had felt sorry for her, but not so sorry that he wanted to hang around to make her feel better.

On the way out he passed an open bedroom door, the light enough to show that it was a kid's room. He left quickly, feeling more than a little shabby.

I can be better than this. I need to be better than this!

CHAPTER TWENTY-TWO

There was something about solicitors' offices. He was sitting on a very uncomfortable seat waiting for a Mr Spencer, whom he expected to be an old boy in a three-piece, so he was surprised to find a young man take the seat behind the desk.

'Mr Taylor. I'm very pleased to meet you. My condolences to you for your loss.'

'Thank you.'

'Right, let's get to it shall we?'

'Yes, please.'

'Right-oh. We need to give you a letter – from Sir Reggie. You can read it now or take it with you. The choice is yours.'

Taking the letter, he folded it and placed it in his back pocket. 'Thank you. Please continue. I know he left pretty much everything to the girl.'

'I think you'll find he actually left her a reasonably modest amount. It's all in the will. It's enough to buy a house should she want to, but as you know, the bulk of the estate is tied up in a trust to protect the house and the... the care centre, to ensure that they can continue for quite some time: Lucy – he emphasised her name – has a right to live and work there and a right to enjoy a salary for as long as she wants to. Having met Miss Lucy, I would imagine that might be a lifetime commitment.'

'Yes, I get that,' he replied, thinking, *fucking told me on that one, didn't he? Little prick.*

230

Shuffling the papers, he read, 'James, I...'

'I'm sorry, but can we skip to the interesting bit? Has he left me anything? If so, what?'

His disdain was beginning to show. 'I suppose we could; you have his letter,' he said almost to himself. 'There's a lot of lawyer-speak, but essentially, he's left you the Porsche...'

He was about to say, 'That was my car', but he stopped himself, remembering that everything he 'owned' had been brought by the old man. 'Sorry, please go on.' He didn't know what to think. He had told himself to expect nothing, assuming the old man had finally done as threatened.

'The sum of fifty thousand pounds...'

James felt something bust inside, and part of him died. It was one thing trying to prepare for the worst but...

'As I was saying, fifty thousand pounds to be paid per annum for ten years, with a lump sum of £250,000 to be used towards a house, and then a further £250,000 to be held until a child...'

James didn't hear the rest. He'd got £50k a year, and he could live off that, maybe save a little. He could buy a house – that much had cheered him a little – but to be tied to producing a bloody kid to get the last bit of cash pissed him off just a little. 'Do I need to sign anything?'

'I'll need your bank details to set up the payments. The money is to be held by us. Should you find a house, we would need to pay the solicitors acting for you.'

James stood. 'I'll be in touch.' Then he turned and left. Once outside, he sat on a bench and removed the envelope, which he tore into quarters which he then threw into the bin beside the bench. He left cursing his life. £50k was okay, he supposed. He hadn't expected anything, really. He began to calm a little, realising that he was actually worth a million – he just had to buy a house and father a sprog to become one. He stopped and laughed out loud, realising that was his father's intention... that he become a grown-up. He turned to head back to the bin, wanting to read the old man's last words.

Relieved to find the bin as he had left it, he pulled the four bits of envelope out, removing the contents which he laid on his thigh.

James

I know that I have failed you as a father. I think you know that losing your mother broke me. That's no excuse, by the way! I was the adult, you the child, and you deserved much better from me. I have lived with that, especially these last 3 years.

We have disappointed each other. If you are reading this it means sadly that we haven't had the chance to make things right – something I wanted to do. Something I thought about most days. Just about every day to be truthful.

I want you to know that having you was one of the greatest joys in my life and that I regret how we parted; I think I needed to find my own peace to be able to seek the same with you. That's not another excuse, but it's the best I have. My life has been a rollercoaster. I like to think, need to think, that I have redeemed myself a little these last few years, but maybe not. That could just be the wishing of a man nearing the end of his mortality?

I hope you are ok. If you are not, stay with Lucy & Frank. There is something special about the place, something special about her. I think you can find some joy there.

Please if you do nothing else, be kind to Lucy. Help her. She doesn't have your money – the money is tied up in the charity. Pretty much all of it, in fact. Lucy and Frank get to live in the house for life, which is what they wanted. She has a home and an income.

My one prayer for you my son, is that you find true happiness and that you live a life worth living. <u>You are capable of so much</u>!

Don't waste a day.

As I know life is just too short, but when you find good things, it is so very precious!

Be kind, be brave, be strong but most importantly be wonderful.

Love, always,

Dad x

James sat crushed and, maybe for the first time, regretful. His dad had cared. He could have cried at the thought of what might have been if they had had a conversation three years ago.

'Are you okay?'

He looked up to find an old lady standing in front of him, her face concerned. He wondered why she would ask him, then realised he was in fact crying. 'I'm fine thank you; I'm just reading a letter from my dad.'

She sat beside him, and he found himself unloading, telling her everything. Well, just about everything. Once he had finished, they sat in silence for a while.

'Your father knows…'

'Do you think?'

'I know.'

'How?'

'It's simple. I'm a Catholic.'

'Practising?'

'We're all practising.' She laughed, and it was a nice laugh. 'I believe your father changed his ways. He made a difference – in his life and to others. My God would know that and would understand that your father did so not to make amends but because he wanted to do good things.'

James felt much happier, relieved even. No, he felt overjoyed that he had returned for the letter and had met this wonderful woman. He stood and helped her up, then bent over to hug her gently. 'Thank you.'

'There's no need to thank me, handsome. Just do what your father did and go live your best life.'

'Can I run you home?

'No, lovely… I like to walk; it keeps me fit.' She smiled again. 'And you never know who you might bump into.'

James watched her walk away, resolving to do as she had urged, hoping this time his resolve would last. *It will. IT WILL – it must!*

***

It was Monday, an all hands to the deck day. The day when the temps would leave for home, once the work was completed. The cleaners were already cleaning the newly emptied cabins. Lucy was here, there, and everywhere. She didn't want to miss a single goodbye. Every group was different, but every group also had one thing in common: they were all kids caring for family members whilst trying to be kids. She hoped they had made a difference.

'Who's up for coffee and a bacon sarnie?'

'Yes, please, Frank.'

They gathered around Frank, who was pouring coffee. Everyone loved him almost as much as they loved the treats he brought with him. It was bacon sarnies in the morning, scones in the afternoon.

Answering her phone, Lucy stepped outside. It was a voicemail from James, apologising for being late but letting her know he would get there as soon as he could. He sounded okay, which was a relief knowing why he had gone into the city. She just wanted him to find some sort of happiness. She had been relieved to find that he and Richard could be civil with each other. She hoped one day they might even become friends.

PART FOUR

CHAPTER TWENTY-THREE

Three months later

Lucy loved this time of year. She was watching James and Richard struggling with the tree. They had just returned with a ten-foot spruce – a perfect tree – and she couldn't wait to decorate it. The cabins had been decorated for nearly three weeks. Each cabin had a small tree with presents under – token gifts to be taken home. This tree had roots. It was a tradition that she wanted to keep going. Their first tree together stood outside, as did their second and third. She hoped to plant a whole Christmas tree forest.

Richard and James had been busy the night before decorating the three trees in front of the house, winding thousands of little bright white lights around them. The trees had looked stunning once finished.

'Looks beautiful. Anyone for a hot sausage roll and a coffee?' asked Frank.

They chorused, 'Yes!' leaving the tree standing, almost upright but secure enough. They gathered around Frank, taking the still-warm rolls.

'Oh my God, Frank, these are wonderful,' said Richard.

'I think it's leaning to the right?' Lucy noted.

'Bit like me,' James said, they all laughed.

Lucy cradled her coffee cup, listening to the three of them. They were her family. She often thought about the last three years, but that life, the life lived before, was becoming a dimmed, distant memory. She couldn't recall too much from those years, but she knew there hadn't been many presents and even fewer trees. At times it felt as if her old life had been lived in black and white, and she was now living in colour.

This Christmas would be the best one yet. They would gather around the tree to open presents. She'd wrapped her gifts last night. Frank had a lovely lighter engraved with all my love Lucy x. She hated to encourage him to smoke, but as he said, the only guilty pleasure he had left was to sit outside with a glass of whiskey and a smoke. For Richard, she'd managed to get hold of a first edition Harry Potter and the Philosopher's Stone. She knew he would love it. He was a man of few possessions and an avid reader, often curled up with a good book. He deserved to own something as beautiful as a first edition. For James, she had bought two tickets for a Queen concert, hoping he might have someone to take. If not, she would jump at the chance of seeing Adam Lambert fronting the band.

After presents, they would follow Frank to the kitchen for breakfast, grateful to put their feet up. They would be closing in three days, reopening the ninth of January, allowing everybody a chance to catch their breath. She hadn't taken a week off in three years. She didn't need time off, not yet. She would holiday when she had someone to holiday with. She'd started to think it might be time to put a foot back into the water. Her only previous dalliance hadn't gone well. She'd lasted three dates, three painful dates, before realising they were just not right for each other. He hadn't taken it well.

'Looks beautiful,' she said to no one.

'Yes, it does,' said James, standing.

'Are you going somewhere?'

'Yep. I have a hot date.'

'Wonderful. Do you know her?' she said, laughing.

'You're a bad girl. I will when I find her.'

'Stay safe.'

She watched him leave. He was a different man to the one who had arrived. He was going to sell the love of his life, his beloved car, planning to swap her for a battered old Land Rover Defender, claiming he needed a 4x4 when out in the woods, but she had seen it as casting off the last of the old and in with the new. The boy becoming a man. He still lived in the house, but he had been talking about buying a little cottage up the road. His love life was still quite hectic – she didn't know if he dated anybody twice – but he was softer than before, even helping Richard to try to find his wife, to no avail.

Strangely, it was Richard who troubled her more than James. On the surface, he was fine, and workwise he was an absolute star. He'd surprised himself. Only yesterday he'd bounced into the room with a huge grin.

'Guess what?'

'What? Must be good news.'

'Good? This is HUGE news. Massive.'

'Go on.'

'Well, if you agree – if the others agree – I've only gone and sold the naming rights to one of the biggest companies in the county.'

'Who?'

'RFXR. They're a tech company – a big tech company with offices in the US and here.'

'How much?' She couldn't breathe.

'Enough to cover us for the next three years. They've also got an option to renew.'

'Oh my God. Does that include teaching?' She uttered a silent prayer; they had been trying to find the funds to employ a couple of specialist teachers, knowing that fifty school days were lost each year by the youngsters caring for parents. The effect on simple reading and writing was a problem for some of the younger kids.

'Yep, and it is enough for the online help once they get back home.'

They'd hugged, she'd cried, and then she ran through the house calling Frank, but later that night, she had popped round to see him – to again thank him – only to find him sat in the dark. A few questions later revealed his anguish at not finding Jackie. Lucy had promised to help, thinking that she would call Mickey to ask for his assistance.

***

The music was loud, the bar was full, and the boys were on top form. He was having a great evening. The girls were making their interest obvious, but then it was not hard to grab attention when you had a footballer in the mix… and James wasn't too shabby in spite of the life he'd lived.

One particular girl caught his attention. She was with two friends, but she wasn't hanging on to their every word. She wasn't joining in with the manic laughter. She seemed a little distant, and he liked that. She looked early twenties and was probably about 5 feet 6 inches without the heels. She had nice legs, but what got him was her eyes. She smouldered. A couple of times he tried to check her body out, but the eyes held him. She had wonderful contact, completely unabashed, he might be the first one to look away… and that didn't happen. Ever.

'Hi.'

'Hi.' How did she get to stand next to him without him seeing her move? She smelled good.

'I'm Rosa.'

'Hi, Rosa, you are very beautiful.'

'Thank you. I have to thank my mum for that. She's from the Philippines.'

'Can I get you something?'

'Sure. How about a taxi?'

'Taxi?'

'For us both.' She smiled.

'Sure.'

They left almost immediately, saying hurried hellos and goodbyes to the lads, who raised a glass in a mock toast to him, mouthing various good wishes.

The journey didn't take long. He followed her through the front door of what appeared to be a classic two-up, two-down terrace. She turned to speak, and he kissed her, his hands cupping her face. She kissed him back, the kiss becoming harder, their tongues exploring. She tasted good, and he hoped he did too. He ran a hand down her back, pulling her to him as she reached for her top, which she pulled off, revealing a black lacy bra. He unclipped it and watched her pull it off. He needed to see her, not just touch, so he pushed her away, her confusion obvious as he held her there. 'You are very beautiful.'

She smiled and dropped to her knees, going for his belt, which offered no resistance. His jeans hit the floor, and he stepped out of them as she pulled down his boxers to free his now very erect cock. He closed his eyes as she took him into her mouth, then slowly opened them, wanting to see her face. This was, he thought, the most erotic moment in any fuck – her on her knees, her breasts touching his legs as she sucked and licked and kissed. He pulled her to her feet – he had to – and they kissed.

She smiled. She had such a beautiful smile.

They climbed the stairs, her in front, holding his hand, leading him. Her arse was in front of his face. She had a perfect arse – hard, tight. He wanted to bend her over and take her on the stairs, but when he reached for her, she laughed and ran into the bedroom, jumping onto her bed. He removed his socks and T-shirt and got onto the bed, looking at her. Her breathing shallowed, and her lips opened, showing her pink tongue and white teeth. He wanted her.

He took a nipple into his mouth, kissing it gently, feeling it enlarge. He trailed kisses down her belly, her skin soft, firm, and warm. He continued to kiss her, pulling her panties to one side and sucking her into him, feeling every part of her. He felt her tighten, felt her spasm. He knew it was time to get the rubber on.

They lay on the bed, sated, staring at the ceiling and breathing hard. He felt her roll onto her side, aware that he was being studied. She was probably deciding if this was a one-off or not. He hoped she might be up for a second or even a third. He sensed this girl was a little special. She wasn't typical. She might even be telling the truth when speaking the immortal lines: 'I don't normally do this.'

He hoped she didn't. It would be nice to find a girl who didn't normally do this.' *I'm such a fucking contradiction, always looking for the girl who does, hoping I find one that doesn't.*

'What are you thinking about?'

'Nothing much.'

'Oi.' She poked him in the ribs, and he rolled over to face her, smiling. 'I was thinking that it might be nice to see you again. That I might take you out.'

'Out? As in supper?'

'Maybe.'

'As in a date?'

'Would you?'

'I might.' She pushed him onto his back, then straddled him. She bent to kiss him, her hair teasing his skin.

'Would you like that?'

'I think so.'

She kissed him harder, reaching for him to check that he was hard enough. She then reached for another condom, ripping the top off with her teeth. He loved how she made something that many struggled with sexy. She reached behind herself to roll the rubber onto his cock, then moaned a little as she guided his cock into her. 'Fuck me,' she whispered into his ear before nipping it sharply. He rolled her onto her back and did as asked.

***

Richard sat outside. Rachel had just left. They'd shared another night together. They had talked about their friendship; he had wanted to ensure that she wasn't under any illusions regarding *them*. She'd accepted they were good mates but with benefits, adding that sometimes it was nice just to share a meal or a movie rather than just sit alone, to have someone to talk to.

Rachel had helped him shop. Some fancy perfume for Lucy, that had cost a small fortune. He'd gone back later to get something for Rachel, who'd been asked to join the family – if that's what they had become – for Christmas lunch as she had asked if she could stay in the cabin having nowhere to go. Then there was a nice sweater for Frank, a rather expensive belt for James, and some treats for the dogs. He was prepared.

Christmas would be very different this year – the polar opposite to last year. A Christmas Day inside was, quite possibly, the hardest day of the year. It was the biggest and most painful contrast to the outside world. He couldn't remember much about past Christmases, but he was looking forward to a special day filled with special people. He had become very fond of Lucy, and he enjoyed the odd chat with Frank, whose reminiscing made for compelling storytelling. He didn't know how much to believe, but if half of it was true, he and Reggie had led extraordinary lives that they had done well to survive. They had become quite close.

James was the strange one. He couldn't quite work him out. He had thought that James didn't like him, but recently, he'd joined him on a drive around the North Norfolk coast looking for Jackie – which had included a very pleasant ploughman's lunch with a pint in the Rose & Crown in Snettisham. James had even picked up the tab. They'd chatted about life, second chances, and it had been a very pleasant afternoon. It was as if there were two versions of James. On his own, he was quite charming and friendly, but once home, he became distant – at least, with him.

Everyone knew he made these trips, and everyone asked how they went, even Rachel. He had pretty much driven the whole coastline, knowing her love of the beaches and the sea. He believed she wouldn't have gone far. Each time he knew the chances of finding her were slim. He could have driven past her house, her safe and sound inside, oblivious to him being so close and yet so far. He wasn't an idiot. He knew that it was a pretty stupid use of his time, but it kept his hope alive.

The night air was now chilly, and he stood checking the skyline. He knocked on her door, shouting, 'Sleep well!' He thought she replied, but he couldn't be sure.

Inside he paused by the map on the wall.

Where are you?

He had highlighted the areas visited. Maybe it was time to go inland or give up?

CHAPTER TWENTY-FOUR

It was always a noisy room, chaotic even to an outsider, but things got done. Jo loved the energy, whereas she knew Mickey would have chosen the café around the corner as his favourite place. She was at *her* favourite place – her desk. It was a place where everything had its place, whilst Mickey's desk could barely be seen, covered by files and clutter. She reached for her coffee.

'No time for that.'

'Why? It's eight-a-clock. What's the rush?' She spoke slowly. She would admit, if asked, to having woken up on the wrong side of the bed.

'We have a body.'

'No – Who? Where?' Adrenalin surged through her, her senses heightening.

'Hall Road. She's young – they think early twenties, maybe late teens – and apparently, it's not pretty. Lots of blood.'

Something curled inside her. She hated death, murder more, but when it was a woman… She had to bite back on the anger that followed, but when it was a young girl, she wanted to save the courts the problem. She grabbed her coffee, pouring it into a to-go cup, and followed him out to the car, drinking as she went.

She drove. 'Who called it in?'

'Her housemate called it in. She'd come home late, stopped out apparently, and she walked in on her mate, dead as a...'

'Okay, I get it!' She regretted biting, but he knew her well. He wouldn't take offence. They made a good team, which is why they often worked together when something big or interesting happened, he'd been delighted when she'd told him about her recent promotion... now a DS, his happiness obvious, she was really very fond of him.

They soon pulled up outside the house. A patrol car sat outside and a young copper stood at the gate. A few neighbours were standing in the street, some in their dressing gowns or wearing a coat over PJs. The young PC looked very relieved to see them.

'Get these people back inside their houses. If they refuse, the other side of the street.' Jo's tone had him jumping. Once by the entranceway, they pulled on the protective clothing. They were the first to enter, since the young copper, outside, had called it in. It had been obvious to him, and to them, that she was dead. That took one look. No need to check for signs of life.

'You okay?'

She nodded. The smell was bad. She had lost a lot of blood, the spray patterns indicating that she had put up a fight but had been stabbed many times.

'Are you thinking boyfriend?'

'Yep, but this looks... beyond fury. It's utter madness. You don't keep stabbing unless...'

'Unless?'

'You're completely fucking psychotic.'

'Whoever did this was as mad as a box of frogs.'

'We are going to get this bastard,' she said slowly, her tone betraying her feelings. 'Let's go talk to the housemate.'

'She's in the car, I think.'

It was a beautiful tree, thought Frank. She'd done a cracking job. He laid his presents under the tree. He loved Christmas, loved the crap movies – sitting with a glass of the good stuff, log fire crackling. Life was good, and he counted his blessings. Maybe Reggie had always known that the girl would be their salvation?

There had been times when he had wondered if Reggie had secretly hoped she might be his. He had banged a few in his time, especially in the early days. His wheels had well and truly come off when he'd lost his Nancy. He held the opinion that the father and son had always been doomed, too much alike to get on. Whilst he stood, he made a list in his head for the hundred and one jobs he had to do in the next few days. He couldn't wait to get stuck in. His love of baking and cooking had come late in life. He didn't regret his life, his decisions. He couldn't. Everything had led him to *this* life. He regretted some of the lives lost, but his balm was that each of them had been 'bad'. Some really quite evil. Some had needed putting down. The past, his past, had been a war between bad and worse.

Returning to the kitchen, he caught the end of the local news. 'Poor little love.' He hoped they'd catch him – and soon. He waved to Lucy as she walked past the kitchen window with the dogs. Both dogs were chasing the thrown balls. He couldn't imagine a life without her. They made a strange family, he thought. Who would have imagined the four of them sat around the same Christmas table? Make that five as another stray had been added, he thought with a laugh.

'What's tickled you, old man?' asked James.

'Life. Just life. What have you been up to?'

'Sowing seeds of happiness.'

'Just make sure that's all you're sowing,' he said, laughing.

'I'll do my best.'

'I know you will, son.'

'Right. Can't stand here like old washerwomen – things to do.'

'You in for tea?' Frank asked.

'Don't know. I might have a better offer.'

'She must need her head checked.'

He heard James laugh as he left the kitchen. It was good to hear the lad happy. He was a different man from the one that had arrived a few weeks before.

***

Mickey gazed out of the window as Jo drove them back to the station. He knew that she would obsess on this one until solved. He would be the good cop this time out. He would be working overtime. She had already cleared the decks with the guv, wanting to check CCTV and visiting the city's bars and clubs. No one had seen her arrive home, and her clothing suggested a night out, not in. They had bugger all to go on.

***

He'd not heard from Rosa since leaving her the night before. Maybe he'd misread her. Maybe this time he'd been the shag. It was a funny thought – thinking he might have been played, that he might have met his match. He'd almost called her a few times, but each time he decided that he would wait for her to make the first move. He didn't want to come over as desperate or run the risk of embarrassing himself. If Rosa had called, he wouldn't have said yes to Dave, who had called him on the off chance he fancied a pint.

'Think of all those lovelies out at Christmas parties.'

So, he had joined him. Dave had been right about the lots of lovely, slightly tipsy girls out for a good time, and one had made it obvious that she was up for it. Her name was Tricia, and she'd wanted a dance. He'd liked her sense of fun, and the incredible tits had helped. She'd stood in front of him, laughing, grabbing his hands and imploring him to dance. It had been easier to agree to her demands than reason with her, not that much could be heard over the noise. She'd moved well, her enjoyment obvious. She was living her best life.

He had followed her home and stood in the background whilst she had paid the babysitter. It had been a little tawdry. They'd gone upstairs, and he'd shagged her quietly as requested. She hadn't wanted to wake the babies. He was now sat on the stairs, with his clothes, pulling his socks on. Casual sex was beginning to feel just a little jaded. It had been his go-to for as long as he could remember – his anaesthetic to life – but maybe it was time to change. It had been soulless sex, a casual encounter with another one-nighter. He was disappointed in himself. It was time to find something worth keeping. He heard the toilet flush.

Shit, she's up. Time to go!

'Are you going?'

'Yes, I thought it best.'

'Don't you want a coffee or something before you go?'

'I'd better get back.'

'You're married, aren't you? Why do I always get the fucking married ones?'

'No. No, I'm not, but I have an early start.' He made it to the door and opened it.

'Will you call me?'

He didn't like the desperation, but then he didn't much like himself. 'Sure,' he replied and left.

He was fairly certain he heard her say, 'But you don't have my number.'

He let himself into the car, grateful for the peace and quiet.

No more… no more. I really need to stop this!

CHAPTER TWENTY-FIVE

A neighbour greeted them as they arrived. She looked like the typical busybody; every street had one. *Good to have in a crisis,* she thought. *Probably a pain in the proverbial any other time.* She carried an air of self-importance as she approached, almost pausing to let the rest of the residents see how special she was. She looked late thirties, a little tired and dishevelled – probably had kids, she thought. *Wouldn't want to be ya.*

Jo listened to her retell how she'd been woken up by the kids screaming. She'd let herself in – they had each other's keys, often babysitting for each other at the last minute. She had crossed herself as she spoke, probably a subconscious reaction to the horrors laying the other side of the rather tatty front door. The garden was overgrown, the hedges almost blocking the pathway. It wasn't a pretty picture. It didn't suggest domestic bliss.

Mickey took her away from the house, back to her side of the shared garden, thanking her for looking after the kids and assuring her that they would both be round very shortly, and yes, a cuppa would be lovely.

'You ready?'

'Yep.'

They entered, having put on protective clothing, neither speaking. The body was in the lounge doorway, on her back, her face untouched but lifeless, her last few moments not reflected. She must have endured agony, she thought. Her chest had been stabbed and cut so many times that it no longer looked like a body.

'Do you think...?'

'Yep.'

'Fuck!' she said, almost resignedly, already processing the mental shift to serial killer.

'So, it's not the boyfriend then.'

'I doubt it.'

'Right, let's go and see what the neighbour knows.'

'I bet she knows everything...'

'Be nice.'

'I'm always nice.'

***

Richard thanked the car gods as his car started. She sounded rough. He knew he would need to change her sometime soon, but he was hoping to get a few more weeks out of her. He'd put some miles on the clock, travelling back and forth around the county. James had offered to help him find something. It was fair to say that he was more into cars than him. He just needed something that started and was safe. He didn't give a flying fuck about anything else. It didn't matter what she looked like.

Rachel jumped into the passenger seat.

'Thanks for this.'

'No probs.'

'It's really sweet of you to help me shop.'

'Haven't I told you how much I love shopping,' he said with a wry grin.

'There was me thinking that you were the one man that did. Oh, the disappointment.'

'Can you live with it?'

'Only if you cook for me tonight,' she said, laughing and throwing in an exaggerated wink.

'I might manage that. So, what are we after?'

'Frank's given me a list. I think he wanted to do it, but he's baking up a storm.'

'It's sweet of Lucy to invite you to join.'

'She's lovely. I really didn't want to go home.'

Richard drove, wondering if he should ask why, or was it best to let her tell her story when she wanted to. He decided on the latter. All in good time.

***

The dogs were walking ahead, enjoying the quiet, having the woodland pretty much to themselves and sniffing every new scent they came across, Flint stopping to roll onto his back.

'You bad boy. What are you rolling in now?' For some reason, he enjoyed rolling in fox poo. Nothing smelled so good, apparently, as rubbing fox poo into your coat.

Ahead, she spotted James. 'Morning.'

'Hi, you.'

'Still hard at it?'

'You know me.'

It was true that she had come to rely on the three men in her life, each of them different. Each of them had a part to play, a job to do. They had become family, her first family. To an outsider, it might not make sense, but to them, it worked.

'In tonight or...'

'I was, but an old flame has called.'

'Lucky girl.'

'I doubt she would agree with that. I was a bit of a dick last time out.'

'Be nice tonight then.'

'I will. I will be on my very best behaviour. What about you? Any suitors?'

'I was hoping you might have a friend,' she said, partly in jest.

James laughed loudly. 'None of my friends would be good enough for you,' he said with sincerity.

'I'll have to download one of those apps.' She walked away without waiting for his reply, wondering if she should do just that. For heaven's sake, she was twenty. She should be seeing boys. She should be out having some fun. Maybe after Christmas, she'd ask Rachel if she wanted to go out for a drink, maybe inviting some of the temps, she thought Shan, Tay, Ames and Jodie would be up for a girls' night out.

***

Mickey was sitting at his desk, Jo pacing the room, talking to herself… they'd just updated Dick Head, now a Deputy Chief based at the Counties HQ in Wymondham. He'd torn them a new arse over their lack of progress.

'Toss you for it,' he said.

'You always win.'

'Heads you go through the phones, calling people, and tails you put your feet up with a coffee and watch the reruns.'

'It's going to be a long night.'

He tossed the coin, cupping his hand to reveal the coin. 'Heads!' he shouted with almost fake glee. 'Lucky me. I get to watch the telly. You get to go and make somebody's night.'

'Thanks for nothing. Be a cop they said. It will be fun, they said.'

'They lied.'

'Ain't that the truth.'

***

The pub was packed. He couldn't see her, so headed to the bar to stand behind a boisterous group, hoping to catch a barmaid's eye. His phone rang, and he looked at the display. 'Not recognized' showed on the screen, so he ignored the call.

Feeling a tap on his shoulder, he turned to find a grinning Lydia. She looked as he recalled: a fresh-faced, pony-tailed blonde with a wonderful smile. 'You look wonderful.'

'What?' She made a face as if to say I didn't hear that. 'Can we go somewhere quieter?'

Leaning in, he said, 'What do you want? I'll get these. You go find somewhere to sit.'

***

Finally, she found a table for two tucked away at the back. She sat and waited, wondering what had driven her to call him. They hadn't met for some four years. She had got engaged and then unengaged whilst he'd been away. He hadn't been particularly nice even when they dated, but there was something between them. It wasn't just the bad boy attraction of her youth; it was that most men in her orbit paled when compared – which she had done with each new date.

Watching him cut a swathe through the bodies to get to her, she smiled. The boys stepped back, and the girls bent towards him, eyes scanning him from head to toe. He had that effect still. He had that effect on her, still. Her body betrayed her thoughts. *The butterflies live*, she thought. *They live… they live… Thank God for that!*

***

Not my usual type, he thought. Maybe that's why she still intrigues me. Slim and not much in the way of tits, but she had something. Last time out he had realised that too late. He had been a prick. A first-class prick. This time, if there was a *this time*, he would commit to just her, to see where it went and what happened.

He sat down, realising that that thought made him happy. The prospect of a relationship was no longer scary. He could hope to commit again, to have one woman in his life. It hadn't worked out last time, that had become toxic. He knew he was bored with one-night stands. Rosa and the other one had proven that for very different reasons. He needed more.

The time flew, the in-between time caught up, the mutual interest explored and confirmed. He felt quite excited; they left together, standing by his car.

'You still have it.'

'Not for long. I'm swapping her for a cottage and a Land Rover.'

'Really?'

'Can I take you home?'

'Yes, please. You can come in for a coffee if you promise to behave.'

'You have my word, my lady.'

The car roared into life; the growl could have come from him. Coming across some roadworks, he floored it through orange.

'Left that late.'

'Not as late as the car behind us. Idiot tried to follow us through.'

'Better to be late in this life than early in the next.'

'It's okay. They met the bus going the other way. They're now reversing very slowly,' he said, laughing. 'Can't believe they tried to follow us… I was pushing it.'

***

Rachel had wrapped her presents and was debating if she should take them across to the house now or wait until Christmas Eve morning. Lucy had invited her and Richard to sleep over Christmas Eve up at the big house. *Bless her.* She thought it would be nice for them all to wake up in the same house come Christmas morning. She'd even asked if she would like her own room or was she sharing? She'd replied that two rooms would be good; they were just friends. She could always pop in to surprise him during the night, or if required, she could jump on her bed to make it look as if they had used both rooms.

Sitting down, she sipped at her wine. He was a walking, talking dilemma. She understood they were *casual.* He had confirmed that a few times, and she had agreed with him, so why the angst? Why did she want to go and hammer on his door until he let her in?

Refilling her glass, she turned the TV on, scrolling through each channel and finding nothing worth watching. She turned it off. Picking up her phone, she texted him. '**Fancy a quickie?**'

She waited and waited, wondering if he would reply. Had she blown it? Was she coming across as very *un*-casual? Was he sat next door wondering how to say no? Would he pretend to be asleep? She'd broken a golden rule: you don't get involved with people you work with. She thought about deleting the text, sending a fun follow-up, when he replied with a knock. She looked up to see him at the patio doors, clutching a bottle of something and wearing only his Christmas boxers. She leapt off the couch to let him in, her heart celebrating.

***

Yawning, he didn't hear Jo come into the room.

'Anything?'

'Nothing. Nada.'

'We have cameras on every street and nothing.'

'We're getting lots of calls, especially about Tricia. The only problem is she was seen leaving with short guys, big guys, bald guys. We've nothing to go on.'

'What about Rosa?'

'Again nothing. Part of the problem is at that time of night the streets are crowded. It's like playing Where's Wally!'

***

Lydia opened the door, turning to face him. She wanted to kiss him, to touch him, but she knew that she would not stop there. She would want more. She would… She shivered. He stood inches away, and she could feel his desire, could read his mind. She hoped he understood the need for slow, very slow, this time. She had fallen for him once, and she knew she was already falling for him again – in truth, she'd probably never been out of love with him. He'd always, and would always, have a piece of her heart. She knew her weakness was troubled men, broken men, or just simply bad boys – and he was the baddest, most broken man she knew.

'Quick coffee and then I'm gone.'

'Promise?'

'Absolutely. One coffee, maybe two, but definitely not three.'

'Okay.' She knew she was smiling; she could feel her face, her skin stretching.

They entered the cottage. It was small but beautifully furnished. The furniture was traditional quality without being quaint, solid oak furniture. 'This is lovely.'

'I like it.'

They continued into the kitchen, the tension palpable as she filled the kettle, selecting two mugs. She knew he was leaning against the hard-top and watching her every move. He was probably hoping for more than coffee. She renewed her promise to take things slowly.

***

Lucy climbed the stairs to bed. It had been a good day. She had just returned from walking the dogs, who'd tried to investigate the squealing coming from Rachel's room as they had walked past. She'd had to call the dogs several times before they'd returned to her with tails wagging. She was happy that they had found each other, although Rachel had sworn that they were just mates.

Stopping at the top of the stairs, she peered out hoping to see James's car on the drive. She thought she saw a flash of lights at the edge of the boundary, but she couldn't be sure. She waited to see if a car would turn into the drive, but none did. She was ready for sleep, counting the days to Christmas – her first without Reggie. The first Christmas had been very magical. It was a day she would never forget. It had been on that day that she had first mentioned wanting to do something to help others. She had watched a movie where people, normal people, had invited strangers into their homes to give them a Christmas. Reggie had listened to her, and to her surprise, he had restarted the conversation the next day when walking through the woods.

Whilst slipping into her PJs she heard a car pull up. A quick check showed James had finally arrived. She was tempted to go and find him to enquire about his evening, but she decided that could wait for the morning.

CHAPTER TWENTY-SIX

The smoke plume gave away Frank's position. He crept up on him.

'Morning, old man.'

'Flipping hell, son, you nearly gave me a...'

'Sorry. Is the coffee on?'

'Sure, isn't it always? Why so early?'

'Lots to do.'

'Thought we were shut?'

'I have a car to see, I hope to find a buyer for mine.'

'You're actually selling the one true love of your life?'

'Yep.'

'Why? I thought you and that car would last forever.'

'It's time, old man.'

They drifted into the kitchen as they chatted, James wishing he could have talked to Reggie like this. Frank was like a much older brother or a stepdad and had looked after him more than once, but...

'You hungry?'

'I'll get something in the city.'

'You'll soon look like a quarter pounder with cheese.'

'Wish me luck.'

'Luck.'

***

Mickey stopped and turned on his heels having spotted the local hack – Steve Woodsmith, an odious little man – quickly heading for the back door. He wasn't in the mood for a chat. He knew Jo would already be at her desk. He couldn't recall a time when he'd been first in. She'd be in a foul mood. They weren't making progress, but at least nothing new was in. That was good. No third vic'. The hat-trick had not been completed.

'You're late.'

'You might be early?'

'Both are true.'

'Did you get coffee?'

'What, am I your coffee bitch now?' he asked.

Without turning, she smirked. 'I think we both know that's a yes.'

'Bitch,' he replied but fondly. 'I'll go. Any joy?'

This time she turned to face him. 'Nothing; unless you count our illustrious leader who wants to talk to the media.'

'I'm only surprised that it's taken this long. Are we needed?'

'Doubt it. You have a face for radio.'

Mickey left, laughing. 'Why do I love you?'

'How could you not?'

***

The Defender chugged into life. She was an old girl, a proper truck.

She's one for the country, not some posh twat living in the city.

James was already fond of her. The Porsche would live long in the memory, but it had become unaffordable, unnecessary even, in his new life. He liked the new raised driving position; next up he needed to buy a house, somewhere to call home, and then he had to find someone to share it with. Maybe he already had? On an impulse, he swung a right to take him towards Lydia's, not knowing if she was home or not. He had the road to himself.

Her car was in the drive. The cottage was a semi, and the neighbouring half looked quite shabby compared to hers, which was a perfect white with pale green, almost washed-out window frames. The door was good old-fashioned wood, and the garden was tidy, picture-postcard perfect. He wondered if that was her hard work, or did she employ an old boy to come and cut the grass and trim the bushes.

Feeling a tad nervous, he knocked. He could hear her shout: 'I'll be with you in a mo!'

He wondered if she'd looked outside to see who it was. If she had done, the truck wouldn't tell her anything. That said, he recalled her family were local farmers. This could even be part of the farm? He had a lot to learn about her. Where did she work? Did she work? Was this her cottage or her daddy's? Another recalled memory came to mind. She liked to ride. He could picture her in jodhpur's carrying a whip. The visual image burnt, and then the door opened, and there she was, a fresh-faced beauty, quite unlike the picture in his head.

'Hi.'

'Surprise.'

'A good one. Come in.'

Feeling like an excited teenager, he followed her. She smelled good and looked good: tight jeans, boots, and a baggy sweater. He wanted to tug that over her head, but he had promised himself to take this slowly… at her pace. He wanted to prove to them both that this wasn't just about...

She had stopped at the bottom of the stairs, and she turned and kissed him, a gentle kiss. She had soft lips, and they felt good. No make-up, and no sticky greasy lipstick. He responded, opening his mouth to her tongue, and someone whimpered – it might have been him. He pulled her close, feeling the heat from her body against his. Her neck bent, and he kissed it. His hands were beneath her sweater, feeling her skin, her flat belly, and her small but perfect tits. He teased her nipple, feeling it react.

'Shall we go upstairs?'

'If you want. We can go outside if you want. I don't care where, as long as you are there.'

'Outside?' she whispered, her tone confirming a question, not a request.

'Do you want to?'

'No. Maybe in the summer?'

'That's six months away.'

'Take me upstairs.'

***

Watching him reverse out, turn, and leave, she stepped into the road, waving until he was out of sight, then returned to her home, closing the door, leaning against it, and smiling. It had been a wonderful afternoon. They'd agreed to meet up again later for supper once he'd gone home to change. She headed for the kitchen, fancying a cuppa. Once made she stood gazing out of the window, daydreaming, thinking about nothing much but very aware that she was smiling. She was happy.

It was a knock on the door that broke the spell. She opened it.

'Hello.'

'Hello again.'

'I thought you were going home to change, and we were going out for supper?'

'I had a much better idea.'

'What?' she'd managed to say as he kissed her again.

'Order in. A curry. Anything. Nothing.'

***

Jo had been back at her desk an hour or so when the calls began to come in following the press conference. Something had tugged at the public's conscience, judging on the number of calls received, but a pattern was emerging regarding Rosa if not Tricia. No one had seen them leaving, but most had seen them on the streets. They had a direction taken, a rough description that ruled out at least ninety per cent of the city's men, and a fifteen-minute time slot to check. It was progress... of sorts.

It was three hours later that a triumphant Mickey shouted, 'Yes!' before adding, 'Bloody hell... *you've got to be kidding me.*'

She turned to look at his monitor, getting up to stand behind him.

'Is that?'

'Yep.'

'Fuck me.'

'Normally, I'd jump at the chance.'

She cuffed him over the head. 'Right, let's go and pay him a visit.'

'Shouldn't we talk to he who can't be...'

'No way. You make that call, and I'll cut your fucking balls off.'

They left, trying not to run, and trying not to draw anyone's attention.

***

The dogs were loving life, chasing through the gardens, happy to be outside, when she saw a car turn into the drive. It would be a little while before she knew who it was. She assumed James had returned.

Accepting, as always, that she couldn't wear the dogs out, she turned for home to spot Frank walking towards her quickly. On reaching her he paused, trying to get his breath back.

'What's the hurry?'

'The police are here.'

'Why?'

'They want to speak to James.'

'Why? What for? What's he done?'

'Nothing that I know of.'

'Okay.' She shouted for the dogs, who joined her quickly.

'You've no idea?'

'None.'

'What have you told them?'

'Nothing other than he went into the city to look at cars.'

'Where are they?'

'Kitchen.'

'Show them to the office. Where's Richard?'

'Not in the house.'

On returning, she checked her appearance and went upstairs to the office, where she sat and waited, a hundred and one thoughts crashing inside her head. Entering her office, she was relieved to see it was Jo who walked through the door first, followed by Mickey. Jo had always been kind. She was trying to help with the search for Jackie, and she had a soft spot for Mickey.

'Please, sit.'

'Thank you.'

'What brings you here?'

She listened, unable to believe that they could think James could do such a thing. His name in the same sentence as those poor girls was pointing at more than the fact that he could help with their enquiries; they thought he was involved. She was sure of it.

'James hasn't come home.' As she spoke, she wondered, *why?*

'Do you have any idea where he might be? This is very important. It could save another life.'

'Believe me, if I knew I would tell you. What will you do? Wait. He mentioned an old flame.'

'Did he give a name?'

She thought. 'No, I'm sorry he didn't.'

***

Frank watched Lucy show them out. He'd tried the boy's number a few times with no joy. He'd overheard their conversation. He didn't believe that James could be involved. Not that. Never that. One moment of drunken madness didn't mean... He was a different man now.

'What can we do?'

'Nothing. Just wait for him to come home.'

'I'll wait up for him. You go to bed, sweetheart. I'll leave him a note to wake me, should I fall asleep.'

They heard a car arrive, and both stepped quickly to the window, but it was Richard and Rachel.

'Do we tell them?'

'We should. Just in case one of them knows where he might be. I want us to get to him first. He should hear it from us.'

***

She was beautiful. He watched her return to the bedroom, carefully carrying a tray with the promised hot chocolate, which she placed on the bedside cupboard. He'd accepted the 'why don't you stay?' invitation.

'What's for breakfast?'

'What would you like?'

He pulled her to him, her kisses tasting of chocolate. She rolled onto her back, smiling, and he bent to kiss her again. He felt her legs parting, and he put a knee between her thighs, then another, keeping his weight off her with his elbows. He snuggled in, kissing her neck, his hands tracing her inner thigh. He could feel the heat, the wetness. He took his cock and entered her, moving slowly, very slowly. Sometime later he would realise that they had made love without words, and his last thoughts before sleeping would be how lovely that had been.

CHAPTER TWENTY-SEVEN

The morning seemed to come too soon. Lydia was sleeping soundly, and he got out of bed without waking her, quietly making for the *en suite*, needing to pee and to pinch some toothpaste. His mouth felt like a dog had slept in it. He didn't hear her come in, but he saw her standing behind him. *She must be on tiptoes,* he thought, but still, only her eyes were showing above his shoulders. He felt the kiss to his back, and he definitely felt her hands reach around him to his cock, which stirred slowly into life, sending shivers through his gut.

'What plans do you have?'

'None. Other than that, I must return home.'

'Do you have to?'

'You could come with me?'

'Are you sure? I'd love to.' Her happiness was obvious in every word.

***

Lucy had also fallen asleep in an armchair. They'd had to force Richard and Rachel to go to bed after they'd updated them. Frank gently woke her, with a cuppa beside her.

'Any news?' she mumbled.

'None.'

She groaned as she raised herself up the chair, her body stiff, her joints complaining at the movement. 'My head hurts.'

'I'll go get some paracetamol.'

The tea tasted good; she took the pills, drinking greedily. 'Have you tried calling him again?'

'No answer. I think his phone has died. I've had Jo on the phone already asking. She's not happy. I have tried to explain that she's barking up the wrong tree, but...

'Is that him?'

They went to the window to see a mud-splattered Land Rover coming up the drive. They watched as it stopped, and then James stepped out together with a rather pretty girl. 'I guess we know why he didn't come home. This could be interesting.'

They were about to go to meet them when another car came into view – a police car. A marked police car. 'Do you think they had one parked down the road?'

'Wouldn't surprise me.'

***

Richard had been intending to work for a couple of hours. He liked to work in peace and quiet, but he stopped abruptly once he saw the police car. He changed direction, heading to the drive, when he was stopped by Frank. He could see James was talking animatedly to the uniformed cops whilst Lucy was comforting a girl. He knew Frank was continuing to talk, but he wasn't listening. He watched as James left the police to speak to the girl. He touched her face and left to sit in the back of the cop's car. He looked ashen and was obviously in shock.

They walked over to the girls, the four of them watching the car disappear down the drive. They stood quite still for a few moments, each processing what had just happened.

Richard was the first to speak. 'What do we do?'

'Nothing we can do.' Lucy sounded broken; she guided the girl away into the house.

'Who's the girl?' Richard whispered.

'Lydia. They've known each other for years. She's a lovely girl, nice family, local farmers.'

'Poor little love.'

'Lucy, I'll call Stephen. He'll know what to do!' Frank shouted as the girls made for the house.

'Who's Stephen?'

'Reggie's lawyer. Tough old bird. Doesn't take prisoners.' He laughed. 'Bad choice of words.'

Lucy turned. 'Why? He's not been arrested?'

'Doesn't matter, love. If Stephen turns up on their doorstep, they'll know to behave themselves, won't they?'

Lucy smiled. 'Thank you, Frank.' With that, she went into the house with a tearful Lydia.

'Anything I can do, Frank?' asked Richard.

'You can drive me to the nick once I've sorted the girls.'

'You think we should go?'

'I think we should. Reggie always used to say hit 'em hard and go mob-handed.'

'You don't think he...'

'No. No way, son. He's been a pain in my arse a few times over the years, but no.'

***

James sat in the car. He'd been invited to go with them, but he'd sensed that if he hadn't, they would have cuffed him in a heartbeat. So, he'd agreed to get into the car. His world seemed slightly surreal. He was still trying to understand the fact that both Rosa and Tricia were dead – and seemingly at the hands of the same person. He couldn't believe that they could think he'd done it. His inner voice confirmed his worst fears. He had been with them both. His DNA would be everywhere. He knew he hadn't killed them, but could he prove it? The question stayed with him all the way to the station as they travelled in complete silence, as did one other question: *If not me, then who?*

***

Something troubled Mickey. Life was never this easy. Well, his life was never this easy, and this would be too easy if James was their man. He had seemed shocked, confused even, when they had first talked to him. He seemed subdued, thoughtful. He might not be speaking, but he could read his thoughts, and he wasn't reacting as expected.

Mickey had explained that he wasn't being arrested, and both had ignored Jo's barely whispered, 'Not yet.'

He explained that they would appreciate his help, preferring to have the conversation here at the station rather than the house. Mickey had noted his first thought was to the girl he'd spent the night with, not himself – that had been interesting and very un-James like.

Earlier, he had almost shared Jo's excitement that they might have solved the 'who', just needing to find the evidence so that tonight the city could sleep soundly in their beds. But now he sat in the interview room with a troubling thought, wondering why girl number three was a walking, talking not-dead girlfriend. The next question added to the uneasiness.

'Can I make a call?'

'We've advised that you're not under arrest, and you can call a lawyer, etc.'

'I don't need a lawyer.'

'What do you need?' asked Jo.

'I want to call Frank.'

'Why?'

'I need him to convince Lydia to stay at the house where she can be protected.'

Jo had been about to reply but stopped. Like him, she had not seen that coming.

'Protected?'

'I don't expect you to believe me... well, not yet, but I know that I didn't murder those women, so that means someone else did.'

'So, you're saying they were killed because of you?'

'I can't think of anything else that makes sense. The odds would be way too staggering to be pure coincidence.'

Jo turned. 'Nice try, posh boy, but I don't buy it.' However, even as she said it, she thought, *what if he's telling the truth?*

***

Reaching for his phone, Richard answered, 'Hi, Lucy. Hang on. Let me get this on speaker. Right, fire away.'

'James just called. He wants us to keep Lydia here.'

'Okay, why?'

'He says she needs protecting.'

Frank put his hand out as if he wanted to stop Richard. 'I should have thought of that. We're going to turn around. He doesn't need us.'

'What?'

'It's bleeding obvious. Sorry, Lucy.'

'What do you mean, Frank?'

'If we accept that he didn't do this, that means someone else did, and that somebody likes to kill the...'

271

Richard slapped his forehead. 'Idiot… Lucy, we're coming home. Stay inside. Can you get Rachel too, please? Let's get everybody in. No one goes out alone. No one.'

***

Lucy stepped outside with Lydia following. The dogs were sniffing excitedly, pleased to be out. Lucy had relayed the conversation with Frank and Richard to Lydia, who was proving to be made of the right stuff. They hadn't phoned ahead, thinking it best to go to Rachel together, taking the dogs with them – safety in numbers.

Thankfully, Rachel was in. She listened to them tell the story, not needing any convincing to quickly pack a bag and move into the big house for the time being. They were soon heading back to the house to be met by Frank and Richard.

'We've locked the doors and the windows.'

'That's a rule going forward. No one out on their own, and we shut and lock all the doors.'

'Agreed,' said Lucy, 'and thank you.'

'Do you have any news?' asked Lydia.

'Stephen is on his way to the station.'

'Is he allowed to be there?'

'Absolutely. He's not been charged with anything. All they know is that...'

Lucy stepped in to protect Lydia's feelings. 'All they know is that James knew both the girls. That's it. That's all they have.'

Lydia smiled. 'Thank you.'

Frank stood up. 'Right, you lot, let's have a cuppa with some of the mince pies I baked yesterday. In the kitchen, the lot of you.'

***

Jo was sat at her desk. Mickey, as he sometimes liked to do, was sitting on it, facing her.

'What you thinking?'

'I don't know what to think. He's either a complete utter psychopath, or he's telling the truth.'

'I think it's the truth.'

'What do we do?' Her tone conveyed the truth accepted.

'No idea, but if it's not him, and I don't think it is, it means our killer is still out there!'

'Wait up.' She sounded excited. 'If it's not him, it's definitely about him. He's the bloody catalyst. The reason why. Agreed?'

'Agreed.'

'Right, so tonight he takes me out.'

'What... are you mad?

'We meet, we drink, and I take him back to mine. You're waiting inside. I kick him out half an hour later, and then we wait and get the bastard!'

'You going to run this past Dick?'

'Nope, you are. We've got time to sort surveillance – we'll need armed response, lots of bodies – but it's our best chance. Maybe our only chance. We need to catch this mother-fucker ASAP.'

Mickey sat. He had nothing better. He had to admit it was the best they had – in reality, it was all they had. 'Let's do it. I'll go and speak to his highness. He'll like it, providing we can make it happen in time. If it works, it might even become his idea.'

'They're the best ideas,' she said with a hint of sarcasm.

**

James listened to Jo, nodding in agreement. He was up for this, even happy to wear the ankle bracelet, so they could keep him safe – she said – though, he suspected that Jo wanted to keep tabs on him! He hadn't kicked off for being brought here as he knew without a doubt that he was the reason two girls were dead. He couldn't think why, but someone wanted to get to him through them, and that meant Lydia was at risk – as were Lucy and Rachel. The question was who? He'd pissed a few people off – actually, there was quite a long list – but the number was dwarfed by those who had hated his old man. Then there was Richard. Had he known all along? Had he been playing a game all along? Had… he didn't want to even think her name given the awfulness, but Lucy couldn't be ruled out, it could be anybody. The world was full of evil people. Somebody hated him enough to kill!

'I need to go home to change.'

'Yes, you do. They might follow you from home.'

'Don't tell anyone.' Mickey sounded concerned. 'We haven't ruled anyone out.'

'What do I tell them?'

'That you are still helping us, and we need a second chat.'

James nodded. It felt a little weird accepting that he had in all probability been followed. He tried to recall his journeys. *Did anyone follow me?*

***

The kitchen was the best place to be, thought Lydia. All five were sitting around the table, the TV on with the sound turned low. Everyone was being very supportive. She was so grateful for the company, for the noise, she appreciated each one of them. Frank was the only one of the four that she knew, the rest were strangers to her, but she felt the love. Richard was wonderful, calming, as was Rachel, and Lucy was unbelievably sweet. Richard had offered to run her home to pack a bag

274

because, as they had all said, she was stopping the night. She was staying with them until this was sorted. To be fair, she hadn't put up much of a fight.

Frank's mince pie pile was disappearing rapidly, as were the sausage rolls intended for Christmas Eve. The dogs were lying at her feet, protecting her. She sat back for a moment, thinking, if only James was here, then this would be a perfect evening. Her phone lay on the table in front of her, and she was willing it to ring. She wanted to hear his voice, hear him tell her that he was on his way, that they had released him. Occasionally, she wondered if… what if it was James. She knew it couldn't be, but what if?

'Lydia, shall we go and get your stuff for the night?'

'Yes, please.'

They were soon sitting in the Range Rover, which Frank had insisted they take.

'Nice car.'

'Yep. Mine's a little older, a little smaller, a little rustier.'

'I think Frank thought we might be safer in this.' She smiled. 'It's all a little scary.'

'Nothing is going to happen to you. Those poor girls were surprised. We're prepared; we're ready.'

'I know.' She started to sob gently and felt Richard pull her to him. He put his arm around her.

'It's okay. How long have you known him?'

'Years. We were part of the same gang growing up. We became friends who dated, but we grew apart. I've just never quite got over him.'

'I haven't known him long, but I think he's trying to be a better version of himself. Frank believes that.'

Her phone rang, and it was James. She listened to him telling her about everything that had happened, how he was allowed home, but they wanted another chat later. She hung up happy to have heard from him. She updated Richard, asking him to put his foot down. She wanted to get back to the house ASAP; she wanted to be there when he arrived.

**

Jo was at home in her modern, minimalist two-bed apartment. Two floors up, it had been a big purchase when she'd bought it. It was one of the many new developments alongside the river, close enough to Carrow Road to hear the crowd during home games. She loved being this close to the city, but the river was a touch of the countryside she also craved – especially on a lazy Sunday off-work day. Mickey was sat in the lounge watching TV. He hadn't been prepared to leave her on her own, even knowing that she was quite safe until she met James later. The team had been prepped. There would be two teams: one would be at a terraced house they'd borrowed from a friend who was out of the country with colleagues, with an armed response unit parked nearby and then Mickey and two other colleagues inside the house. The second team would be split between the bar and the car park.

The borrowed house was perfect. It was situated at the end of a small cul-de-sac, with a parking space in front, so there was nowhere to hide. Anyone approaching would be spotted yards away. They would park cars outside, forcing any newcomer to park at least fifty yards down the road. Again, buying time to react.

Finally, she had found something suitable that she could wear over a stab vest. She looked in the mirror, and she looked okay. She had to remind herself that she wasn't going on a date, but in her defence, she had to look the part. She had to look like someone James would want to shag. She heard the doorbell. 'Can you get that? It's probably the tech guys.' She was ready to be fitted with comms. She loved moments like this. One of the reasons she'd joined the force was to make a difference. She hadn't been good at the mundane stuff, but luckily, someone had believed she could go further. Tonight, she intended to prove everyone right. She would catch the bastard. He needed putting away.

Mickey knocked on her door. 'You ready?'

'Almost.'

Standing in front of the partially opened door, he asked, 'How you feeling?'

'I'm good... I'm fine, really I am. Stop worrying.'

He turned his head away after spotting her in the mirror. 'James is meeting you at nine. I'm going in with you, then leaving you to it. We'll have two in the bar just in case, and they'll leave just before you. They'll stop and talk to our man outside, the one on the door, two on the route back to his car. They'll follow you to the car park at a discreet distance. We have two cars in the car park, and they'll follow you to the house.'

'Sweet. So where will you be?'

'I'll be in the house waiting for you after I leave the bar. I'm not leaving you alone.' He whistled as she stepped out. 'Looking good!'

She smiled, but it felt forced, and her gut tightened. It wasn't every day you hoped to come face to face with a maniac with a knife.

'You okay? We can stop this now.'

She'd been about to say over my dead body. 'No way. We're getting the bastard. Where are we meeting again?'

'Gonzo's. We've been through this. Are you sure?'

'I'm fine. I'm just getting prepared. Remind me why there again.'

'It's small, but we can control the access. We can surround you with bodies, and it's a short walk to the car park. The owners have agreed to close for the night, and we're having a private party. We don't yet know where he watches from. It could be that he follows him to the car park and waits. We're going to check every car that arrives, rechecking them through the night. We have to believe he either waits at the car park or follows him to the bar. We think the car park is the most likely place, but a private party will keep him outside.'

'It's good of them.'

'Who?'

'Gonzo's.'

'Imagine the publicity; if we pull this off… I've promised them that we'll have a big old party in the new year.'

'Let's hope we have something to celebrate.'

After the soundcheck, they left, and she found herself checking out every single man walking towards the city. They parked, and he squeezed her hand. 'I only have one worry.'

'What's that?'

'Being fast enough.'

'Don't worry about me.'

'I wasn't.' He laughed. 'I'm worried about…'

'Twat.' She dug him in the ribs.

***

It had been a strange day; his emotions were all over the place, but he was putting on a brave face for everyone else. Especially for Rosa and Tricia. He hadn't forgotten that two girls lay dead, their only crime to have met him. He was quite prepared to risk getting hurt to save a third girl from being murdered. He owed them that much.

He'd told Lydia, who had taken the news very badly. He knew that she hadn't been impressed with the fact that he'd shagged both the dead girls so recently, but she had come round a little. Now she was really upset that he had agreed to act as bait. He'd taken her to one side to tell her, then he had spoken to the rest of them whilst sat around the kitchen table. It had been obvious to him that none of them was the killer, he'd never doubted that he was surrounded by good people – people who cared about him.

The reaction had been immediate and loud, each trying to explain why this was a bad idea. He could barely hear anything being said through the noise.

What if tonight he became the subject?

What if he didn't wait for him to pull?

He didn't have the answers, but now, suited and booted, he was ready to leave. He too wore a stab vest brought to him by his protection for the night. Rob, a young cop in his early twenties, who could have passed for Jason Statham's better-looking younger brother. James had thought his look a tad forced, but the girls didn't think so – especially Lucy, who seemed very taken by him.

Walking into the kitchen, he found Rob the centre of attention. He felt invisible for a couple of seconds. He'd been about to cough theatrically when Richard saw him.

'You good to go, mate?'

'I think so. You up for this, Rob?'

'Absolutely.' He stood. 'Ladies.'

They left, having been wished good luck and told to stay safe. Each of the girls had hugged him, with Lydia and Lucy kissing him. Lucy asked Rob to look after him as they left the building, heading for the car. He felt choked, hoping to be back home ASAP.

'Nice people.'

'They are the best.'

'What's the story with Lucy?'

'Take it you're not local?'

'Nope. Moved up a few months ago.'

'It's going to take more than a trip into the city to tell you everything you need to know about her. Just take it as read that you would need to be on your best behaviour if you didn't want to answer to Frank, Richard, or me.'

'Don't worry, mate, Frank's enough on his own. He might be the wrong side of seventy, but you can still get a sense of the man he was.'

'What do you mean?'

'Nothing, but you can tell by the way he carries himself – and the size of him – that you wouldn't have wanted to upset him when he was younger, and he's very protective of Lucy, which I like. I have three younger sisters, and I'd kill any man who upset them.'

'So, you're here on your own?'

'Yep, me and a grotty bed-sit until I sort something.'

'Surprised she hasn't invited you to Christmas Dinner,' he said with a hint of sarcasm.

'How do you know she hasn't?' he said with a wink. 'That's my reward for getting you home in one piece.'

'Best you look after me then. Frank cooks a wonderful roast!'

***

Jo was stood at the bar, and Mickey was chatting inanely, no doubt trying to keep her mind busy, giving her no time to think about what might happen later. She loved him for it, but that didn't stop her wishing that he'd just shut up… be quiet, to let her think.

It felt strange, standing in an empty bar. The bouncers on the door had been kitted out with stab vests, but they were under strict orders not to get involved. Mickey had suggested using their colleagues, but she had argued that it was best to keep them if they were up for it. Too many changes and they could scare him off. They had been very up for it. One was an ex-cop retired from the force, and the other was a nice lad, keen to play his part, both understanding that they were decoration only. They weren't expecting anything to happen here or at the car park; they remained convinced the action would be at the house.

Hearing footsteps, she turned to see James walking towards her. He looked like he was bricking it. *Hallelujah.* She was going to have to sort him out. They had planned to stay for an hour before leaving, so she had an hour to sort him. She would need to see the excitable James leaving the bar – the man who had pulled the *sure thing.* A man about to fuck her would look very different to the one standing before her!

Motioning to the side, she took him to a corner table. During the next hour or so, colleagues would be arriving in pairs to keep up the pretence of a private party.

'You okay?'

'I'll be fine.'

'You don't look it. When we leave here…'

'I know. I know what to do!'

He sounded upset. She wasn't his greatest fan, and he knew that. 'We really appreciate this. It's our best chance to catch this bastard.'

'That's why I'm here. You might not think I care, but I do. Those girls were somebody's daughter… somebody's…'

He sounded genuine, sincere, and her attitude changed, softening a little. She took hold of his hand, and her voice softened. 'We will get him. With your help, we will stop him.'

'I hope so. I really do. If another girl…'

'Do you want a drink?' She signalled to Mickey. 'Two cokes.' They waited for him to return.

'No news. Lots of cars in and out. Not many single guys, and no one fitting the profile. They are keeping an eye on anyone returning to their cars, but there is nothing yet.'

'I'm convinced nothing is going to happen until we get to the house: that's how it's gone down so far – he waits for James to leave.'

'You've got to be prepared for nothing to happen; he might take the night off.'

James groaned. 'God, I hope not. If not tonight, then when?'

Rob joined them. 'I was thinking we should put some music on? This is meant to be a party. Just in case they are waiting and watching.'

'Good idea. Will you be at the house later?' Jo asked.

'Nope. I'm following you to the car park, then following you on the route before leaving you to it once you're inside. Thought I'd head back to the house after to help out.'

James raised his glass, smiling sardonically. 'That's very noble of you.' Then thinking about those at home, he added, 'Thanks, mate, that's good of you.'

***

Frank called the dogs to him. 'I'll take these bad boys out for a walk before they pee on my floor.'

'I'll come with you.'

'Thanks, Richard. Will you girls be okay?'

Rachel looked around the room, pausing briefly on Alison and Paul, their protection detail, both tucking into freshly baked sausage rolls and coffee. 'I think we may need more food, but other than that we're okay.'

Both cops looked up in embarrassment. Alison was the first to speak. 'These are just too good.'

'Please stay in front of the house where we can see you,' added Paul. 'Just in case.'

Frank and Richard left by the front door. Every light was on, both inside and outside, illuminating the way. They heard footsteps behind them to see Rachel running towards them carrying a flask and a bag. 'Coffee and rolls for the poor buggers by the drive.'

'I'd forgotten about them hiding in the woods.'

'This must be costing a fortune?'

'You can thank Dick Head for that.'

Richard laughed, almost choking on his reply. 'Who's Dickhead?'

Frank stopped. 'He's the Deputy Chief – John Head, but known to everyone behind his back as Dick. The name suits him because he's a prize knob. However, he wants this man caught – and quickly. Reggie knew him very well, back in the good old days.'

They'd reached the car parked in the trees along the drive, the occupants, both men were well wrapped up. It was a bitterly cold night, so they were overjoyed to take the flask and food from Rachel. After the usual pleasantries were exchanged, they headed back to the house, calling the dogs.

'Looks stunning.' Rachel sounded a little emotional.

'It is. It's a view that never gets old. I hope you're enjoying your time here?'

'I am, Frank. I can't think of any place I'd rather be.'

Frank placed an arm around her. 'We're very happy to have you here. Let's go home. It could be a long night.'

Richard walked behind him, calling the dogs in. Flint stopped, peering into the distance. He growled a low growl from the back of his throat, then barked three times. He didn't make a lot of noise usually, but he had a good warning bark. Richard stopped and looked past the dog. He listened, but hearing and seeing nothing, he called Flint to him.

***

John Head sat behind a desk; he'd come in to show support to his troops. He liked to remind them that he cared, that he hadn't gotten too big for his boots. He listened to the update from Mickey.

'Let's hope so. Keep me posted, please.'

He terminated the call, fighting the impulse to join them. He wanted a result tonight. This needed to end now, with no more murders. He loved his city, and he was proud of its police force. The murders had shocked the people, and emotions were running high so close to Christmas. This story needed an ending, and he couldn't think of anything better than 'Apprehended'.

***

Checking her watch for the umpteenth time, she was happy to see that it was almost time to go. The comms had been busy, with nothing to see reported time and time again. There was no one suspicious on the street outside, on the road back to the car park, or in the car park itself. They'd picked St Andrews as it was a one-way system out of the city and close to the bar, but within half a mile, they could go in one of three directions, so whoever it was had to be close by. Maybe on one of the side streets. It was the best they could do; they didn't have the manpower to cover everywhere, hence the focused approach they'd used.

Mickey came over. 'Right, I'm off. I'll see you back at the house. The rest are ready; you'll be well covered. Do what she says, okay.'

James nodded, he and Jo standing ready to go. The bar seemed deserted as the last of the couples left, and she looked around them. It was a surreal experience being stood in a bar on their own.

'Give them two minutes. They're checking with the guys on the door that the coast is clear, then walking back to the cars. We will follow with our guy out front following us. We have the car park covered. I just need you to step outside as if you know you've pulled the girl of your dreams.'

'I'm not that good an actor,' he said, smiling.

'That's what we need.' She hated to admit it, but when he turned the charm on, she could understand why girls melted.

'Let's go.'

They exited, hand in hand, and she laughed as if she was walking out with the funniest man on the planet. *She* was that good an actor. James whispered something in her ear whilst they paused, appearing to chat to the doorman. With 'Goodnights' hanging in the air, they left, heading down the slight hill toward the car park.

As they walked hand in hand, they kept up the pretence of a couple ready to have a good night. At one point, by a shop window close to the car park, she stopped and pulled him towards her to fake a kiss.

'Steady on, old girl.'

'Don't flatter yourself. If we're being watched, we want them to know it's us. I might repeat this by the car.'

'I do hope so.'

'You're doing okay. How are you feeling?'

'Truth?'

'Yep.'

'I'm shitting myself. It's as if I'm in a really bad scary movie. I keep expecting someone to jump out screaming, with a raised knife.'

They turned to cross the road, and the traffic was eerily quiet. Ahead they could see the couple who had left before them, standing by the car park entrance sharing a smoke, which they extinguished when heading inside ahead of them, all four taking the stairs. Comms chatter was busy, reflecting the anticipation they all shared, the possibility of violence hanging in the air. She wanted to shout for silence but couldn't. It was good to know nothing seemed untoward, which was what they'd expected but...

***

The multi-story car park was quiet except for the screech of tyres as someone left the floor below. He couldn't help looking left and right as they walked. Each step felt scary. It felt strange holding her hand. He knew she wasn't a fan, but he also knew that she would risk her life to save his, and that was quite an adrenaline rush on its own. He stiffened, hearing footsteps behind him, only to see the chap that had been standing outside with the bouncers go to his car, his phone out. Only he knew if he was actually talking to someone. It could be just a reason to sit in his car.

True to her word, once he'd opened the door for her, she hugged him, pretending to kiss him whilst she scanned the entire floor. Nothing could be seen, so she got in the car, urging him to get in. Once sat, he asked, 'Time to go?'

'Yep, I'll give you a heads-up as we go. It's beginning to look like he's going to pay me a visit after you've gone home. Keep to the MO.'

'Okay.'

The car started first time, and he patted the instrument cluster. 'Good girl.'

'Do you always talk to your cars?'

'Nope, but I've only had her for a couple of days.'

'What? Fuck and bollocks! Fuck, fuck, fuck!' Her tone was rising with each word.

'What's wrong?'

'Two fucking days.'

The penny dropped. He berated himself for not thinking sooner.

'Okay.' She explained to the team listening what the problem was, saying that they would stop the car by the exit, and James would get out to lift the bonnet to check the engine before heading home. She was hoping they would be visible to anyone waiting for them to pass.

'You're assuming he didn't follow me in?'

'I don't know. We don't know. If he followed you from home, we are okay.'

'How else would he know?'

'Tracker maybe? Your car? Your phone? We should have thought of that.'

'I think he follows me in, then waits for me to leave... I don't think he's in the bar, the clubs. They're too busy – we could leave and not be seen. I think we're good. I think he follows us, checks where we park, then waits for us to leave.

'I hope you're right!'

'I know we are. Nothing else makes sense. There's only one way into the city from home, with loads of side roads. I pretty much always use this car park.' It sounded, even to him, that he was trying to convince himself.

They left, the mood in the car having changed. They wound around the car park before heading for the exit. He wound his window down, grateful for the blast of cool air. 'I'll pull over just there, before we hit the street.'

'Take your time; we have to hope he has eyes on us. We need him to see you've swapped cars. He could be in a parked car, he could be down the road, or he could be following us.'

He parked with the hazards on, getting out to lift the bonnet and fiddle with the wires, hoping the pantomime performance did the job. Dropping the bonnet with a loud bang that reverberated around the houses, he returned to the car.

'That should do it.'

They left in a puff of diesel smoke. 'Let's hope so.'

***

Suddenly the comms burst into life, the last car reporting that he was four cars back, meaning there were three cars between them – anyone of which could be the killers. She checked the mirror, trying to see the driver behind her. Every sense was heightened. There was an awful lot riding on this. It had been her call. A trickle of sweat ran down her back. Suddenly, a car pulled out of a side road, almost hitting them, and she noticed a young couple laughing. She envied them in that moment, oblivious to what was playing out in front of them. Just short of the roundabout, there was another parked car, its roadside indicators flashing. She turned as they drove by. She couldn't see the driver, but she saw the car pull out behind them.

'Are you still behind?'

'I'm five cars back now.

'Mickey, is everything good at the house?'

'Yeah, good this end. Everyone in position.'

'Just remember we expect this to go down once James leaves, not before. So don't get trigger happy. We don't want to scare him off by body-slamming the neighbour walking his dog. Got that?'

'Yes, boss.'

'We're pulling into the street. Check anyone following us, but don't scare them.'

'Pull up over there. The house with the white door. You can park outside.'

Once stopped, she took a deep breath. 'See the van in front?'

'Yep.'

'Armed response. They're ready to save your arse if needed, but when you leave, I want you in your car and gone. Got it?'

'Yes, boss.'

She placed her hand over his. 'I don't want you over worrying. The boys with the toys are five feet away, there's a car behind you that will follow you once you leave, and we will have Rob and the team at the house. We have this locked down. Besides, it's me he wants, not you!'

'Why do you do this?'

'I'll tell you tomorrow – hopefully.' She exited the car, joining him. The door was a few feet away, and they stepped towards it, key out. Within seconds, they were safely in the house.

***

James relaxed once inside, feeling safer in the house, and happy to see a huge cop on either side of the front door, their backs against the wall so they couldn't be seen from outside. The house was in darkness, and he watched as she turned the lights on. She called him into the front room.

'You alright, lad?' He almost jumped out of his skin; it was Mickey, standing in the shadows.

'Come here.' She pulled him to her. 'We need to keep working this. We have to assume we are being watched. We're going into the kitchen, and I'll make a coffee, then I'm taking you upstairs – lights on.'

'How long before I leave?'

'I'd say five minutes after we turn the lights on,' she said with a laugh.

'You're so funny,' he said, trying not to laugh, which made it worse. His guts were churning.

They were soon upstairs.

'This is surreal.'

He lay on the bed, looking up at the ceiling and listening to her checking in with everybody. Nothing was happening, then there was a whispered, 'Man approaching opposite path, heading towards the house. Didn't see where he came from.'

'Everybody standby.'

The wait was excruciating; he uttered a silent prayer, praying for everyone involved.

'He's gone past the house; do we follow him?'

It felt the right call. 'Agreed, proceed carefully but at a distance. We're finished up here. Heading downstairs.'

Standing, he felt sore, and he could feel the beginnings of a headache. He rubbed the back of his head, rotating and stretching his neck.

'You okay?'

'Yep, it's not me I'm worried about; you could be here hours waiting with nothing to show for it.'

'Let's hope not.'

He followed her down the stairs to the front door. Once again, a cop stood either side but out of sight. He hugged her. 'Good night, I'll call you tomorrow,' he said aloud, and then he whispered, 'Good luck. You really are quite impressive close-up.'

Watching him leave, she looked up and down the road before going back inside, shutting but not locking the door. She turned the hall lights off and went into the kitchen, needing a coffee. Mickey was sat at a small table in the dark.

'I need a coffee.'

'I'll make you one. I stopped on the way for a few essentials thinking this might be a long night.'

'I'll do it. You need to stay out of sight. Any news?'

'Nope. One of ours is following him, and I've alerted Rob that he's on the way home.'

***

As he turned into the drive, it was obvious that everyone was up and waiting for him. Every light was on. He drove past a car parked amongst the trees. He waved, but he wasn't sure they'd seen him. No one had followed him, apart from the boys in blue behind. Glancing in his mirror, he could see that they had pulled over to talk to their undercover colleagues. He stifled a laugh and groaned. *Undercover.*

He pulled to a stop in front of the house, glad to be home but wishing he could have stayed with Jo and Mickey. Someone was waiting for the chance to strike and kill.

Switching the engine off, he climbed out of the car and saw Rob gesturing wildly. He had no idea why. He saw Rob leave the rest standing by the window, and now everyone was shouting at him. He saw Rob run out through the kitchen door.

He turned, hearing running, feet on gravel, and someone was screaming. It was high-pitched and didn't sound human. He could hear the dogs behind him barking, sounding like they wanted to rip somebody's face off, then he fell back, aware of somebody flying through the air at him, the fall knocking the wind out of him. The screaming changed, becoming words, and he felt his chest being thumped, again and again, then a hot bursting pain at his neck when whoever had sat on him was swept aside by someone. *Rob,* he thought. He could hear the dogs biting, barking, and helping to drag his assailant off. Everything was in slow motion. He tried to sit up … struggling with the effort, and then finally he saw them, Rob and his assailant. He closed his eyes in disbelief. *It couldn't be. It's not possible.*

Finally sitting up, all he could see was Rob's back. He was pinning her to the ground, shouting over the screaming. He stood. He had to know. Frank had pulled the dogs off; everyone stood a few feet away. Richard came to his aid, asking if he was okay. He was soon joined by Lucy on his other side. He felt a little drunk, lightheaded. They were talking about blood – his blood, he realised – and he held his hand to his neck, feeling the warm sticky mess. The night was cold, and he shivered. The police, his protection, had sprung into life, their car now parked across the drive, the blue light on and swirling through the trees.

He had to know. Before he did whatever they were asking, he had to know. He pushed them off and walked towards her, crashing to his knees when he saw her face. It was her. She'd changed her appearance – she looked awful, almost unrecognisable – but it was her. It was Sarah, and she lay screaming obscenities, squirming, frantically trying to throw Rob off her. He sat back on his heels, his head a hornet's nest of *why. Why would she? How could she? She was dead. I watched her die on a kitchen table.*

***

The call didn't make sense, and so she'd asked Rob to repeat. Mickey joined her, picking up on her reaction, mouthing, 'Everything okay?'

She asked, 'Is James okay? Thank Christ for that.' She continued to listen, thinking no one could have foreseen this. 'Does he need medical treatment? Okay, bring her in. We'll meet you there.'

'What's happened?'

'I'll update you in the car, but we've got her.'

'Her?' His voice raised; his surprise obvious.

'Yep. Do you remember the solicitor's wife, Sarah Horton, who ran away with James?'

'Yep.'

'She's back.'

'What? Really?'

'Apparently so.'

'I didn't see that coming. What's next?'

'Can you sort this lot out, thank them, etc. and I'll meet you at the station?'

'Sure. What about James? You said hospital?'

'He's fine. Apparently, it's a nasty cut to his neck. The paramedics sealed it, but they have taken him to hospital to get it checked. Might need a few stitches.'

***

It was a bumpy ride in the back of the ambulance. Lydia had insisted on accompanying him to the hospital. She hadn't had time to calm down, to process anything, other than the fact she was very grateful that he was alive.

'What do you want for Christmas?' His voice was still shaky.

'What?'

'Just one shopping day left, and I need to get you something.'

'How about a nice quiet Christmas Day at home with my family.'

'How about we split the day and wake up with my family.' He liked that idea. They had become his family. Frank, Lucy, and even Richard were family.

'I'd like that. Wake up at yours, have dinner and then supper with my folks, then home to mine to sleep.'

'Best meal of the day... supper. Cold meats and pickles with a huge pork pie.'

'Deal.' She leaned over to kiss him, whispering, 'Don't screw this up, pretty boy. No third chances.'

'Promise... but I might have trouble sleeping.' He laughed.

The paramedic turned away, smiling.

***

Richard turned to Lucy, putting his arm around her, and together they walked back into the house, followed by the dogs. Frank and Rachel were already seated at the table, cuppas in hand.

'They've left?'

'Yep. She screamed all the way into the car. I think she screamed all the way down the drive, too.'

'I still can't believe it, and I saw the whole thing.' Richard sat beside Rachel. 'You okay?'

'Me? I'm fine. Although I don't think any of us will sleep well tonight.'

'Well, I'm going to bed,' said Frank. 'I need my beauty sleep.'

'Goodnight Frank.'

'You two go to bed. I'll wait up for James,' said Lucy.

'He could be hours yet; you know A&E,' said Rachel.

Richard took her hand. 'Come on, let's get to bed. Night, Luce,' he said, adding as they left, 'shout if you need anything.'

Lucy called the dogs to her and stepped outside, already missing Rob but happy knowing that he'd accepted her invitation to join them for Christmas. The night was cold, and she pulled her jacket around her, the dogs exploring, sniffing the ground, just happy to be out. It was almost Christmas Eve – probably would be by the time James returned. She looked up at the sky, and there was hardly a cloud. She saw bedroom lights being turned off – that would be Frank, the mother hen, turning lights off, drawing curtains, and shutting doors before he shut his own. She felt at peace, at home, and she looked to the sky, whispering, 'Thank you.' She often spoke to Reggie late at night before rolling over to sleep.

CHAPTER TWENTY-EIGHT

According to his watch, it was now officially Christmas Eve. He thought this a waste of time. He'd told Jo, and he'd told Dick that Jo had been right that she was as mad as a box of frogs. They were wasting their time; this wouldn't be prosecuted. He'd met a few nutters over the years, some just pretending to be – they were easy to spot – but Sarah Horton was a class apart. Something had fried her brain. They would probably need to talk to James to understand why. Once they understood why, then they might reach her, but he doubted it. She was on a different planet!

The lads who had brought her in said she screamed the whole way in and didn't shut up. Now she sat opposite Jo, smiling but not saying a word. Nothing reached her. She was hiding. He knew Jo wouldn't give in; she would want to break her. She needed to, not wanted to. She was the most driven cop he'd ever worked with – his favourite partner. He was sufficiently self-aware to know her strengths were his opposites. The biggest question was why did she like working with him when the chance allowed?

***

This was proving to be the most frustrating hour of her life. Sarah sat opposite and either ignored her or screamed in her face, spitting at her regularly. She didn't know which was the most frustrating. When she screamed, she wanted to cover her ears or leave the room, and when she hid behind that face, she wanted to slap her – and slap her hard. She'd asked Mickey to take advice. She hadn't arrested a looney tunes before, and so it was important they got this right.

There was nothing behind the eyes. Vacant didn't do it justice. It was as if she'd come alive just long enough to try to kill James.

'James is alive.' No reaction, not even a blink.

'He's probably home now. James that is... Christmas tomorrow. Family dinners. Presents.' Again, nothing. No reaction.

She leaned closer. 'He has a new girlfriend, and she's very pretty.' Pushing her chair back, she stood. 'I'll leave you to it. I'll be back later, once I've slept. They may move you.' She walked to the door, nodding to the uniformed cop by the door.

'Wait.'

She returned to her chair, hardly daring to breathe. Sarah looked like she wanted to laugh, like she was trying not to. Her voice came out in a whisper, and Jo had to lean in. She couldn't be certain, but she thought she said, 'Fooled you once.'

She laughed. It was a high-pitched laugh.

'Fooled you once, I'll fool you twice.' Then she started banging her head on the table; Jo pushed her head back, shouting for help.

***

At last, Lucy saw headlights on the drive, and she leapt up, calling the dogs to her. She didn't recognize the car, but it had to be them. The car pulled up beside her. It was a local taxi company, and she was pleased to see James and Lydia in the back. He looked okay. Tired but okay.

Lydia paid the taxi driver, they both got out, and Lucy gently hugged him.

'It's okay, I won't break.'

'What have they said?'

'He's a lucky man.'

'I am at that. Thanks to the vest. Without that, I wouldn't be here.'

'Let's go in. We need to get you two to bed.'

'Oh, I nearly forgot,' he said playfully. 'Rob sends his regards, and he thanks you for the invite to dinner.'

It was a good job they were outside as she knew she would be blushing. She felt warm inside… happy. He was coming tomorrow. She'd better tell Frank!

***

The car park was deserted apart from them. Mickey was dog tired, ready for bed, but he could see she was wired.

'You've got to let it go.'

'She's fucking playing with us. I know it.'

'She's a basket case, complete looney tune. She doesn't know what day it is.'

'You think?'

'I know. She's away with the fairies. God knows how she held it together to get here. She needs help, but my gut tells me she isn't going to find normal any time soon.'

Jo hugged him. 'Thank you. Can I get you an early breakfast?'

'Go on, I fancy a big old fry up.'

***

It was the dogs barking that woke Frank. He was a light sleeper at the best of times, and his bedside clock showed that it was almost eight am. He swung his legs, throwing the duvet off. He hadn't slept in this late for months. The last time he had, he'd been a bit poorly.

Standing up, he sat straight back down, his head spinning. He'd got up too quickly. *Steady on, old boy, you're not as young as*

298

you used to be. He stood again, feeling a little better. He had a lot to do. He was planning a nice supper tonight – cold cuts and pickles – and he had loads to prepare for tomorrow. He was looking forward to the next day. As he dressed, he wandered over to the window. The sun was out, and it was a dry day, though last night's frost covered just about everything. It looked beautiful.

Taking the stairs, he found Lucy in the kitchen. She had started breakfast. The bacon was sizzling, the toast was in, and the coffee was on; he was a lucky old sod. Life was good – better than he deserved if he was honest.

'You're up early.'

'No, I think you're up late.' She offered her cheek for him to kiss. 'Hungry?'

'Could eat a horse. Where are the rest?'

'Richard's popped into town with Rachel. Last-minute dot com.'

'Any sign of James?'

'I thought I'd take breakfast up to them; can you pour the orange juice and the coffee?'

'So, I hear we have company tomorrow.' He watched her blush, and she looked even prettier. 'I'll have to take him to one side.'

'Why?' She sounded concerned.

'I'll need to have the chat. Check his intentions and...'

She laughed. 'I think he's nice. Honest. I think that what you see is what you get.'

He threw a piece of bacon to each of the dogs. 'I hope so. I really do,' he added quietly.

CHAPTER TWENTY-NINE

They were all gathered in the dining room, apart from Frank who was busy in the kitchen. The dining room was seldom used. It was a big, formal room, and the table could seat twelve with ease. The huge tree in the corner was the centrepiece, and the floor underneath was covered with presents. They had agreed to open them after they had eaten. Rob had arrived, apologising for the presents hastily bought the day before.

The mood was light and happy, and Lucy was beside herself with joy. She had walked the grounds earlier, wishing Reggie a Happy Christmas. She'd even had a little cry as she had reminisced. Reggie had given her this life, and he had become her family, but she'd made a promise to visit her mum tomorrow. She hadn't been to say hello for a long time, and it was time that she did.

'Penny?' asked Rob.

'What?'

'You were miles away.'

'I'm sorry, Christmas does that to you. Did you speak to your family?

'I did. I had to explain where I was and with whom.'

She giggled. 'Oh, dear. Am I forgiven?'

'Only because I promised to call them later with a full update.'

Frank entered. 'Right, my lovelies, dinner is ready. I just need a little help.'

'Richard, James, Rob, please take your seats. We have this,' said Lucy.

She was followed by Lydia and Rachel, Rachel shouting as she left, 'You lot are doing the washing up!'

Frank returned, carrying the duck, which he laid in front of James. 'Can you do the honours?'

Lucy was close behind, carrying a huge joint of beef, which she placed in front of Richard, followed by bowls of vegetables: they had to make another trip to the kitchen. Once finished, the table was laden. She wasn't one for table pictures, but once Rob had lit the candles, it was a work of art.

Taking his seat at the far end, Frank poured himself a glass. 'I know I'm probably breaking with etiquette – this should be at the end of the meal with a nice glass of port – but I wanted to say that you lot are very special to me, and I love you.' His voice was breaking. 'I know that he's up there somewhere looking down on us, wishing he could be here. To Reggie!'

The rest stood, raising their glasses. 'Reggie.'

***

The day passed by in a blur. James and Lydia had said their goodbyes after lunch, leaving in a whirl of hugs and best wishes. Richard and Rachel had offered to walk the dogs after tea, and they'd been gone quite a while. Lucy and Rob were curled up watching telly – some old movie that seemed to be on every Christmas. Frank dropped into an old armchair in the kitchen with his second glass of port. *It really is a Wonderful Life,* he thought, and he raised his glass in a silent toast.

***

It had been a good day, a very good day, although he had missed the family back home in Durham – especially his sisters. He had felt bad cancelling the journey home, but with only two days off, he would have spent most of that in the car. His mum had been fine, putting on a brave face, no doubt as this would be the first Christmas apart. Dad had understood, being a retired copper himself – an old school sergeant who he thought was secretly quite proud of his eldest having chosen the same profession after getting a first in Cognitive Psychology. He'd opted to study in San Diego, California for the third year, returning to the UEA in Norwich for his final year.

Once qualified he had options – lots of options – but following in the old man's footsteps appealed. Not up north, though. He'd fallen in love with his adopted county – the beaches, and the city – so he'd applied to join Norfolk Constabulary. The first few months had been hard, with his uni' mates disappearing all over the world. New friends came and went, but he was doing a job he believed in, working with some wonderful – and some not so wonderful – people. Life was good, but finding himself here, sitting beside this beautiful girl, in this glorious house, was definitely a pinch yourself moment.

Lucy stirred. She had tucked herself into him, and now, she sat up. 'That was good!'

'Yes, it was.'

'Do you want a cuppa?'

'Coffee, please. I think I might need a cup or two to be ready to hit the road.'

'You don't have to.'

'Don't what?' He sounded a tad apprehensive, which he was. He didn't want to spoil this before it started. He didn't think she was into one-nighters. He had been, but he hoped this might turn into something else, something more.

Lucy smiled, and it was a nice smile. 'We have lots of guest rooms. I'd feel happier if you slept here tonight. I might even bring you breakfast in bed if you're a good boy.'

'Thank you, I'd like that.' He reddened, thinking just how much he would like that.

Lucy stood, pulling him to his feet. 'Let's go make that coffee.'

He followed her into the kitchen, and she stopped very quickly, turning to face him and putting a finger to her lips. He looked past her to see Frank asleep in his armchair. He watched as she pulled a cover off a sofa to lay over him, standing to blow him a kiss. She then turned, taking his hand and whispering, 'Sorry, coffee might have to wait.'

'No probs.'

'I love that old man. He and Reggie saved me.'

'From what he told me earlier, they think you saved them.'

They climbed the stairs hand in hand; she opened a door, and he stepped in behind her, immediately knowing it was her room. She turned, kissing him.

CHAPTER THIRTY

James cut the call. He had a decision to make. He knew what he had to do, but would he? If he told Richard, he would have to tell everyone… and that scared him more than he would admit to.

He'd only made contact with the tracing agent on Christmas Eve. He hadn't expected to hear anything for days, maybe weeks, maybe never, but now he knew where she lived. He had an address. He wished that Richard had thought of this. It had been too simple. He searched online on how to find a missing person, surprised to find lots of agencies offering to do just that. He selected an agent, filled out a simple online form, and £180 later, it was job done.

It had been an innocent question that had started this. He'd asked Richard what he wanted for Christmas, expecting 'anything other than socks', but he had paused before replying.

'One thing mate: just one thing. I want to find Jackie.' His voice betrayed his emotions, and in that moment, he had decided to try to find her. He owed him that.

The house was empty. Lydia had left earlier to go and see her parents. He'd been invited, but he had declined, wanting to pop home himself. He showered quickly, dressing even quicker, almost as if he did everything quickly, he wouldn't stop, and he wouldn't chicken out. He knew that it would be easy to give up the address. Just the address.

The Defender didn't enjoy being driven hard down the country lanes. He was bouncing up and down, and from side to side, but he wouldn't take his foot off the pedal. He needed this done – the sooner the better. He saw Richard's car in the drive, which was good. He was hoping he might be outside or at least on his own. Everyone was back at work preparing for the first guests of the new year. It was a hive of activity, and he found Richard at his desk. Thank God, he was alone.

'I've got some news for you, bud.'

Richard looked up. 'Hi, what?'

James sat on a desk, noticing that he had a desk between him and Richard. Was that through choice or a subconscious survival decision?

'Spit it out. You've got me worried.'

James was trying to find the words, the best words, to start this, his rehearsed speech forgotten. 'I've found her.'

'Her? Who?'

'Jackie. I have an address.'

Richard sat motionless, obviously trying to process. Then he leapt to his feet to hug him. 'Oh my God, how? Where is she?'

'She's got a house on the coast in Aldeburgh. I've got the address.'

Richard stepped back. 'How on earth?'

'I employed a tracing agent.'

'A what?'

James explained, and Richard looked like he was going to explode with joy. Then his face changed. 'What's wrong?'

'It's truth time.'

'Not with you?'

'In a few hours, I'm going to face the truth. Will she slam the door in my face or listen to me? I've always understood when looking for her that the ending might not be a happy one. It might not be the ending I want.'

'When are you going?'

'Now.'

'I think it might be best if you take a little time to prepare, to calm down, maybe shower, shave, change, etc. Go and observe before charging in. Maybe write a note before you go?'

'Do you think?'

'I do. For all you know, she could be living with someone or seeing someone. You don't want to upset her. I think it's best to take a note, so you can leave it if that's the best thing to do.'

Richard sat on the desk again. 'Okay, I think you might be right.' He stood again, giving James a hug. 'I can't tell you how grateful I am, mate. I'm forever in your debt.'

James left with Richard sat at his desk again, fingers typing furiously. James was kicking himself. *Coward. You fucking coward...*

***

It was lunchtime by the time he'd finished writing the note, the rejected efforts filling his bin. Lucy had come to see him, as had Frank, both overjoyed for him, but like James, they also counselled caution, which he knew was to protect him from disappointment. Both had offered to ride shotgun. Chatting to Rachel had been easier than he had feared. She reminded him that they were mates, that she cared for him, and she hoped it all worked out for him.

He read the note for the third time. It was what it was. He tucked it into an envelope and wrote across the front 'Jackie' with 'PRIVATE' scrawled underneath. He sealed the letter and tucked it into his back pocket. The clock said '12.39', and he could be on the road by one pm. He smelled his armpits, thinking, *yep, I need a shower.*

***

At last, he spotted Richard walking towards the cars. He had been waiting ever since he saw him leave the house to go and get ready. He'd changed his mind twice whilst standing there. Conflicting thoughts crashing. One moment it was an easy call to leave things as they were, nothing was broken. But immediately, he knew that the ending might be happier if he went armed with the truth.

'Richard!'

Richard turned and walked towards him, a nervous grin on his face. 'Hi, bud. Is this the send-off?'

'I need to tell you something.'

'Go on.'

James sighed, thinking *fuck me, this is hard.* 'It wasn't you; it was me.'

'What are you going on about?'

'Lucy. It wasn't you. You didn't attack Lucy.'

'What? Who the fuck did?' It was obvious that he'd worked it out when he stepped back and stood a little straighter. 'Why? Why tell me now?'

James stepped towards him, talking quickly. 'I had to. I wanted you to drive to her knowing that you're a good man...'

He didn't see the punch, the power flooring him. He sat on the ground, rubbing his face. *I had that coming.*

'Get up.' Richard bent down to pick him up, pulling him to his feet. 'I think it's best that you leave. Just go.'

'Okay, I'll go, and I'll tell Lucy.' He stepped away. 'I am truly sorry.' He stopped after a few feet. 'This won't make it any better, but I wasn't attacking her, I just wanted to ask her out. I want you to know that.' He'd got halfway to the house when he heard: 'Stop!'

Turning, he found Richard walking towards him. 'Don't.'

'Don't what?'

'Don't tell Lucy. In fact, don't tell anyone.'

'Why?'

'She doesn't need to know; the truth could hurt her, and I don't want her hurt. This has become family to me, this is my home, and she's become a sister. God knows what would happen if you...'

'Okay. Whatever you want.'

'I'm going to go. I hope sometime soon I can say thank you for having the balls and the decency to finally come clean, but right now, I can't. Right now, I want to hit you again. To be truthful, I want to beat the crap out of you, but then they would know.'

'I was always going to tell you if you found her. I was fed up with the lie.'

'Me too. Me too. I'll see you later.'

'Good luck.' He watched him get in the car and drive off, thankful that he had found the courage to tell him the truth. He felt the first flutter of freedom, his old life now behind him. Now, he could start living again.

For the first time, he was free from the past, free from his many mistakes.

***

Richard swung out onto the main road. The drive would take about an hour and a half, even in the piece of shit he was driving. His mind was scrambled. He'd lived with the fear that he might be a monster for too long. Now, though, he could begin to imagine that he was the man that she had said he was. A good man. He'd been pretty awful to her at the time, managing to convince himself that he was protecting her. He hoped she could forgive him. What if she wouldn't speak to him? He had the note, but he'd written that before his chat with James. She might slam the door in his face.

He was driving on autopilot, and he wound his window down a few inches, hoping the cold would keep him focused on the road ahead.

It had been a funny few months. In many ways, he had been blessed: the money left by Jackie, meeting Lucy, the job which he loved, the place was special, and even James had come through twice. He began to forgive. Everything happened for a reason – or so he was told. He believed that in part, but that didn't excuse bad choices. He wondered if Jackie would, in time, join him, or would he join her? He hoped it would be the former, but that was a big ask. A very big ask.

His phone pinged, and he looked at the screen to see a text from Lucy, probably wishing him good luck. He would pull over shortly and reply whilst setting up directions to take him to Jackie. She was now about thirty minutes away. He hadn't eaten since breakfast – he didn't think he could. His stomach was churning. He looked around the car for something to drink and found a half-full diet coke. He emptied the bottle in two gulps. His phone pinged again. This time Rachel had texted, and he felt for her, sat at home knowing he was going to see Jackie. He had felt for some time that she was finding the whole friends thing a little harder than he was.

Spotting a layby ahead, he pulled in, quickly replying to both girls and typing in the address into Google maps. The reality smacked him in the face, and questions flashed through his mind. He felt nauseous, and so he pushed the car door open, sprinting to the hedge before throwing up. His throat burned, and his guts hurt. He stood wiping his face on his hankie, which he then looked at briefly before throwing into the hedge.

Returning to the car, he decided to find a filling station, needing mints and water – and maybe something bland to eat – before knocking on her door.

After filling up at a nearby station, he selected a Mars Bar, a packet of mint gum, and a bottle of water. Leaving the little shop to a cheery 'Happy New Year', he raised his right hand in greeting, his mouth already full of chocolate. Once back in the car, he finished the Mars, drank half the water, and popped three pieces of gum into his mouth before setting off.

Following Google's instructions, he soon pulled up at the start of her road, where he parked, counting houses until he got to hers. He felt a little flushed, so he wound the window down until it was fully open. No one stirred. There was a car outside her house – a recent 5 series. *'Nice car. I wonder who owns that?'*

He didn't have long to wait as the front door opened, and he watched, barely able to suck air into his lungs. He slid down into his seat, feeling just a little stupid, watching as a thirty-something guy stepped out holding a toddler's hand, and then he saw her, and everything stopped. She looked happy. She was speaking to them, waving as they got into the car. She blew them a kiss as they drove past him, seemingly in slow motion. He didn't know what to do, so he started his car and turned, wanting to catch them up to see where they were going.

A short while later he parked as the BMW turned into a driveway, the front door opening. He watched as a pretty blonde walked to the car, taking the youngster out of the back. She hugged and kissed him, and Richard watched as they chatted away, the man joining them on the way into the house, and the blonde kissing his cheek as they entered. It was pure relief that coursed through him; he couldn't move for a few seconds.

***

Having showered, she was now sitting on her bed styling her hair, various clothes laying on the bed. She had narrowed it down to two options, favouring the dress, but the trousers promised a warmer, comfier evening. She hadn't been out for a few weeks, so she had been looking forward to a night out with the girls from work. She had a part-time job with the local council, working in the account's office.

She stopped singing along to Mr Bublé when she became aware of someone knocking on her door. Turning the dryer off, she stood up and tiptoed to her window facing the road. She could see a car parked outside that she didn't recognize, but she couldn't see the person knocking on her door. Cursing, she picked up a robe and put it on as she went to see who it was, checking her appearance in the mirror before she opened the door.

Everything stopped as if time had been frozen. She wanted to scream, she wanted to shut the door, she wanted to... She stopped thinking. It was freezing, and she only had a thin robe on, but it felt like she was burning up. She felt strange. She tried to speak, to form words, but nothing came out.

He smiled, and it was a nervous smile that she knew well. If there had been any doubt before, that was now dispelled in a heartbeat. He looked good, and she hated that he did. He shouldn't. He looked different, but he was still her Richard. No, he wasn't her Richard – he hadn't been her Richard for three years. All these thoughts took moments. In them, she could have told their life story, their past, and their future without speaking, without breathing. She knew that she would remember this moment for the rest of her life. Everything hung on what happened next. She stopped thinking, no thoughts, no emotion, and everything calmed.

'Hi.'

It was his voice that rebooted her, like a switch being thrown, and she felt the surge fire through her body from her feet to her brain. It was all too much, and she collapsed. She would have fallen to her knees, but he caught her before she reached the floor.

He was talking to her, but she had no idea what he was saying. She felt him pick her up and carry her to the sofa. He sat her down, kneeling in front of her.

'Can I get you anything? Tea? Something stronger?'

Words still wouldn't come, so she nodded yes.

'Tea?' was met with another nod.

She watched him in the small kitchen as if from a distance. Nothing made sense. How had he found her? She had led a quiet life in another county, living in a town – a village really – that they had never visited, and yet here he was. Her rational brain was asking different questions. What did she want? What did *he* want? Was she safe? She dismissed that one immediately, thinking, *don't be daft, he wouldn't hurt me.*

She'd had three years to think about what had happened. She had never given up on him, never believing the lie. Had she done so, it would have made a lie of the years they had spent together, and she had always known that he had loved her.

'Here you go. Be careful, it's hot.'

Sipping slowly, she checked him out. He didn't look like a newly released prisoner. She had expected a haunted look, a bruised look, someone who'd had the joy beaten out of them, but he looked good. Nervous, yes, but otherwise, good. Words were still hard to come by; she felt her heartbeat finally start to slow.

'Thank you.'

'You're welcome. You probably have a thousand questions. Would it help if I just told you a few things?

The nod said 'yes, please'.

'Before you start, do you want to check the cupboard beside the fridge? Hopefully, there's some Scotch left. The glasses are in the cupboard to the left.'

Again, she watched him in the kitchen. 'When did you start drinking Scotch?'

She raised her voice. 'It's nice after a walk on the beach. Especially this time of year.'

He sat on the floor, sipping at his drink. She gulped hers down, the fire burning her throat, and she coughed. He laughed. She wondered what her life had been like yesterday, the day before, knowing he was here, then she wondered what would tomorrow look like?

Would they walk the beach?

She was already hoping, and he hadn't spoken yet.

She told herself off. *For heaven's sake, just shut up.*

Listen to what he wants to say!

They had drunk most of the bottle – it had been almost full before they'd started. She'd had to stop him for a couple of minutes to text a couple of the girls, apologising for the late cancellation, but something had come up. She listened as he told his story. He hadn't complained, and he didn't seek pity, he just told the story – his story. Some of it broke her heart, but he was now talking about Reggie and Lucy, Frank, James, Rachel, and the dogs. She was overjoyed that he had found happiness. He was still speaking, but she'd been far away for a few seconds, trying to visualise his life these last three months. She tried to replay the last few seconds – something had sparked a physical reaction. She had to ask him to stop and repeat himself, and then she heard him, each word sinking in, each word making sense, each word making her want to scream with happiness.

***

313

Richard had dreaded this moment. Her reaction would shape his, *their,* life. He had imagined this moment many times, trying to be honest with his hopes. He still hadn't known what he truly wanted, what he hoped for whilst driving here. The least would be a kind of peace, an acceptance, a closure of sorts, but having sat here, having talked to her, having enjoyed her company, he started to hope that they might find each other again. Everything considered this had been so easy, and that had to tell you something about them, about their past, didn't it?

Her happiness was obvious, and she took his hands in hers. 'Can you remember any of this?'

He thought carefully before he answered. 'Sometimes I think I do, but sometimes I wonder if it's my memories or me remembering bits and pieces I've been told or overheard. It's hard to know the difference. I'm told I may never recall the past, and the best advice I've had was from Frank, who said, 'Son, make today worth remembering.'

'I like the sound of him.'

'You'd like him. You'd like them all.'

'I hope so.' She hesitated. 'How do you feel about James?'

He puffed his cheeks out. He knew his next few words were hugely important. 'Don't get me wrong, part of me hates him. Part of me wants to kill him. I punched him and put him on his backside when he told me.' Her face was impassive, non-judgmental. 'All I could think of was the damage he'd done, but I've learnt that forgiveness is possible, that people change. I've seen kids looking after parents. I've seen the best of people. He's a very different man than he was.'

'So, are you?'

'Am I in what way?'

She poured herself another shot. 'Well, you're definitely more handsome, more interesting.'

Feigning outrage, he laughed. 'More interesting?'

'You are. You're still Richard, but more ...'

'You like me slightly drunk?'

'You didn't do drunk very often, but yes.'

'Think I need a coffee. Want one?'

'Yes, please. That would be nice.'

He pulled himself off the floor, joints aching, and went to the kitchen. By the time he'd returned, she was sleeping. He placed her coffee on the table beside the sofa and drank his as she continued to sleep. He didn't want to wake her. He decided to carry her upstairs. She was easy to carry, and she put her arms around his neck as he took the stairs carefully.

'My knight.'

Once upstairs, he laid her on the bed, covering her with the duvet. She was sleeping once more, and now he had a choice to make. He decided to sleep on the floor. He'd slept on worse. He took a spare pillow, dropping it beside the bed. He removed his trousers and shirt, then lay down, falling asleep very quickly.

CHAPTER THIRTY-ONE

Richard woke slowly, his head hurting, it took a few seconds to work out where he was and that someone was banging on the front door.

He looked for his watch but couldn't see it.

He sat up, his mouth dry, beginning to recall images from the night before.

The banging continued, he leaned over the bed, to gently shake the sleeping Jackie. 'I think somebody wants to come in.'

'What?'

'I think somebody is at the front door.'

She sat up quickly. 'Oh shit!' She leapt out of bed, checked her appearance, and left, bouncing off the doorframe. 'Fuck that hurt.'

He listened to her walking down the stairs, he heard the door open but couldn't make out the conversation. She sounded stressed but happy considering the circumstances. He heard a 'thank you', then the sound of the door shutting.

'William! William, no you don't, come here!'

He heard her running up the stairs.

'William, don't!'

He swung out of bed, pulling his trousers on, trying to find his shirt when the bedroom door banged open to reveal a happy, flushed William.

'Helloooooooooooo!'

'Good morning. You must be William.'

William shyly nodded his head, and Jackie entered, picking William up for a hug.

'Sorry, Mummy.'

Richard mouthed 'Mummy?' his brain scrambled; he questioned his own sanity.

Jackie nodded, tears forming, and she started to sob.

William pushed back to look at her, then turned to him with his arms outstretched for a hug.

He stood and walked to them very slowly, his eyes asking the question.

She nodded 'yes'.

Printed in Great Britain
by Amazon